Second Edition

Chosen Family

Ellen M. Levy

(Author of *Romance at Stonegate* and *Struggles in a Boston Marriage*)

Halo
PUBLISHING
INTERNATIONAL

Halo Publishing International
7550 W IH-10 #800, PMB 2069,
San Antonio, TX 78229

Second Edition, October 2024
ISBN: 978-1-63765-676-1

Halo Publishing International is a self-publishing company that publishes adult fiction and non-fiction, children's literature, self-help, spiritual, and faith-based books. We continually strive to help authors reach their publishing goals and provide many different services that help them do so. We do not publish books that are deemed to be politically, religiously, or socially disrespectful, or books that are sexually provocative, including erotica. Halo reserves the right to refuse publication of any manuscript if it is deemed not to be in line with our principles. Do you have a book idea you would like us to consider publishing? Please visit www.halopublishing.com for more information.

Dedication

The book is dedicated to my mischievous sister, Nancy, who loved Deborah and Miriam as if they were real members of our family.

TABLE OF CONTENTS

Addendum

Glossary

Preface

In Deborah and Miriam's era, families were defined as two parents and their children. In the twenty-first century, lesbians and others in nontraditional units select a family of choice. This book is the story of how Deborah and Miriam created a family unit, built of relatives and friends.

Many people are welcomed into Deborah and Miriam's chosen family. Miriam's sister Hannah and her family follow the typical family structure, tied even closer because they share the family business. Marjorie, Miriam's oldest and dearest friend, and her relatives become a natural extension of their family when they include Deborah and Miriam in all the Jewish holidays. When Susan and Helen, their friends from New York, move in with Deborah and Miriam, they are good friends and employees, but gradually they too become part of their family.

With the addition of those few people and those connected to them, the family has expanded to about a dozen people. And what about their friend/savior, Mrs. Berkowitz, her husband, and their four daughters? And Leah, the child in a wheelchair living just a few doors away? And there are their close friends, Marilyn and Julie, and Chava and their childminder, Rachel, and her family. They count too.

As you read *Chosen Family* you will learn how all these people, each with their own challenges and joys, become part of Deborah and Miriam's world. As each faces pain and excitement, Deborah and Miriam react as if they were blood relatives. And others, such as Deborah's writing mentor, Dr. Hubbard, and Sylvia's biological mother, Ruth, are part of their universe.

If the criteria for being family is that they are loved, then all those mentioned above fit the definition. And it does not really matter what they are called. These folks are all important to Deborah and Miriam, and therefore are included in this book.

Acknowledgements

$\mathcal{A}$s with all my books, it takes a team to bring my story to life. I first want to thank my mentor, Fay Jacobs, who has inspired me to be a better writer. After beginning her first review of this story, she sent it back to me with instructions that I needed to learn the mechanics of writing, for which I had been relying on her. I panicked, fearful that I couldn't do justice to her demand and that she was giving up on me. Much to my amazement, as I channeled Fay, much as I channel Deborah and Miriam to write the script, I learned I was able to call on hidden talents in tightening the script. Thanks to her, I now consider myself a better writer.

A person on my team who deserves extra credit is my friend Phyllis Guilliano, who has read and edited each book multiple times. She questions my assumptions as she edits, and I am grateful to her for her perspective and talent. Also, Julie Greenbaum listened to the entire book twice, tracking missing details and encouraging changes with great skill. My sister, Nancy, reviewed the Jewish aspects of the books, correcting and adding as needed.

Also important were the other listeners, who allowed me to read the book out loud, working with me to smooth out missing parts, questioning motivations, deleting awkward phrasing. Barbara Heir listened to the entire manuscript, offering much to this creation. My good friend Sara Fleming added her perspective along the way, as did my entire Writer's Circle, led by Dana Finnegan and Becky Bohan.

Last in the process, but certainly not least, is my friend and layout designer, Sara Yager. Her attention to detail amazes me as she adjusts photographs or page design, and she fixes things I cannot even see, smoothing out all the rough edges. She created the cover and is fully responsible for the beauty of the book.

I also thank Elizabeth Andersen, copy editor, and Sherron Smith, proofreader. I am pleased to credit Hugh Mangum Photographs, David M. Rubenstein Rare Book & Manuscript Library, Duke University for providing an extensive collection of photographs of people in the early 1900s, from which I selected many of the characters.

It is a pleasure to work with such a talented group of people to bring my stories to you.

Family Tree
(Ages in December 1914)

LEVINE
MANHATTAN; GREAT BARRINGTON, MASSACHUSETTS

Mr. Levine — Mrs. Levine
(43) (41)

Deborah   Milton   Anna
(23)   (18)   (16)

Sylvia
(2)

The Levines are a loving New York City family with a country home called *Stonegate*, where they escape city life for a small town in the bucolic Berkshire Mountains. Their younger daughter, Deborah, lives in a Boston Marriage with Miriam and their child, Sylvia.

Family Tree
(Ages in December 1914)

COHEN
BOSTON, MASSACHUSETTS

Bubbie (Grandma)
(died August 16, 1914)

Mrs. Cohen
(died July 27, 1914)

Hannah Cohen
Goldman (26)

William Goldman (30)

Miriam (22)

Sarah (6 months)

Sylvia (2)

Mr. Cohen's successful Yiddish publishing company on Boston's Newspaper Row afforded the family a single-family home near their temple. Upon Mr. Cohen's death, his two daughters, Miriam and Hannah, along with their partners, take over and greatly expand the business. Deborah and Miriam turn the family home into a loving community haven for their enlarged family of choice.

Family Tree
(Ages in December 1914)

GOLD
MANHATTAN; GREAT BARRINGTON, MASSACHUSETTS

Mr. Gold (51) — Mrs. Gold (40)

Ruth Gold Bernstein (23)

David (20)

Beth (18)

Michael Bernstein (24)

The Golds are a successful cosmopolitan New York family who value material possessions above all else. Ruth, their older daughter and childhood friend of Miriam, hastily marries Michael and moves to Manhattan.

Family Tree
(Ages in December 1914)

BERKOWITZ
MANHATTAN; LENOX, MASSACHUSETTS

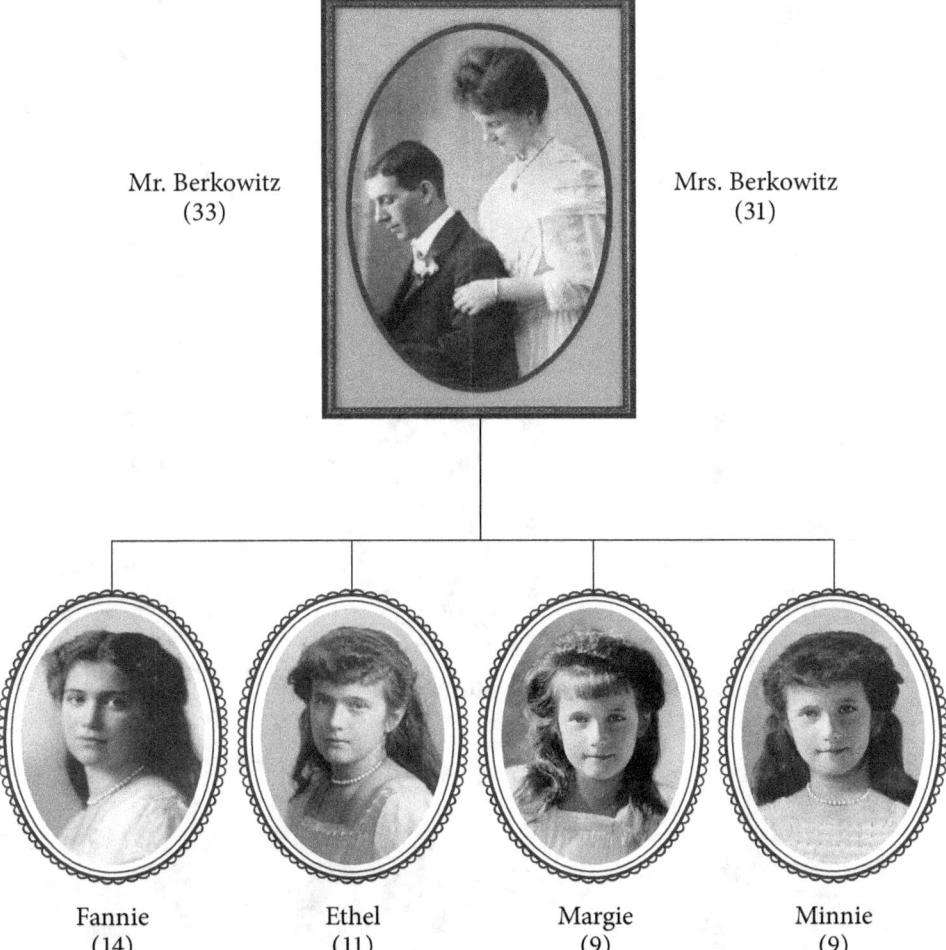

Mr. Berkowitz
(33)

Mrs. Berkowitz
(31)

Fannie
(14)

Ethel
(11)

Margie
(9)

Minnie
(9)

This colorful young family of four daughters lives in the same building as the Levines in New York City and nearby in Western Massachusetts. The sage Mrs. Berkowitz becomes a reliable confidant and advisor to Deborah and Miriam.

Friends

(Ages in December 1914)

Chava (24)
Deborah's friend

Esther (25)
Chava's girlfriend

Marjorie (22)
Miriam's best friend from childhood / employee

Susan and Helen, (24, 26)
Friends from Barnard / employees

Micah (23)
Marjorie's boyfriend

Aaron (18)
Marjorie's brother / employee

Mildred (11)
Orphan Train girl

Marilyn and Julie (25, 26)
Lesbian friends

For Deborah and Miriam, securing a family is paramount. Following the loss of their beloved Bubbie and Miriam's mother, they pull their friends into a tighter circle. These courageous friends become part of their new and unorthodox family.

Other Characters

(Ages in December 1914)

Elizabeth (16)
Daughter of Suffragette

Mrs. Stern (37)
Mother of 3 girls / Cohens' cook

Leah (13)
Neighborhood girl in wheelchair

Rachel Stern (17)
Lowell Mill girl / childminder

Rebecca Stern (16)
Rachel's sister / employee

Rivkah Stern (14)
Rachel's sister

Sadie (20)
Volunteer at Denison House

Benjamin (15)
Rivkah's boyfriend

Along with their friends, Deborah and Miriam surround others in their orbit with love, respect, support, and ways to grow.

DANGER

FROM INFECTION OF

DIPHTHERIA

WITHIN

Entrance to or exit from these premises is prohibited without permission of the Medical Officer of Health.

CHAPTER 1

Sarah

December 1914

"What do you mean you're home early because of diphtheria?"

"They sent all the volunteers home because several folks at the settlement house are sick."

"This is serious, Miriam," Deborah said shrilly. "Some people die from diphtheria."

"I know." Taking a deep gulp and carelessly dropping her heavy blue coat onto the chair, Miriam said, "The truth is, one little girl at Denison House died today."

"Oh no! That's horrible. Did you know the child?"

"Yes. She was the sister of one of the children I tutor."

Deborah looked at Miriam, surveying her for signs of illness. Her sweet face looked as lovely as usual, though her typically bright eyes had no luster. "Do you think you've been exposed?"

"Maybe. The little girl who died came into the tutoring room last week, looking for her sister because she wasn't feeling well," Miriam said, her voice shaking. "The nurse at Denison House told us we'd already be sick if we got it from the child who died, but I'm scared. It is spreading quickly throughout the building and all of Boston. Just being there today has put me at risk."

"This is frightening. I'm scared for you."

"And for all of us, especially the babies. Diphtheria seems to hit children hardest."

"What shall we do? Should we contact the doctor? Do you need to go to the hospital?"

"Not right now."

"How would you know if you have it?" Deborah asked, her eyebrows wrinkled.

"The nurse explained our necks would become thick and swollen or we'd get a croup-like cough that sounds like a seal barking."

"I'm concerned for your welfare," Deborah said softly. "I'll take care of you. We'll get through this together."

"I'll be fine. But I worry about Sylvia. Maybe I should isolate myself. I can stay in our bedroom and you can move into her room."

"That's a good idea. I'll sleep in the bed next to her crib."

"I'm glad we got her an elevated wicker crib. I didn't think she'd still be in it at almost three years old, but it seems safer than putting her in a bed. I'd worry she would fall out of a bed. Special children need that extra safety."

"Look at you, concerned about Sylvia when you've just been exposed to a serious illness. But I do think it's a good idea you isolate yourself."

Deborah offered to talk to their cook. "I'll tell Mrs. Stern to deliver all your meals to outside your door. That way she'll not be exposed."

"And she'll not pass it on to Sylvia," Miriam said.

Deborah shook her head. "How long do you need to isolate?"

"I've no idea," Miriam said.

Changing into a nightdress, Miriam headed into isolation with a pile of books.

Deborah explained the situation to their housemates, Helen and Susan. The couple, their old friends from Barnard College, had come to Boston to help Deborah and Miriam run their publishing business. Not only did the arrangement assist Deborah and Miriam, but it meant Helen and Susan could live together as a couple, something they could not do without revealing their relationship to their families in New York. The four women and Sylvia made a lovely family unit, and now Deborah was especially thankful for their friends' presence.

"Any symptoms yet?" Deborah asked at Miriam's door just before bedtime, glad Miriam couldn't see the stress etched on her face.

Luckily the answer was "No."

Deborah panicked the next morning when Miriam announced she had a significant sore throat. Deborah tried to remain calm, brushing strands of her dark, unruly hair off her face. Peeking in the doorway, she thought Miriam's skin looked paler than usual. "What can I do for you?"

"Nothing right now. Luckily, diphtheria is often not serious in adults, and I'm 21 now. So even if I'm sick, my biggest concern is protecting our fragile Sylvia. I'm worried her medical problems will make her more susceptible."

"And what about your niece, Sarah? She's only six months old and she's here every day."

"I worry for her too. Could you ask Rachel to care for the two babies at Hannah and William's home for the next few days?"

By the afternoon, Rachel, the young woman they had hired to work as a caretaker for the children, transferred the young ones to Miriam's sister Hannah's place. By now, it was clear Miriam was ill with a fever and a hoarse voice.

Deborah stayed home from work and paced the floor outside their bedroom, asking questions about Miriam's health through the slightly open door. Then Deborah heard a barking cough, convincing her this was diphtheria.

"Shall I send for the doctor?"

"I guess so," Miriam said weakly.

Deborah wasn't able to reach the doctor directly on their still new telephone. His wife explained he was visiting other sick patients and he'd get to Miriam as soon as possible.

Two hours later, Deborah stood outside their bedroom door as the doctor examined Miriam. She tried to hear their conversation but heard nothing except for Miriam's raspy cough and the doctor's muffled voice. Deborah waited for the diagnosis she was certain she'd hear.

"Diphtheria, but a mild case. I've given her some antitoxin, but I've no worries about her full recovery."

"Thank you, Doctor," said Deborah, tears running down her face.

The doctor explained Miriam would be as good as new within a week or so. He asked about the other members of the household and was pleased Miriam had isolated herself. He encouraged them to keep the children away from Miriam until the last of her sore throat.

While Miriam improved, Hannah suggested Sylvia stay at her home, though Deborah worried about Hannah managing the two children. Rachel, as often was the case, was the answer to her concerns. Their wonderful childminder offered to stay late at Hannah and William's house, caring for the two girls until they were ready for bed. Because Rachel regularly put Sylvia to bed for naps, the child was quite calm about this change in her routine.

Hannah's new self-assurance, gained from being married and a parent, made it manageable. By the second night she sent Rachel home early and put the two children to bed by herself. Parenting was becoming natural to her.

But during the night, Hannah awakened to Sarah's cries. Once in the baby's bedroom, she was shocked to see her infant red-faced and covered in sweat.

She picked up the feverish child, listening to the cough she recognized as the sound of croup. Holding the child tightly in her arms, she scurried into the bedroom, awakening William from a deep sleep.

"Sarah is sick, William," Hannah cried. "I am certain it is diphtheria. We must get her to Children's Hospital. Do you think we can find the new location on Longwood Avenue in the dark?"

Assuring her he could find his way, William dressed quickly.

"I do not want to take Sylvia with us to the hospital and expose her further to this illness," Hannah said as she put on an old, loose fitting dress, hiding the fact she didn't have time for proper undergarments.

"But Sylvia has already been exposed. She was sleeping in the same room as Sarah for two nights and she was with her all day."

"You are right. We must tell Deborah and Miriam what is happening. They need to decide about Sylvia."

"We can stop by their house on the way to the hospital," said William.

"It is the middle of the night. Do you think we should wake them?"

"Yes, I do."

Hannah dressed her own baby first, bundling her tightly, and handing her to William. Then she picked up Sylvia, wrapping her in a blanket. Sylvia squirmed, but fell back to sleep. After putting on their heavy winter coats, Hannah and William, holding the children, walked carefully in the dark to the car. Hannah shivered yet barely noticed the cold night air as she sat with the two babies while William maneuvered through Boston's silent streets.

When they arrived at Deborah and Miriam's home, William walked quietly to the door, knocked, but heard nothing. Then he rang the bell. Immediately lights flickered on the second floor and Deborah appeared.

"Sarah is sick with diphtheria and we are taking her to the hospital," he said matter-of-factly. "Do you want us to take Sylvia with us to have her checked?"

"Is she showing symptoms?" asked Deborah, pulling her messy dark hair away from her face and tightly wrapping her shawl around herself.

"None. But she was sleeping in Sarah's room."

"How sick is Sarah?"

"She has a high fever and a bad cough."

"If Sylvia has no symptoms, give her to me. I'll bring her to the hospital tomorrow if she shows any signs of illness."

As Deborah lifted Sylvia from William's arms, she said, "I hope they're able to get Sarah's fever down quickly. I'll come in the morning, hopefully without Sylvia, to see how Sarah is doing."

Sylvia slept through the transfer to her own bed as Deborah stood over her, gazing at their sweet little girl. She loved her beautiful, round face and slightly slanted eyes, pleased she was sleeping so comfortably. When Deborah exited the bedroom, she found both Susan and Helen standing by.

"Sylvia seems fine," said Deborah, "but Sarah is sick, probably with diphtheria, so Hannah and William are taking her to Children's Hospital."

"Oh dear. I hope she'll recover quickly," said Susan.

"I hope so too." Deborah took a deep breath. Then she talked to her friends, making plans for tending to Sylvia until Rachel arrived in the morning.

Deborah was so happy to have Rachel, now eighteen years old, to help with the children. It was fortunate meeting Rachel at the settlement house where Deborah volunteered to help her write her story about her year working at the Lowell Mills. They stayed in touch, and Deborah and Miriam were delighted to have Rachel take over child care after Miriam's mother and her grandmother, Bubbie, both passed away. Their losses still made them ache, but their memories sustained them as Rachel helped to keep the family intact.

Deborah headed back to the bed next to Sylvia, sleeping fitfully, quietly checking the baby about once per hour. She hoped Miriam, asleep in the next room, wouldn't wake since there was no reason to worry her.

In the morning, after checking Sylvia thoroughly, Deborah stood outside Miriam's door explaining what had happened during the night.

"Hannah must be so scared. Do you think I'm too sick to be with Sylvia?" Miriam said, her voice still hoarse.

"Yes, my love. You need to rest. Susan and Helen will watch Sylvia while I go to the hospital to check on Sarah. I'll stay with Hannah and William for a while, then come back to check on you and Sylvia."

"Don't worry about me. I'm just concerned about Sylvia getting sick."

"I don't think being a Mongoloid makes her any more susceptible to this illness than other children."

"I hope not."

Trusting Sylvia was in good hands, Deborah drove to the hospital. On Longwood Avenue, she was impressed by the new medical building, with its striking architecture and large dome. This modern building was situated with a farm just outside its doors, with cows clustered close to the entrance, a striking contrast of old and new.

Once inside the lobby, she faced the dramatic circular stairs leading to the upper four levels. The floors glistened all the way up to the ward in the Hunnewell building, but she discovered they'd moved Sarah to an isolation room.

The antiseptic smell in the corridors overpowered Deborah. She found the correct room, with both Hannah and William dozing in chairs near Sarah. Not wanting to wake them, she went directly to the baby's crib. Sarah, recognizing Deborah's face, made a noise reminiscent of Miriam's raspy cough. Deborah tried to offer a smile yet was pained to see how sick the baby was. Hannah awoke to the sound of Sarah's bark.

"Thank you for coming, Deborah," Hannah said, yawning.

"How's Sarah?"

"Her fever is the same, but as you can hear, the cough is worse, she has a runny nose, and her neck is swollen. And now she has yellow spots on her skin and sores in her mouth. The doctor was pleased we brought her in so quickly so he could start the antitoxins right away, but I am really scared."

Deborah put her arms around Hannah, holding her while she wept. William woke up, frightened by Hannah's sobs.

"Did something happen?" he asked.

"No change, William. I am sorry to scare you."

"I am glad to hear that," he said, still fearful.

They'd sat for hours, afraid to hold Sarah for fear of catching the disease. They worried about becoming too sick to care for their own baby. Sarah was too weak to cry much.

Deborah sat with the concerned parents, trying to comfort them, though worrying about Miriam. She went to Sarah's crib before leaving, quietly reciting the *Mi Sheberach*, a Jewish prayer for healing.

Deborah arrived home to an almost empty house, with only the sound of Miriam's cough filling the silence. Susan and Helen had gone to the publishing shop, and Rachel had taken Sylvia to Denison House, the settlement house where her mother, Mrs. Stern, was using the kitchen to prepare food for everyone.

Deborah checked regularly on Miriam, who didn't seem to need her. During the afternoon, she headed to the shop, greeted by Marjorie, Miriam's sweet childhood friend and now a shop employee. Marjorie, dressed in a soft green dress with lace trim, leaned in, wanting to know all the details about Miriam and Sarah's health. After assuring her both were being well cared for, Deborah gave the others a similar update, then helped everyone to prioritize their projects. She was pleased to feel needed. Due to Miriam and Sarah's illnesses, she announced the printing and publishing shop would shut for a couple days, to ensure no spread of the disease.

Deborah arrived home to find Miriam napping and coughing, but claiming to be no worse. The next morning, with Miriam no sicker, Deborah stopped by the hospital again.

Hannah greeted her with a grin. "Her temperature is down, and she's on the way to recovery. She's sleepy and weak, but I saw a smile, which thrilled me."

After just a few minutes, Deborah headed home, anxious to tell Miriam the good news.

By the third day, Deborah persuaded Hannah to go home for a few hours to take a bath and change her clothes with William taking his turn later. Over the next couple of days both Sarah and Miriam improved.

On day five, Deborah arrived home from work to find Miriam in the kitchen.

"What are you doing downstairs?"

Miriam smiled. "I was hungry. I think it's a good sign. And I want to report that my sore throat is gone."

Deborah quickly moved to put her arms around Miriam in their first hug in days.

"Don't get any ideas," said Miriam, smirking. "I'm not ready for anything more than a hug."

Deborah relaxed and smiled too, pleased the illness was passing and Miriam's humor had returned.

Assuming Miriam was no longer contagious, Deborah moved back into their bedroom. Despite Miriam's insistence she was only ready for a hug, as they held each other tightly a spark passed between them. Deborah stroked her lovingly as Miriam initiated tender, intimate kisses. As they touched each other's bodies, their breathing became heavy. Their arousal was gentle, with puffs of excited breath. Miriam led them to a gentle session of loving, with quiet relief in their bodies and hearts.

In the morning, Deborah and Miriam traveled to Hannah and William's house to surprise Sylvia. Somehow Sylvia had escaped the dreaded disease. When Rachel arrived to care for Sylvia, she was surprised to find Miriam recovered. Deborah drove them all home, but Sylvia resisted being taken from Miriam. Instead, Miriam joined them in the playroom, where they both helped Sylvia practice walking independently, which she'd not yet perfected.

Miriam was finally strong enough to visit Sarah and Hannah at the hospital and when she and Deborah walked into the sickroom, Hannah burst into tears. The sisters embraced, relieved both patients were recovering and grateful for

Miriam's self-imposed isolation. By the end of the week, Sarah was home and, except for a slight lingering cough, was her regular sweet self.

Gradually everyone except Miriam returned to work, focused on sending notes to their customers, explaining the shop had been shuttered for illness. They hoped to eventually catch up.

While recovering, Miriam worried about her weekly volunteer work at Denison House, fearing the young children she tutored might feel abandoned. She penned a note, asking about the health of the residents and explaining her own illness. Deborah delivered the letter and returned with messages of hope for Miriam's return and tempting information about a new child for her to tutor.

Deborah shared that the child Miriam was to tutor, an eight-year-old girl named Florence, was rejected by her family. Prior to being at Denison House, she had lived at the Experimental School for Feeble-Minded Children, the same place where they had taken Sylvia for a consultation. Little Florence was far behind on her lessons, and Miriam was immediately interested in tutoring her.

Deborah invited this girl to their home, fascinated to hear how she had fared at the school. Florence explained she was placed at the school with an unknown illness. Once there, she was cured by a doctor, who attributed her bad behavior to a serious case of pellagra, a skin disease that also had mental changes.

Deborah wondered whether it was Sylvia's doctor, Dr. Kingsley, who had saved this child. Could Sylvia have a similar illness, possibly causing her to be Mongoloid? Could she too be cured?

Curious and a tiny bit hopeful, Deborah invited Florence to continue coming to their house so she could write this girl's story for the Denison House Newsletter and so Miriam could tutor her. In her heart, Deborah also hoped to find a cure for Sylvia.

Deborah soon learned that Florence's symptoms had no similarities to Sylvia's. Once Florence's swollen hands and intestinal disorder had subsided, so had her frequent outbursts. Deborah listened with great interest to the wonderful care she received at the school, trusting the good doctor who remedied Florence's illness was the same person guiding Sylvia's development.

(SEE ADDENDUM "FLORENCE: THE GIRL WITH PELLAGRA")

"I'm so relieved you are well," Deborah said softly, sitting in their bedroom wing chairs one evening. "I was so worried about you. I don't know how I'd manage if you died from diphtheria—or anything else. I've come to rely on you."

"I worry about you too. I don't know how either of us would do without each other. It's as if we're two halves of a whole." Miriam said, sighing.

"It's so good we found each other. How would either of us have coped with everything we've faced since we met?"

Miriam attempted a smile. "You have been incredibly important to me, with both Mother and Bubbie dying this past year. But life is lonely without them, and it's not enough—having Hannah as my family. I'm looking for this year to be a time of expansion, a time to increase our connections with others."

"Wait a minute. Miriam. What are you talking about? We have so much more than we have had in the past. We have a child, a thriving business, and some friends who are like us. What more do we need? You're not thinking again about how we need to have a houseful of children to be a real family?"

"No. I wasn't thinking of that at all. Not that I wouldn't like it, but no, I'm thinking of how we need to create a new family."

"What a foolish idea. We can't make up for the loss of Mother and Bubbie by adding others," Deborah huffed.

"We can get closer to those around us, and we've made a start. My friend Marjorie and her family feel a bit like family since we've been spending the Jewish holidays with them. And the Berkowitzes already feel like family even though they live far away."

"New York is not far, Miriam."

"No. But it's too far for us to keep up with their four girls regularly. Children change so quickly. Each time I see them they seem so different."

"You're right. They do. Even my sister and brother seem changed each visit even though they aren't children anymore," said Deborah.

"So, let's work towards increased connections with those we love."

Life went on at home as if they'd not faced terrible sickness and fear. As they lit the candles for their Chanukah holidays, Deborah and Miriam reflected each night on the miracle of health, hoping the coming year would bring wellness and happiness to their chosen family.

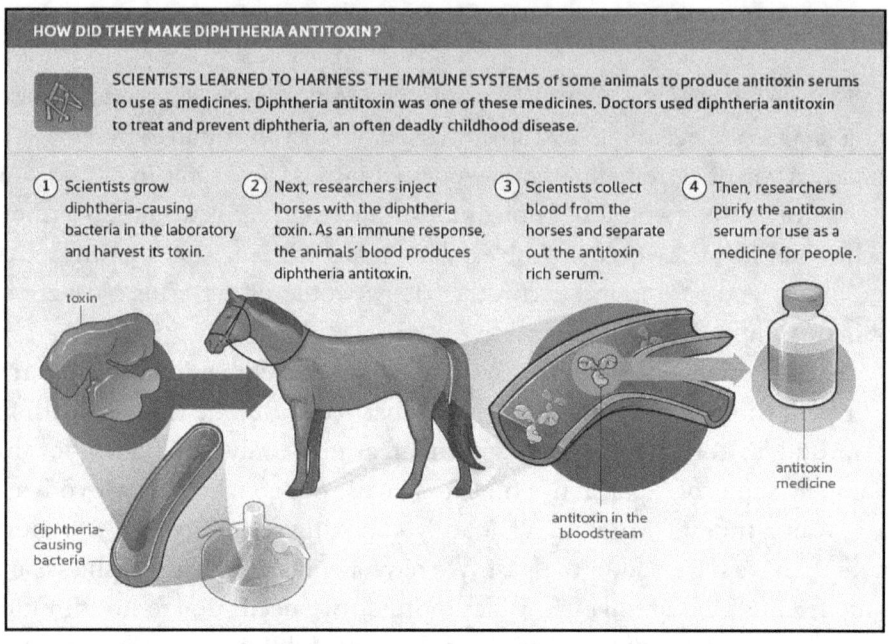

HOW DID THEY MAKE DIPHTHERIA ANTITOXIN?

SCIENTISTS LEARNED TO HARNESS THE IMMUNE SYSTEMS of some animals to produce antitoxin serums to use as medicines. Diphtheria antitoxin was one of these medicines. Doctors used diphtheria antitoxin to treat and prevent diphtheria, an often deadly childhood disease.

1. Scientists grow diphtheria-causing bacteria in the laboratory and harvest its toxin.

2. Next, researchers inject horses with the diphtheria toxin. As an immune response, the animals' blood produces diphtheria antitoxin.

3. Scientists collect blood from the horses and separate out the antitoxin rich serum.

4. Then, researchers purify the antitoxin serum for use as a medicine for people.

toxin

diphtheria-causing bacteria

antitoxin in the bloodstream

antitoxin medicine

Boston Children's Hospital, 1914

CHAPTER 2

Dr. Hubbard

January 1915

*A*fter Chanukah, Deborah was grateful for Miriam and Sarah's recovery from diphtheria. She thought about how life could otherwise have taken a horrible turn and was lost in troubling thoughts when she received an interesting letter, which changed her focus.

"Miriam, look what was in the mail. A note from Dr. Hubbard," Deborah said, not realizing Miriam had left the room. She tore open the letter.

January 8, 1915

Dear Deborah,

I'd like to inform you that your article, "Parents of Young Women," will be published in the popular magazine, "Ladies' World." Also, I've submitted another of your articles to this same publication, and I'm hopeful it too will be accepted.

I've reviewed the other articles you sent, and I continue to be impressed with your writing talent and your remarkable insight into the topics you explore. I believe many of your articles could spur wonderful conversations among young girls at Barnard College, so I'd like your permission to assign some of them to my students.

I'd also like to invite you to be a guest speaker to discuss your writing. Would you be available within the next month? The bonus will be that we can finally meet face-to-face.

Please continue to send articles.

Sincerely,
Dr. Grace A. Hubbard
Associate Professor of English, Barnard College

Deborah paced around the living room, which still looked just as it did when she met Miriam's family, over four years earlier. Dressed in her usual tailored skirt and blouse, unlike the popular frilly style of many girls of the times, she dropped onto the well-worn, comfortable velvet couch and stared at the letter.

Miriam arrived with their two-year-old in her arms, and Deborah told her about the letter. She talked quickly, with Miriam straining to understand her.

"It's exciting," Miriam said. "You seem as thrilled as when you first saw your name in print in Dr. Hubbard's book."

"I can hardly believe she values my writing enough to invite me to speak to students who are close to my age. What an honor!"

"I'm so proud of you. When do you think you'll go?"

"There are no Jewish holidays until *Tu Bishvat*, which falls on a weekend at the end of the month, so anytime is fine with me." Deborah rambled on about what she would say to the students, hardly noticing Miriam.

Deborah packed carefully for her visit to Barnard College, excited until a large printing order arrived the afternoon prior to her departure. "I can't leave you to do this without me," she said, wide-eyed.

"Certainly you can," Miriam said, smiling. "You can't get out of your talk so easily, nor can you disappoint Dr. Hubbard."

Deborah was comforted when Miriam suggested inviting Fannie, the oldest daughter of their mentor, Mrs. Berkowitz, to help them during her school vacation the next week. Mrs. B. always seemed the answer to their challenges, so it seemed fitting to select her daughter.

"What a great solution. You're so clever, dear."

"I'll call New York and ask Fannie to come to Boston," Miriam said, pleased to have an excuse to use their relatively new and still mysterious telephone.

On the train to New York, Deborah reviewed the large pile of articles on her lap, some to discuss with the students and others to share with Dr. Hubbard. In the stack was an article about their old friend and often nemesis, Ruth. It made her anxious to think about writing a book about this challenging young woman, so she wrote a letter to Mrs. B. about her concerns.

January 18, 1915

Dear Mrs. B.,

 As usual, I'm writing you about a concern. Miriam is convinced it would be rewarding for me to write a book about Ruth, her self-centered camp friend who introduced us and who ultimately gave us her unwanted child. Miriam innocently thinks the book would be a testament to the young woman who bore our daughter, Sylvia. I'm not convinced. Miriam seems to have forgotten how difficult and selfish Ruth is, though I'm acutely aware of that fact.

 When I think back to when Ruth rejected her newborn and we stepped in to care for the baby, I remember we had no thoughts of keeping the child. It was only after she decided to put her Mongoloid infant into an institution, that we considered it. I recall writing to you about the enormity of this responsibility, finally deciding to take on Sylvia's care, despite my initial reluctance.

 The book has become quite an issue between us. Miriam hopes to someday share Ruth's story with Sylvia, although I wonder whether Sylvia will ever comprehend. Miriam wants me to highlight Ruth's good qualities, yet the first article I've written is not complimentary at all and I've not shown to it Miriam.

 Now, Miriam has requested that I discuss this potential book about Ruth with Dr. Hubbard, the professor at Barnard who is helping me publish articles. I'm on my way to New York right now to be a guest lecturer in her class, which is quite a thrill, but it makes my stomach clench to think of discussing this book. If I continue to be honest, everything I write would belittle Ruth, no matter how hard I try. Also, I fear that someday Ruth will read my story and feel betrayed. It isn't my intention to hurt anyone.

 I want to please Miriam, which is why I am considering writing this book. What do you think?

 My trip to New York will be quick, so I doubt I'll have time to visit with you and your family. I'll let you know if I can fit in a short visit.

Love,
Deborah

If Dr. Hubbard thought the idea for a book was viable, Deborah needed to take her task seriously, even before hearing from Mrs. B. She needed to meet with Ruth while she was in New York. Having never spent any time alone with Ruth, she hoped a visit would provide insight into her central character. *Oh my—I'm beginning to think like an author.*

Deborah reread the article she'd written and took out a pen to write another about Ruth, hoping she could be more empathetic. She found it impossible. She wrote what was in her heart, but it wasn't flattering.

RUTH'S FRIENDSHIPS

Ruth has always been insecure about her friendships. She has a wonderful ability to attract others, yet none of the young people who flock to her gatherings become real friends. None of them invite her privately to their homes, nor to join them on shopping trips. She is never included in small gatherings of young girls who share their innermost secrets with one another. At Ruth's parties, the others politely listen to her ramblings, but at others' parties, no one pays attention to her.

Ruth has no insight into her own shortcomings. She does not understand how her focus on herself pushes people away....

Deborah's heart pounded. Despite her best effort, each story was full of criticism. Her concerns about writing a book denouncing this girl made her chest hurt. She struggled about whether she could pretend to write something positive, while actually chastising Ruth on every page. Deborah didn't want to disappoint Miriam, but she didn't think herself capable of writing fiction.

Deborah thought of her invitation for tea with Dr. Hubbard the next day, an opportunity to meet before her appearance in the classroom. How many new articles should she share? Could she ask about the other submissions Dr. Hubbard had made? Should she mention Miriam's idea of a book about Ruth? Deborah felt like pacing the floor. Instead, she sat quietly in the comfortable train seat, with her hands trembling and moisture collecting around her neck and under her arms.

Mr. Levine met his daughter at Grand Central Station. She spotted him immediately, recognizing his professional lawyer suit, even on his day off.

"Welcome home!" he called out from a distance. Deborah knew she wouldn't mention she now considered Boston her home.

He approached with a hug and warm greeting. On the way to their luxurious apartment on Riverside Drive, Deborah's father asked questions about the publishing business. Deborah was pleased to talk about the shop and to ask his opinions about business matters. They'd developed a satisfying new relationship recently, both putting aside the lengthy strain between them after he learned of her relationship with Miriam.

At home, Deborah found her mother cheerful. There was no lingering sign of her mental breakdown almost a year earlier. All seemed normal, except that her brother Milton was absent much of the time, busy with classes at Columbia College. He excitedly awaited his eighteenth birthday, which meant he could enlist in the army and fight in the war, should it reach American shores. At nineteen he'd be eligible to fight abroad in Europe.

Deborah also looked forward to spending time with Anna, her younger sister, who loved being the center of attention. At fifteen, her world was full and exciting. Deborah expected to hear many stories of adolescent drama.

On Thursday Deborah donned the new outfit her mother surprised her with for this special occasion. "This is lovely, Mother. It was sweet of you to buy me new clothes. I really love the white shirt and tailored dark skirt. They fit perfectly."

"I'm pleased you like it. I must tell you, dear, your regular clothing is looking a bit tattered and stained."

"I wear my dresses every day at the shop, and I've not bought any new clothing since moving to Boston. Thanks to you I'll look stylish in front of Dr. Hubbard's class this afternoon."

Deborah took a deep breath before saying, "I'm really nervous about today. I'm not a college student, and I'm afraid I'll sound ignorant in front of all those educated girls."

"I'm certain you'll do a wonderful job. You're bright and articulate. You'll impress them by being yourself."

"I appreciate your faith in me. I hope I do as well as you predict."

Deborah got a ride from the family's driver the short distance to Barnard College, remembering the first time she entered the huge ornate gates at the school's entrance. She also thought of the other times she had passed through them when volunteering for *The Bulletin,* the Barnard College newsletter, and for suffrage meetings. So much had changed in her life since then.

Deborah was now settled with Miriam, they had a wonderful daughter, and they owned a thriving Yiddish publishing and printing business with Miriam's sister, Hannah, and her husband, William. And most importantly, at the moment, Deborah was now a published author. She glowed, thinking of how fortunate she was.

As planned, they met in Dr. Hubbard's office, down the hall from the room where Deborah would lecture. "You must be Deborah," said Dr. Hubbard. "It's a great pleasure to finally meet you."

"The pleasure is mine, Dr. Hubbard," Deborah said, shaking her hand, hoping the professor didn't notice her moist palm. She was surprised by Dr. Hubbard's appearance. Somehow, she'd expected someone younger, taller, and more severe. Instead, she saw in the older woman with graying hair a resemblance to her beloved Bubbie. Although Dr. Hubbard's features were dissimilar, she had the same warm eyes and soft figure of Miriam's grandmother. The professor was more polished in her dress, but Deborah could imagine Dr. Hubbard putting on a house-dress and welcoming everyone into her home with tea and cookies. This familiarity helped Deborah feel less nervous.

Deborah looked around the room, as Dr. Hubbard walked around her wooden desk to sit in her leather seat. Deborah's eyes landed on a framed letter. "Dr. Grace A. Hubbard has the distinction of being listed in *Who's Who in America in 1914*." Deborah certainly had an impressive woman as her mentor.

While drinking tea in the crowded lunchroom at Fiske Hall, Deborah relaxed. They found a cozy corner for an animated discussion about Deborah's writing. Dr. Hubbard spoke of the submissions she'd made to magazines and asked Deborah to write articles on topics related to parenting, which might appeal to other publications. Just before they headed to the lecture, Deborah gathered her courage and brought up the idea of writing a book.

"What a splendid idea! I'd be pleased to advise you on this project. Have you thought of a topic?"

Deborah began talking about Ruth, but they needed to cut the discussion short to get to the classroom for the lecture. Once seated at the front of the room, Deborah was wringing her hands and sweating profusely.

"Be calm, my dear. You'll be a great success today. Just answer the queries I pose to you and I'm certain you'll stimulate interesting questions from the students. After all, many of them aspire to be as successful in their lives as you already are."

Even after Dr. Hubbard's kind words, Deborah's palms remained damp. She looked around at the young women—mostly in white shirts, tailored dark skirts, and hair piled on their heads—and was pleased she looked the part of a college girl, thanks to her mother.

Seated in front of the students, Dr. Hubbard introduced her, and then asked, "How old were you when you knew you wanted to be a writer?" After a simple answer, during which Deborah relaxed, the professor moved to a more difficult question. "How do you write objectively when the subject is something that moves you deeply?"

Deborah forgot her nervousness, answering, "I'm not objective. Everything I write comes from my heart. Certainly, I try to evaluate other perspectives so I can explain a rationale for my opinion, but what I state is my personal view of each topic I write about."

A student raised her hand, not waiting for the allotted time for questions, and asked, "Do you ever write something which is a stretch of the truth?"

"No, I never have, but I'm facing a challenge right now, regarding truth versus fiction. I'm wondering if it's possible to convert fabrications into something believable. I struggle with this regarding the book I'm about to write."

The student responded. "I'm so impressed you're writing a book. Please tell us more."

"I haven't started yet, but I've been asked to write about a person I don't respect. I may need to change her characteristics in order for readers to empathize with her."

"Why would you write about someone you don't like?" came a voice from the rear.

"I've been asked by a good friend to write this book to gather information about this girl's decision to give up her child."

"Is this the child you write about?" asked another student.

"Yes, but the point is I need to make her a sympathetic character the reader will want to hear about."

"Maybe you should make her into a villain," said another voice. "Anyone who gives up their child would certainly be one."

Dr. Hubbard stopped the personal nature of this conversation by asking the students if any of them had written about someone they considered a scoundrel. After a short discussion of this topic, she returned the focus to Deborah.

"Please tell us, Deborah, about your writing practice. When do you write? Do you have patterns as to the environment you choose, such as only in daylight or in total silence? What can you tell us?"

Deborah happily responded, pleased to have the topic switch from her discomfort about Ruth to more concrete questions. She was no longer perspiring.

The hour passed quickly in lively conversation, leaving Deborah no time to worry. After the last student had left, Dr. Hubbard said, "The discussion went perfectly, just as I predicted. I knew you would be appreciated. And you and I can discuss your conflicted thoughts about your book topic."

"Ruth's a challenge to write about, without sounding mean-spirited."

"Then we shall talk about this through letters, once you've sent me a sample of your first pages."

"It will be a while. I really need to write about her as she is, then see if I can make her a more pleasing character."

"You've set yourself quite a challenge for your first book, but I've great faith in your writing, so I look forward to reading whatever you write."

Glowing, Deborah shrugged her shoulders and said, "Thank you." As she walked out, she thought about telling her family in New York and everyone back in Boston of her great success as a guest lecturer.

On her way back to Riverside Drive, Deborah settled into the back seat, ignoring the driver her father had sent. She shivered, wrapping her scarf tighter around her neck. She read in the newspaper that the day before had been only three degrees, one of the coldest days in recorded history. To take her mind off the chilling temperature, she pulled out paper to make notes about her experience, but her fingers were too stiff. She decided to wait to write back in her old bedroom.

Deborah's Journal, January 31, 1915

What an exciting day I've had; I never felt so important. Talking to Dr. Hubbard's class was one of the highlights of my life. I was thrilled to hear the students talk about my articles as if I was the smartest person they ever met. Even though I'm practically their age, they called me "insightful" and "wise," words I never heard in reference to me before.

And Dr. Hubbard was wonderful. She treated me like a peer, not a girl who could have been her student. Her excitement about my articles, as well as her encouragement of my continued writing, makes me feel accomplished and capable.

I really love the idea of writing a book, though I don't know if I can manage to write about Ruth. I'd like to write about practically anything else, but Miriam wants it so desperately I'll give it a try.

Miriam dreams of having a child who will ask normal questions about the girl who was her mother, but truthfully I don't expect Sylvia to ever ask those questions. Her comprehension is far behind other children her age, though I don't want to spoil Miriam's hopes. I know how much she wanted to be a mother. It's in Miriam's heart to have a houseful of little ones running underfoot. I hope Sylvia will be enough for her.

I'll visit Ruth tomorrow if she'll see me. Maybe visiting her will make it clear to me whether this book is possible.

Barnard College tea time

The Ladies' World March 1915

CHAPTER 3

Ruth

February 1915

"I'm glad you agreed to meet with me while I'm in New York," said Deborah, brushing snow from her coat at Ruth and Michael's front door. Avoiding Ruth's gaze, Deborah focused her attention on the apartment's fancy furnishings and Ruth's coiffured hair, barely noticing Ruth's overzealous smile and piercing eyes.

Ruth, greeting Deborah with a hug, said enthusiastically, "I've never spent time alone with you, so I was delighted when you suggested getting together, but I worried you wouldn't get here because of all the snow."

Deborah, undeterred in her mission, felt a pang of guilt, knowing Ruth would feel differently if she knew the real reason for this visit. "I'm pleased to see you," Deborah said quietly, hoping Ruth wouldn't notice her hesitancy as she mouthed this partial lie.

Ruth, as usual, was oblivious. In a singsong manner that lightened every word, Ruth said, "I don't have many visitors, so I'm pleased to show off my lovely home to you."

As they walked through the house, Ruth chatted nonstop, commenting on each cherished possession. Deborah barely had time to examine one item before Ruth described the next. Ruth consistently mentioned the store where it was purchased, often commenting on the high cost with a frequent refrain: "I just had to have this."

Deborah was awed by the extravagant furnishings. Michael was still in school so it was likely everything was purchased with family money. Shopping was obviously her favorite pastime.

Deborah asked about Michael, but Ruth dismissed him, making statements such as "He's not interested in the finer things in life" or "He's so rarely here, he hardly notices my new purchases." Ruth referred to her husband as "a wild young man," making him sound immature. Her comments made Deborah wonder if he was still engaged in their marriage.

Deborah steered the conversation to Ruth's background, asking, "Which items are from your childhood?"

"I don't have pleasant memories of my youth, so everything is new."

"I'm sorry to hear that."

Ruth seemed pleased to discuss her difficulties. "I really shouldn't say anything, but … when I was young, my parents weren't usually present. My father worked a great deal so we could buy whatever we wanted. My mother was always at meetings, more interested in her friends than her children. My brother David was always an odd boy, withdrawn and bookish. Even now, he doesn't seem interested in having friends. Beth, my sister, follows my mother's tendencies; she's interested in fashion and making a good impression."

"And what about you? How would you describe yourself as a child?"

"I was lonely and never had friends. The happiest time in my life was at camp. All year I looked forward to the summer when Miriam and I would chat in our cabin until past 'lights out.' I was glad to have a real friend."

Deborah looked directly at Ruth, willing herself not to fall back into her pattern of internally berating Ruth for her self-absorbed manner. She benefited by keeping the focus on Ruth, gaining perspective on her.

After the tour of Ruth's belongings ended, they sat down to tea, served by her cook in elegant gold-rimmed cups. As Ruth passed bite-sized biscuits of freshly baked buttery pastry, she commented about how she should resist because she'd put on several pounds. Deborah noticed Ruth's waist was no longer narrow, but despite her comments, Ruth ate several treats.

As Ruth continued her irritating patter, Deborah wondered if she'd ask about her welfare, or Miriam's. Ruth did not, nor did she mention Sylvia. It amazed Deborah that she never acknowledged this baby existed, or that she'd been the girl to bear her. Deborah couldn't imagine being so detached. It made her question how Ruth really felt about giving Sylvia away.

Ruth continued the one-sided commentary about herself until Deborah tired of this self-indulgence and said she needed to return to her parents' home.

"Please visit again anytime you're in New York," Ruth said, smiling.

Deborah held her breath, afraid Ruth would ask to return to Boston, but she didn't. Deborah bundled up to protect herself against the cold and maneuvered carefully to avoid the large piles of snow on the walkway. All the way home she thought about Ruth's self-centeredness, wondering if she could tolerate her a bit more for the sake of the book Miriam wanted her to write.

On Deborah's return to Boston, Hannah and William picked her up at South Station train depot. Deborah loved the vast station, with its magnificent, vaulted ceilings, huge arched windows, and mosaic marble floor. In the car, Deborah talked excitedly about her successful experience at Barnard College as Hannah and William listened intently but silently.

At home, Miriam greeted Deborah with open arms, embracing her as if they'd been apart for more than a few days. They sat in the parlor, Miriam anxious to hear about Deborah's time in New York. Deborah talked on and on, first about her experience as a guest lecturer, telling Miriam as many details as she could remember. She left no space for Miriam to ask questions or comment, but just rambled on. Deborah did not notice Miriam's eyes glazing over during her long monologue. When she finally took a breath, Miriam made a few supportive comments and then asked about Deborah's time with her family.

When Deborah discussed her parents and siblings, Miriam was more engaged. "Being with my family was lovely. My father constantly praised me for the wonderful job I've done supervising the printing shop. I'm glad he's proud of me but I told him the business requires a joint effort between you, Hannah, William, and me working together to get anything done. Nevertheless he has it in his head I'm the reason the business is running so well."

"I think you're what holds us together, though I'd never admit it to the others," said Miriam.

"How sweet of you to say," said Deborah, not revealing she too believed there was some truth to her father's statement.

Miriam asked, "How did you find the rest of your family?"

"Though I saw Milton only a bit, our time together was enjoyable. He's a fine young man with wonderful scruples. I respect him, yet I worry about his interest in fighting for our country, should we become involved in the war overseas. Anna was as delightful as always; she lights up a room."

"I admire the way you've shifted your relationships with both your siblings. You no longer think of them as children."

"They aren't. Well, Milton isn't. I suspect Anna may always have a youthful exuberance, even as she reaches maturity."

"Let's hope. That would be a fine quality."

Deborah then told Miriam about her visit with Ruth. "You won't believe who I saw while in New York ... Ruth."

"I'm so surprised. Usually you can't tolerate her more than a few minutes."

"She does talk on and on about herself. I was interested in what she said, knowing I could use it in the book you asked me to write."

"I'm glad you're taking my advice and writing about her."

"I'm trying, but I'm not certain I can do it. First of all, I feel horribly guilty. She knows nothing about why I'm suddenly interested in her. I don't want to misrepresent myself and lead her on."

"I doubt she noticed," Miriam said.

"Now look at which of us is being critical. There is a second reason I'm unsure about this book. I'm worried I can't make it readable."

"What do you mean? Your writing is always easy to read."

"It's not about my writing skills; it's about the subject. I don't know how I can make Ruth likeable enough for anyone to want to read about her."

"Deborah, don't be so nasty."

"I'm not. I'm being realistic. Ruth is extremely self-centered; you've said that yourself. I was appalled she didn't ask a single question about you or Sylvia when I saw her."

"Were you surprised?"

"No, not really."

After a moment of deep thought, Miriam asked, "Would you feel comfortable asking Ruth to talk about her decision to give up Sylvia?"

"Miriam, I can't do that."

"But don't you wonder what her thinking was then, or what she has thought about it since? It must be the hardest thing she ever did."

"I'm not certain it was difficult for her. She's shown no interest in the child."

"She hasn't given us a hint about her feelings, but she had to feel something. After all, she carried the baby in her body and then gave birth to it," Miriam said, sighing.

"It is not an 'it.' It is our daughter you're talking about."

"I know." Deep sigh.

Suddenly, Deborah sat up straight, realizing she'd focused only on herself in much the way Ruth might have done. "I'm sorry. I've not asked you one single thing about your time while I was gone. How's Sylvia? How's everything at the shop?"

Miriam, realizing this conversation was difficult for Deborah, allowed the subject to change. After she caught Deborah up with all the comings and goings of the past few days, they headed to bed. After all, they had several days of loving to make up for.

Miriam's Diary, February 8, 1915

*I wonder why Deborah changed the discussion so abruptly when
I questioned Ruth's feelings regarding Sylvia. She clearly didn't want
to talk about it or even think about it. I'll bring up this topic again at
another time.*

*I'm so proud of Deborah. I always knew her writing was exceptional,
but Dr. Hubbard has helped her to believe in her own talents. The
experience of speaking to a group of students made her feel important.*

*Also, I'm pleased she's decided to write a book. I suggested she write
about Ruth because I hope she'll explore Ruth's decision to relinquish
Sylvia to us instead of to an institution. I hope Deborah learns things that
will help us explain our daughter's history to her when she's older. It will
be wonderful to have a tale for our child about the girl who bore her.*

*I'm very happy being Sylvia's mother, and I'm ashamed I look
at other families with envy when I see them coordinating the needs
of multiple children. I always imagined myself tucking a houseful of
children into bed after a wonderful day of play.*

Deborah wrote a bit every day, finding many gaps. "Do you think it would
be appropriate to write to Ruth for the missing information?" she asked Miriam.
"I'm concerned she'd read my interest in her as another gesture of friendship."

"She probably would, but your concerns are interfering with this project.
Maybe you should tell her you're writing about her. Honesty is usually best,"
Miriam said.

"What could I possibly say to her?"

"The truth. But you can phrase it so she feels honored you chose her, rather
than embarrassed you think her so selfish."

"How about this? 'Ruth, I'd like to write a book about you because you're
such an interesting person.'"

"That sounds a bit unbelievable if you just blurt it out," Miriam said. "What
if you say: 'Ruth, after talking to you at your home, I was fascinated with what
you told me. It made me want to learn more about you. I was thinking someday
Sylvia might want to know about the girl who gave birth to her.'"

"Do you really think Ruth will want Sylvia to know she was her mother?"

"I've no idea but maybe you could ask her. It is odd we never discussed
this with Ruth when we took Sylvia, nor since."

Deborah pursed her lips and took a few moments to think this over. "Telling someone I'm writing a story for her child would please most people, but probably not her. I really don't think she considers herself to be Sylvia's mother, though maybe I'm wrong. I'll avoid that topic until she really trusts me."

After more discussion, Deborah decided to ask Ruth if she could write a story, rather than a book, about her.

Deborah's Journal, February 15, 1915

Writing to Ruth feels an important step. I must phrase things carefully because, should Ruth reject the idea, the whole project would be at risk.

I'll show the letter to Miriam, who has become a fine editor, with many suggestions about how to improve my writing. I remember my frustration when Miriam refused to give me feedback, yet I read her wrong. It wasn't reluctance but fear her suggestions wouldn't be adequate. I'm grateful we discussed this, and I can now turn to her for her honest critique.

I wonder why Miriam chose a time like this to talk about Ruth being Sylvia's mother. She must have been thinking about it while I was gone. Otherwise, why would she interrupt my excitement about my speaking engagement to bring up such an issue? I hope she drops the topic.

Deborah waited anxiously for Ruth's response to her letter. Over two weeks later, a large package arrived in the mail, and Deborah realized why Ruth had taken so long to respond. Ruth had practically written a book herself. Ruth had, as Miriam assumed, been flattered with the attention. She wrote many stories about her childhood, detailing many things of little interest, but giving Deborah a great deal of material. The book was suddenly real.

Deborah's continued correspondence with Ruth was extensive. She sent questions to Ruth, who'd send back another packet of answers. Deborah worked night after night to place Ruth's experiences into a cohesive story.

Then Deborah felt she needed to talk with Ruth directly. "I've gathered a huge amount of material for the book," she said to Miriam as they walked in their neighborhood, pleased for an evening without blustery winds. "But I want the story to reflect Ruth's personality, not merely her words."

"How will you do that?"

"I'm afraid the only way would be to talk with her directly. Do you think we could invite Ruth for another visit?"

"I never thought I'd hear those words come from your lips."

While awaiting Ruth's visit, Deborah and Miriam had several conversations about Ruth. Deborah questioned whether Miriam thought of Ruth as part of their family.

"I've been thinking about your desire to create a new family. You don't want Ruth to be part of our family, do you?"

"She's sort of like a distant cousin," Miriam said. "But then, she is the actual mother of our child."

"I don't think she gets family status for birthing Sylvia. She's never behaved like a mother."

"No, she hasn't. I think our friends, Susan and Helen, feel more like family than Ruth does. They know much more about us and support us in ways she never could."

"Settled," Deborah said. "Ruth is not, and will never be, part of our family."

When Ruth arrived in Boston on a cold winter's day, Deborah picked her up at South Station, leaving Miriam at home to care for Sylvia.

"How wonderful to see you, Deborah," Ruth said in her typically upbeat manner.

"Nice to see you, too." Falsehoods were becoming easier because there was now a bit of truth to this comment, though not the way Ruth heard it.

Deborah struggled with the three valises Ruth had packed for her short stay. Ruth took the smallest of the cases, making a show of how difficult it was to manage. Deborah handled the other two and didn't offer to help poor weak Ruth.

Once in the car, Ruth began her patter. "It's been so nice to get to know you. In the past it was just Miriam who was my friend, but now you're my friend too."

Deborah was glad she had to focus on the driving because it would've been hard not to look at Ruth incredulously. How could Ruth see this as a friendship? Ruth had not learned one thing about Deborah. Ruth never noticed this, but for the purpose of the book Deborah was pleased Ruth felt comfortable with her.

Once at the house, Miriam took over, asking Ruth leading questions, including "How's Michael?" and "Have you heard from any of our old friends from Great Barrington?" Ruth needed little prompting to talk. Deborah listened intently to every word to familiarize herself with the cadence of Ruth's speech. She wished she could write down Ruth's comments to quote her exactly.

Susan and Helen were pleasant to Ruth, but after dinner that first evening, Susan knocked on Deborah and Miriam's bedroom door. She entered their room and quietly asked, "Would you two mind if we spent evenings on our own this week? We weren't able to have our usual conversations with you over dinner since Ruth took over. We'll have dinner with you as usual, but then we'll excuse ourselves, as we did this evening, if that's all right."

"I'm sorry," said Miriam. "I know she can be difficult. It'll be fine with us if you spend time on your own. After Ruth's monopolizing the conversation over dinner tonight, I'd be tempted to do the same if I could."

Over the next couple of days Ruth paid no attention when Sylvia entered the room and made no comments about the child, as if she didn't exist. Ruth seemed upset when Sylvia required attention or when Deborah or Miriam noted something especially adorable about their child. When Miriam remarked about how Sylvia had the same nose as Michael, Ruth stopped talking and stared at Miriam as if she'd no right to mention it. Her look of disgust was disturbing.

The four days dragged on. Either Deborah or Miriam came home from work early each day to entertain her, yet Ruth had a way of making them feel guilty for working. There were no thanks when they went out of their way. It was too cold to go outside, according to their fragile house guest, so they found indoor activities to interest Ruth, such as a puzzle, handiwork (which Miriam disliked and Deborah didn't do at all), or a game. Unless Ruth was winning, she often forgot to take her turn until prodded. And through everything Ruth talked. And talked.

After breakfast on Ruth's last day, Miriam surprised both Deborah and Ruth when she asked directly, "Ruth, would you be willing to talk with us about your decision to give up Sylvia?"

Ruth became pale and didn't notice Deborah's eyes widen.

"I don't think there is anything to discuss. I wasn't cut out to be a mother, though I didn't know until after the baby was born."

"But wasn't it difficult to give up your child?"

"Not really. If my parents and Michael weren't making me feel badly about not wanting the baby, it would have been easy to do."

"So, Michael wanted to keep the child?" Miriam asked.

"I really don't want to talk about this. Could I have another cup of tea?"

"Ruth, I'd really like to discuss this further," Miriam said with surprising determination. "Would you rather discuss this with me alone?"

"I'll go tend to Sylvia," Deborah said as she left the room, not waiting for Ruth's response.

Miriam nodded, noticing tears forming in Ruth's eyes. "So, was Michael upset with you for your decision to give up Sylvia?"

"Michael is always upset with me. I think it started then, but I'm not certain."

"Oh, Ruth, I'm so sorry."

"It isn't a good marriage, but it would have been an even worse marriage had I kept the child." Tears were streaming down her face now.

Miriam reached out and held her hand. "Why do you say that?"

"I really didn't want to be a mother to that infant. I'd have no patience for a child with problems. If she was normal, maybe I could have found some way to love her. I really meant it when I said I wasn't cut out to be a mother. I'm too selfish. I couldn't tolerate a child's needs being in the way of my getting what I want."

Miriam gulped, amazed Ruth had insight.

"Maybe that was because you never had enough love growing up."

"I didn't. Remember all those talks we had at camp? I really never felt loved and I wouldn't know how to love a child, especially one who needed me as much as that little girl."

"I'm impressed with how well you know yourself, but sad you feel this way," As she held her breath, Miriam asked, "Do you ever wish you'd not given up the baby?

"No, Miriam. You never have to worry I might want her back."

After an audible sigh, Miriam asked, "But what about Michael? Does he want you to take her back?"

"No. He really wants nothing to do with me or with any baby. He doesn't love me. He just stays with me because it's convenient. His parents pay all our bills while he's finishing school, and I run our household. He thinks he has an easy life. But it's devoid of love."

"I'm so sorry."

"I'm used to it, though I'm very lonely. I've no real friends, other than you and Deborah. I don't know why no one cares about me."

Ruth burst into sobs and Miriam held her. Miriam considered for a moment telling Ruth why no one could stand her for long, then decided Ruth didn't really want to hear the answer. Miriam held onto Ruth, wondering if this pathetic young woman was ever going to find happiness.

After a few minutes, Ruth said, "I need to go wash my face. I'm sorry to have burdened you."

"That's what friends are for."

Going back to their room, Miriam found Deborah waiting to hear about their conversation.

"Ruth's a sad person. Her marriage is very difficult. She has no friends and no love."

"Tell me more."

"No. I think I should keep her comments in confidence. You just need to know she'll never want Sylvia back."

"That's a relief. That has been a nagging concern for me since she became ours. Are you certain?"

"Absolutely. The good news from my conversation with Ruth is that I no longer need you to write a book about her. I now know enough about her and her motivation to give away Sylvia."

"That's why you wanted me to write a book about Ruth? I thought you wanted a story to tell Sylvia when she is older. That's what you said."

"Deborah, I thought a story for Sylvia was what I wanted. Now that I know her feelings about giving away her baby, I feel satisfied."

"So, what were her feelings?" Deborah asked.

"I can't say anything further because I need to respect her privacy. What she told me was not anything unexpected, but I don't feel comfortable sharing her words with you."

"I can abide by that as long as I no longer have to write the book and you aren't upset by what she said. I don't want you carrying a heavy burden and not sharing it with me."

"No. I'm not upset, and I'm as relieved as you are about her never wanting to take back Sylvia. But the unfortunate news is that Ruth will remain in our lives. I cannot abandon her."

"You really know how to be a friend."

This was the end of the conversation. Deborah was left wanting more, but respected Miriam's protection of Ruth's privacy. Although Deborah was shocked Miriam dared to discuss giving away her baby, she was pleased the discussion was over. Deborah and Miriam were exhausted, and glad it was time for Ruth to leave.

After delivering their guest to South Station, Deborah and Miriam were unusually quiet, not talking much on the way home, nor at dinnertime. They carried on normally with Sylvia, but other than that they both craved stillness. Ruth had stimulated their world during every waking hour, and they both needed to re-establish peace.

At bedtime, Miriam spoke softly. "I'm tired after spending the past few days listening to Ruth's nonstop talk."

"I agree," said Deborah with a sigh. "I have often wondered how Michael handles it."

"Maybe he doesn't. Maybe that's why he spends so many evenings out with his friends and why he has a wandering eye. Ruth spoke of him as young, but I think he may be looking to escape her presence."

"I actually feel bad for him," said Deborah.

Miriam smiled weakly. "I never really liked him, yet his lot in life is tough. If he didn't get her pregnant, his life would be much happier."

"And he never ended up with a baby even though it sounded like he wanted to keep her."

"Maybe he shouldn't have married her. He did the right thing by her, but then she gave away their child. I can't imagine how he tolerated her making that decision," Miriam said.

"We're the lucky ones to benefit from her mistake."

Miriam nodded. Deborah sighed, then continued. "I can't believe you brought up the topic about her giving away the baby."

"Our baby. I just had to ask. I thought Sylvia might ask questions someday and we'd want to tell her as much as possible."

"Tell her Ruth gave birth to her? I don't want her to know Ruth was her mother."

"But she has a right to know, the way any child would. If we were ever to have another child, it would be unfair to tell the other child but not tell Sylvia about her parents."

"Wait a minute. What are you talking about? Another child? It was a tough enough decision to parent Sylvia. Just because I said yes to her doesn't mean it was a decision to parent other children. What are you thinking?"

"I thought you love being a parent," Miriam said with a sweet smile.

"I do. I love Sylvia with all my heart, but remember, I never wanted children at all. Having another one would be overwhelming."

"Even if I did most of the work?"

"Miriam, stop right now. I don't want to have this discussion. I don't want another child. We have a daughter with special medical needs and a business that is overwhelming. There is no way to fit another child into our lives."

"We'll stop talking about it for now, but someday I may want to discuss this again."

"I don't think there is anything to talk about. My answer is 'no.' We're so fortunate. We have each other and a wonderful child thanks to Ruth, so let's be grateful."

"I am" was all Miriam said, though Deborah suspected there were many more words waiting for permission to be said.

"I think we should show our happiness with each other if you're not too tired," Deborah said, hoping to steer the conversation in a new direction.

"I'm not too tired for some loving," said Miriam, putting aside her concerns and taking off her nightdress as she climbed into bed.

Deborah willingly took off all her clothing and glided into the bed next to Miriam.

"I've an idea," said Miriam, with a twinkle in her eye. "Remember how exciting it was, all those years ago when we described out loud all the actions we thought Ruth and Michael were taking in the woods soon after they met?"

"I'll never forget that experience, which might have been the night she got pregnant. What do you have in mind, my wicked girl?"

"I think we should describe others having relations while we act out what they're doing."

Deborah had a quizzical look, narrowing her eyes. "And who do you think we should describe? Ruth and Michael? Hannah and William?"

"That sounds awful. I don't want to think about my sister and her husband in bed." Miriam made a face and shook her head.

"So, what if we talk about what we're doing and feeling?"

"How's this?" said Miriam as she began taking action. "I'm running my hands along your breasts, noticing your soft curves and watching your nipples become hard."

Deborah smiled. "And when you touch my breasts, I'm feeling the arousal in both my nipples, and between my legs."

"I can feel the warmth and wetness between my legs also. Now, I'd like you to place your lips on me down there."

Once their lips were occupied with nuzzling each other's woman's parts, there was no more conversation, just groans. The talk had aroused them both, and they enjoyed the togetherness.

Deborah's Journal, February 28, 1915

Four days with Ruth felt like two weeks with anyone else. She asked me questions, but as soon as I started to answer, she interrupted me mid-sentence and talked about her own experience. Ruth's idea of friendship is having someone listen to her. I felt lonely when I was with her, like my life didn't matter.

I can hardly imagine what it's like to be Ruth. She must feel empty. One-sided conversations don't lead to closeness.

I'm so grateful to have others in my life who care about my opinions and who want to please me. Miriam is exceptional at listening attentively and responding to my needs, so I feel appreciated. I value my friendships, which are based on mutual respect and admiration. I feel fuller for what others offer me, and hopefully I add to their lives.

I'm concerned about the topic Miriam brought up about having another child. I'm not surprised to hear she longs for more children, but I hope she understands I don't share that desire. And where does she think this child would come from, given we can't bear children together? I guess there are enough unwanted children in this world, that she would have no difficulty finding a needy child to parent. Yet it might not be Jewish, which I'm certain would be a significant issue for her. I sincerely hope she drops this idea.

Miriam's Diary, February 28, 1915

Having Ruth here this week has made me think about the choices I made in the past. I'm embarrassed I selected Ruth as a close friend. I wonder if she was different when we were young, though I doubt it. I must have been insecure to choose someone who doesn't know how to be a friend. Did I select her as a means to be popular? Did I compromise my own values? I certainly didn't choose her based on her principles.

How could someone who birthed a child show no interest in her? I wonder if she would have felt the same way had Sylvia been a normal little girl. Ruth hardly seems fit to be a mother.

Ruth is the loneliest person I've ever met.

Ruth and Michael's parlor

CHAPTER 4

William

March 1915

$\mathcal{L}$ife went back to normal after Ruth left. Deborah and Miriam gathered Sylvia into their arms after work each day, grateful to Ruth for enriching their lives through the gift of this little girl.

William and Hannah were always in good moods, despite their exhaustion, when they arrived at Deborah and Miriam's home each afternoon to pick up their daughter. Sarah's gleeful laughs put a wide grin on William's face as soon as she was in her father's arms.

William enjoyed the food Mrs. Stern had waiting for them each day, especially because Hannah had still not mastered the art of cooking. With sensitivity, he mentioned his pleasure that Hannah was not stressed by the responsibility of providing a meal after a long day at work.

Discussion over dinner was typically a continuation of concerns about work, so no one got a break from their workday until dinner was over and they all parted.

"I want to talk about anything except publishing or printing," William said on the way home one day.

"That is fine, but I want to say I was very proud of the way you handled that difficult customer today," Hannah said.

"I do not know why everyone is making such a fuss. I was quiet and listened, as I usually do."

"You are always a good listener, but when you repeated back what the customer said, you made him feel you were really listening."

"I always pay attention when people speak, and I repeated his words to make certain I understood everything he said," said William with scrunched eyebrows. "I was not doing something deliberate to calm him down."

"But you did calm him down. He was agitated with everyone else who spoke with him, but when you took over, he settled down. I admire your skills."

"Okay."

"Maybe you should say, 'Thank you for the compliment.'"

"Thank you although I do not think I deserved extra praise. Can we talk about something else?"

Hannah shook her head and gave up trying to explain this to him. "What else is on your mind?"

"Have I told you lately how happy I am?" William said with a smile.

"That is nice to hear, especially after such a tough day."

"Enough about our workday."

"Okay. Now tell me why you are so happy."

"I am fortunate to have found you," William said. "You make me feel like a regular person, not so awkward and clumsy. And you are bright and sweet."

"And pretty?"

"Yes, That too—and you are a wonderful mother."

Hannah sighed deeply. "Parenting did not come naturally to me at first but once my sister and the baby nurse taught me what to do when Sarah fusses, I began to feel more secure."

"You certainly seem confident to me."

"Thank you. And you have certainly been part of my feeling assured. You offer me steadiness, and even though you had little experience with babies you are a natural. You soothe Sarah, even when she's fussy, just like you did with the customer," Hannah said.

"Enough about the customers!"

"Sorry."

"I am pleased Sarah responds so well to me. I do not do anything special. Maybe she just likes how I smell."

"I do too!" she said with a coquettish grin, which William interpreted correctly as a desire for intimacy. They put Sarah into her bed quickly and headed directly to their bedroom.

William awoke the next morning, thinking about work. While Hannah fed the baby he asked, "How do you think your father would react if he saw how the publishing company has progressed since he died?"

"I think he would be proud of us, especially you," Hannah said.

"Why me? Everyone else works as hard as I do."

"Because you are what holds us together. Think about it. You are the only one who learned the business directly from him. You are the one who taught every one of us. We could not have managed without your direction."

"Your father was really the genius behind everything. Combining the publishing and the printing gave us an edge on all the competition. It was his idea to assist people to create their books or newspapers and then print them here, too. He did not want them to send their materials out to someone who was familiar with Hebrew but not Yiddish. Many people do not understand the difference between both languages, though they think they do."

"My father could not do it all without your help, and now we couldn't either!"

"You flatter me too much. Maybe I am not so wise, just old. Sometimes I feel like an elder, even though I am only thirty." William waited a minute and then said, "Even with Susan and Helen working with us, we remain behind all the time. How would your father manage all this work?"

"I think he would not take in more than he could accomplish in a reasonable amount of time. He wouldn't want his customers to wait for their work to be finished. He was more concerned about his customers than his own success. I'd like to honor his interest in his customers while we continue to grow."

"You are right," William said. "But he only had his small family to feed and clothe. We now have a much larger family to support with this business. I've been thinking about this a great deal, and I have a suggestion."

"What is it?"

"I think it is time we separate the publishing and printing functions. That way we could focus on each part of the work and not hold up the printing customers while we edit work for publication and vice versa."

Hannah thought about this for a moment.

"William, please discuss this with Deborah and Miriam. After all, we all own the business together. I admire you for coming up with a potential solution, though I do not understand how this change will help us."

The meeting between the four business owners took some surprising turns. They all agreed they wanted to honor the original intention to put the customer's needs first while also finding ways to grow the business. When William suggested the idea of separating the publishing and printing aspects, he was met with immediate opposition from Deborah and Miriam. Hannah would have joined them, except she had had time to think about this since he introduced the idea a few days earlier.

William was surprisingly steadfast in his position, posing ways to accomplish this most easily. He proposed that publishing skills required the kind of writing and editing expertise Deborah and Susan possessed. They could assist customers in creating exceptional manuscripts. By focusing on that part of the work, rather than be bogged down with the details of the printing tasks, they'd be more effective.

On the other hand, Miriam, Hannah, Helen, and he were skilled in the printing side of the business. It would be easier to train others in typesetting and other duties required in the printing of materials if they couldn't accomplish everything on their own. They discussed the many people out of work who could potentially be competent printing employees.

"We could hire only females," suggested Deborah. "There are many bright, capable girls who have difficulty finding employment, especially in jobs requiring their brains."

"How would you feel about that, William?" asked Hannah. "Would you prefer to work with men?"

"I always got along better with girls," said William shyly.

Suddenly they were all talking as if this was a real possibility. None of them wanted to make any sudden changes, but they all agreed to keep their eyes open for potential employees for the printing room. They could certainly use more help even if they didn't follow through on William's plan.

"William," Deborah said a few days later. "I want to sincerely thank you for this great idea. Now that I've thought more about this, I must agree I'm much more efficient as an editor. I'll be more productive if I'm not doing typesetting."

William nodded in agreement, then blushed, embarrassed by the compliments yet proud he'd made a significant contribution to the business.

Their first new employee wasn't a girl, as they'd planned, but Marjorie's younger brother, Aaron. Still finishing high school, he offered to make afternoon deliveries. Aaron expressed interest in being an apprentice to the business once he graduated, and this seemed a perfect solution. They'd pay him a tiny salary for his delivery job, and his apprenticeship would be less expensive than hiring another employee. This became their plan, finding young people who wanted to learn the printing business as an apprentice before being hired permanently.

"Who else do you think we could entice to work with us?" Deborah asked at their weekly meeting.

"Rachel, our childminder, has a sixteen-year-old sister, Rebecca, who has been doing piecework but is bright and capable of much more," Miriam said.

They agreed Miriam should ask her about her interest.

The next day Miriam said to Rachel, "Do you think your sister, Rebecca, would be interested in a job at our shop?"

"I'm certain she would. She hates working in the sweatshop making dresses, and she would be a great asset for you."

"Please invite her to the office to discuss this."

"She cannot take off time from her work or they'll fire her. She's there for long hours every day so I don't know when she could come."

"Have her stop by our house early one morning or after work," Miriam said.

"You wouldn't want her before work; she's there before 7:00 a.m. every day. If she comes after work, she might look quite haggard."

Miriam thought about this a moment, hating that the sweatshop workers had such a difficult schedule.

"We'll understand and not hold it against her."

"I'm certain she'll be thrilled," said Rachel, "but I've a question. Do you think there would be a spot for my sister, Rivkah, too? Although she's only 14, she might be useful."

"I remember Rivkah from Denison House. I tutored her. She's bright and sweet. Isn't she still in school?"

"I'm afraid not. She stopped going. She's actually a bit of a wild one. She doesn't work and spends most of her time with her boyfriend, Benjamin. I think he is a bad influence on her, so my mother would be pleased if she had something to do to keep her out of trouble."

The thought of an unruly fourteen-year-old at work made Miriam nervous. "We don't need any issues, and we couldn't watch over her. Do you honestly think she would be an asset to us, Rachel?"

"Well, I guess not. I wouldn't want you to take on a problem, and I think she might be one."

"In what way is she a problem, Rachel?"

"I'm not certain, but she and her boyfriend sneak around, like they are hiding something. I don't want to be unkind, but I think he is taking advantage of her."

"Is he forcing her to do things she doesn't want to do?" Miriam wrinkled her face.

"I suspect she is complicit in the intimacies he offers. She always has a dreamy look when she returns from being with him, and often her clothing is askew or her hair unkempt."

"She does sound like a challenge. I'm certain you are worried about her. Selfishly, I think we should start working with your sister, Rebecca. I don't think we can deal with the challenges Rivkah offers, but feel free to talk with me about her if you have further concerns."

"That is very sweet of you, Miriam."

Rebecca visited the office the very next day, excited for this opportunity. She talked about the sweatshop. "Piecework is boring and repetitive, and no matter how hard I work, I will never make a good wage. Here I could have a future, learning a real trade, and I'd love to work with all of you."

She cried when they offered her the job.

In their next meeting, Deborah said, "William, you've now trained several people. I think we should name you our official trainer."

William shook his head, but they all encouraged him to take on this role. "Hannah, will you help me? We can make a list of everything to review with new employees."

"I'll be glad to assist," Hannah said, "although you know a lot more than me." The two of them worked each evening to create instructions for every machine and for each duty to give to anyone they hired who could read.

The next week, William shyly told the group, "It was easy to train Rebecca. People we hire need to be able to read. It is important for this business." After discussion, they agreed literacy would be required for all employees.

William, pleased with the work he and Hannah did writing down training instructions, decided to add drawings of machine parts. He enlisted Helen, the artist of the group, to draw for his new training manual. As he put this document together, William became increasingly confident.

On Deborah and Miriam's way home from the shop one day, Deborah said, "I love seeing how self-assured William has become, not at all like his former hesitant self."

Miriam smiled. "I wonder if it's William's new official role as our trainer, or maybe it's being a parent. Since Sarah was born last June, he's matured. He told me stories of his being teased mercilessly as a child," Miriam said. "Maybe his experiences made him more sensitive as a father."

"We may never know what caused the change, but I find it becoming."

Miriam grinned. "That's a strange way to describe it, but I think you're correct. It suits him well. And I'm very happy for the support he's been to my sister. I don't think either of them ever had friends before they found each other. I never thought that mattered to my sister, but now that she has someone besides me in her life, she seems so happy. She's changed, too."

"She does seem different these days. Marriage and parenthood have softened her."

"They're quite a pair; two people who never fit in. But together they're stronger and happier than either was alone. I'm so happy they found each other." Miriam smiled.

"And I'm happy we found each other as well." Deborah and Miriam exchanged glances, touched their hands together for a moment, and then quickly returned to their chaste public behavior.

"Hannah and William are both extremely bright, and they have great ideas for the shop," Deborah said.

"I've come to like William's idea of splitting the work. My father was pleased when he combined the publishing and printing, but I think the time has come to seriously consider changing things. I want to make him proud," said Miriam.

Deborah's Journal, March 31, 1915

I'm pleased Miriam is coming around to William's idea about splitting the business. I feared she'd want to continue things the way her father had done them. She's much more flexible than I'd be if he were my father.

I really enjoy working with William. He has become much more vocal now that he knows us well. It was wonderful to hear him suggest such a monumental change.

William is an amazing man with many noteworthy qualities, including a keen intelligence. He's steadfast, a solid rock for Hannah, and actually for all of us. He has always been more committed than any of us, putting this business ahead of anything else in his life, even before he became part of our family. William could never be anything but honest. I suspect he wouldn't know how to lie or deceive. I've learned he's funny too, something I'd never have guessed when I first met him. I'm not always certain he knows he's being funny as his humor comes without a smile. I'm pleased he's part of our family and our business.

That night, Deborah sat at her desk and wrote a short piece about William. She made educated guesses about Mr. Cohen, and assumptions about William as his employee. Maybe someday this would be an article to submit to Dr. Hubbard.

FAILURE AS A STEPPING-STONE

Failure is a necessary step towards growth. Without taking risks, a person cannot develop self-confidence.

As a young man, William was afraid to fail. He was chastised often, so he feared taking any steps, afraid his actions would lead toward intolerance. Getting the job at Mr. Cohen's printing shop was his first step in developing a sense of worth. With Mr. Cohen's gentle lessons, William learned to try things without worry of failure.

At his job, William was never blamed for mistakes. Instead, he was taught a better way to proceed, to produce more success. Without judgment, he began to trust himself, which helped William appear more capable and feel more assured ....

Before she went to bed, Deborah thought about what she had written, as it applied to her and her family. Would she too need to fail to grow? And Miriam? And then she thought of her little girl, who would probably face failure throughout her life. Would her daughter ever be capable of growing from her mistakes?

CHAPTER 5

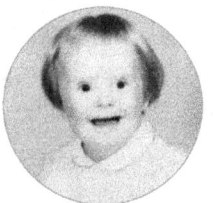

Sylvia
April 1915

The month of April began with Passover. This year Deborah, Miriam, and Sylvia, as well as Hannah and her family, were invited to Marjorie's home for the first two nights of Passover. Marjorie's family set an extra table to accommodate the additional guests, with her mother claiming it was always a joy to fill their home for *seders.* "Let all who are hungry come and eat" was written into the seder.

As the week-long holiday approached, Deborah and Miriam fretted about what they'd feed Sylvia, because she wasn't willing to eat *matzoh,* the staple of these eight days when bread products were not permissible. There were plenty of other foods to interest her, so they managed. The seders were meaningful and noisy events, with children's voices adding joy to the services and the meal.

Happily, Passover ended just before Sylvia's third birthday on April 16, so they were able to make a regular cake, rather than one with matzoh cake meal. Her birthday was a cheerful event. Hannah and William bought Sarah and Sylvia matching outfits, and the two children were adorable in their "sister" clothes. Although Sarah was only ten months old, she noticed the matching dresses, pointing back and forth between her cousin and herself. Sylvia was oblivious to the similarity but happy with all the attention.

In the midst of the celebration, a package arrived addressed to Sylvia.

"Did your parents send Sylvia another gift?" Miriam asked. "That's sweet, though why would they send a second present?"

Miriam unwrapped the package to find an adorable dress with matching shoes and tiny hat to match. She gasped when she saw the card.

Deborah took it, not recognizing the handwriting. "From Ruth! I can't believe it. She never sent a present or even a card in the past. I'm surprised she knew it was Sylvia's birthday." Deborah shook her head in amazement.

"Deborah, certainly, she knew the date. Remember, Ruth was the one who was at the hospital, crying out in pain on this date, three years ago."

"Until this year she never even acknowledged Sylvia's existence. What did you two talk about that would cause this change?" she asked Deborah.

"We talked about Ruth's experience having a child."

"I'm shocked." Deborah shook her head.

"Let's show Sylvia her new outfit and tell her it was from Ruth. I guess Ruth wants to be part of her life."

"I'm not so sure. Maybe she feels guilty for ignoring her."

"Deborah!"

"I need to stop berating her, but it has become a habit," Deborah said.

"One that I think you should change. Maybe she is trying to make up for her previous behavior."

"You're the most forgiving person I've ever met. After all, you not only forgave Ruth for her selfish behavior, but you excuse me for my awful behavior."

Miriam said, "I think this is the easier one."

"I'd better behave."

Miriam sent a thank you note to Ruth.

Sylvia was quite short for her age. Deborah and Miriam had learned her blond hair and small features, atypical of a Jewish child, were common for a Mongoloid. Sylvia was plagued with frequent earaches and repeated respiratory infections as Dr. Kingsley from the Experimental School for Feeble-Minded Children had anticipated. When sick, she was compliant with any treatments they tried, except castor oil. When she saw the spoon coming toward her mouth, she began to spit even before it hit her lips. That was the end of castor oil as a remedy.

One evening, soon after her birthday, Miriam was singing a favorite song while putting her to bed when Sylvia suddenly stiffened, arched her back, and wet the diaper Miriam had just changed. As Miriam noticed Sylvia's eyes turning white, she screamed loudly. "Deborah, come quick. Something terrible is happening to Sylvia."

Deborah, Susan, and Helen all came running. Susan announced, "I'll get the doctor," as she ran to the kitchen to call the number written on the special list above the telephone.

Deborah and Miriam, tears running down their faces and terror in their eyes, held their little girl, comforting her as she went from stiff to limp. Helen put her arms around both mothers until Susan returned, saying the doctor would be there shortly.

It felt like an hour until he arrived, though it was actually much less. Miriam described what happened and the doctor quickly explained. "She had a seizure. I'll give her belladonna and she'll get some rest. I'll come back in the morning to see if she's okay. Don't worry if her pupils become huge, which often happens with this treatment."

Neither Deborah nor Miriam got much sleep that night, waking frequently to check on Sylvia. Happily, she had no more fits during the night.

Early the next morning, the doctor arrived to check on his patient. Sylvia seemed fine, having slept well after the medicine. "I'd like to give her something called bromide, which recent research says is effective with epilepsy."

"So that's what she has? Epilepsy?" Miriam asked.

"Yes, it is common in children like Sylvia."

Miriam became quiet, thinking about this label, added to that of Mongoloid idiot.

"Thank you for taking great care of her," said Deborah as the doctor was leaving.

As soon as they were alone, Miriam said, "I think we should take her to see Dr. Kingsley at the Experimental School. We always feel better after we get his opinion."

"I'll call there today to make an appointment."

Even though the stern woman at Dr. Kingsley's office was usually dismissive, she understood the frantic nature of their call and made an emergency appointment for them that day. They asked Susan and Helen to let everyone at work know what had happened, and they told Rachel they'd be gone for the day.

During the long ride to the school in Waltham, Sylvia seemed herself. "Maybe we're making a mistake, taking her all this way if she's fine," said Miriam.

"She wasn't fine. She had an epileptic seizure," said Deborah urgently.

Miriam nodded and said nothing further, clasping Sylvia tightly.

While waiting in the office, the receptionist asked how the child was feeling, surprising them with her kind attention. As they sat back, Deborah picked up an article written by Dr. Walter E. Fernald, MD, the physician whose photograph they saw in the lobby of the school. She also looked at a copy of the Annual Report of 1914. "They really see themselves as progressive. I think we were both foolish to resist coming here."

"We're here now, which is what really matters," Miriam said.

Dr. Kingsley, as usual, was very comforting. "Sylvia looks wonderful. You're doing a great job with her" were his first words.

"The local doctor thinks she had an epileptic fit. She's not well," Miriam said, frowning.

"She's fine, Miriam. Many children who are Mongoloid idiots have seizures, and we can usually control them with bromide. Also, there's a new drug, discovered a few years ago, called phenobarbitone. Don't worry so much. This can be handled well."

"Bromide is what the local doctor gave her," said Miriam.

"Then she'll be fine. Since she's here, I'll check her, but I'm more worried about your frantic looks than about Sylvia."

Dr. Kingsley examined Sylvia thoroughly, reassuring them that she was healthy several times before they finally relaxed. Miriam proudly announced Sylvia was drinking independently from a cup and had started to name objects, which pleased the doctor. He was also encouraged that Deborah and Miriam were following the music program he had recommended on their last visit. He discussed setting up a calisthenics program for her and suggested they meet with the specialist.

As Dr. Kingsley walked the girls to the next building to introduce them to the calisthenics person, Deborah wondered if he always accompanied the parents or whether he was giving them special treatment. Could it be because they were two girls without a man involved?

Dr. Kingsley offered them some insight into his motivation when he said, "I'm really proud of you two for taking such wonderful care of this little girl. I rarely see parents so determined to improve the health of their child. Usually they want to drop off their problematic youngster and enlist us to provide the care. I admire you two."

Miriam and Deborah smiled at his kindness. Thinking of how special this doctor was, Deborah was reminded of the question she had been wanting to ask since writing an article for the Denison House newsletter with the little girl who had previously resided at this school. "Dr. Kingsley, do you know a child named Florence, who lived at this school until recently, when it was discovered she had pellagra?"

"Why yes. I was the one who diagnosed her. How do you know about her?"

Deborah explained their Denison House connection with Florence and their assumption he was the one to set her course straight with appropriate treatment. Dr. Kingsley was pleased to hear the girl was doing well, and they cheerfully discussed Florence's good fortune to have met him.

Deborah and Miriam's grins turned to apprehension as they entered the next building. This space was quite a shock, drab and more basic than the main building. Miriam gasped as a large cockroach ran past them.

Their attention shifted when they entered a large hall, filled with equipment and a large number of children being helped by workers. They looked around in astonishment at children with unusual features as if their faces had been blown up like a balloon and then deflated. Some had tongues hanging out of their mouths; others were teetering on shortened legs or seated in invalid chairs. Neither Deborah nor Miriam could speak when they both noticed a child who looked a lot like Sylvia.

As Dr. Kingsley brought them toward a worker in a far corner, they noticed several other children resembling Sylvia—short of stature with slanted eyes. Deborah wondered if they too had simian creases across their palms, as they had been taught was distinctive to Mongoloids. One of these children had drool covering the front of her shirt, and another had an open mouth, much like Sylvia's when she was tired.

"This is Mr. Frank." Dr. Kingsley said. He will teach you exercises to do with Sylvia. She's younger than most of the children here, but I'm certain that with your guidance she'll be able to do some of the same drills. I'm leaving you in good hands."

Miriam panicked. "Do you need to leave? Couldn't you show us yourself?"

"Mr. Frank is the expert. I'm good at the diagnosis and treatment, but he's in charge of the calisthenics programs. When you're done, please stop back at my office."

Mr. Frank taught them a variety of movements to do with Sylvia, focusing on increasing her muscle strength, helping her posture, and improving her balance, so she'd fall less often. Though they were strengthening exercises, Sylvia would enjoy the games.

Back in Dr. Kingsley's office, he explained that, typically, once a child has one seizure, she is likely to have others. Her biggest risk was falling and hurting herself, but since Sylvia was rarely alone, there should be little to worry about.

When they got home, Deborah spoke as Miriam cradled Sylvia in her lap. "I'm so glad we went today. Dr. Kingsley always puts me at ease. He tried to calm us about the fits, but I can't help but think of his comment that once there was one, there'll usually be others. I'm more worried than ever."

"I'm worried too because I never knew anyone with fits. I did hear about a girl who had one in my school. She left school and never came back. I don't know what happened to her."

"I'll go to the library to learn everything I can," said Deborah, comforted there was something she could do.

"I'm pleased you use the Boston Public Library to our advantage."

"I'm grateful to have an excuse to go there. I must admit I always wander around after I do my research, usually going up to the room with John Singer Sargent's *Triumph of Religion* paintings. I'm secretly hoping to find Sargent there, working on one of his murals. If ever I saw him, I'd head straight to Hannah and bring her to the library."

"You know he's her favorite artist, and she'd be thrilled to watch him paint," Miriam said, smiling.

"I think he must paint late at night, so no one can catch him in the act. But I'm ever hopeful."

On Deborah's trip to the library two days later, she found the book, *The Borderlands of Epilepsy*, 1907, by Sir William Gowers, which explained that it's often challenging to distinguish epileptic from non-epileptic disorders.

When she got home, Deborah read to Miriam from a note she'd written while reading the book. "What looks like epilepsy is not always epilepsy."

"I don't care what it's called. I care that Sylvia isn't stricken again," Miriam said.

Deborah read more. "A single attack doesn't justify a diagnosis of epilepsy." Miriam wasn't soothed.

Deborah's Journal, April 20, 1915

Miriam wasn't calmed by my research. I must admit I was until Miriam brought up her concerns. It doesn't matter what it's called; it only matters whether it happens again. We'll both be more watchful of Sylvia from now on, yet I wonder how long we can keep up this vigil. There will come a point when we'll need consistent sleep and trust she'll survive the night. Rachel will watch her diligently when we are not with her, and she seems to know just what to do for her. I'm incredibly grateful that we have her to guide Sylvia's growth.

I'm concerned Sylvia might be plagued by fits forever. I know what an outcast she'll be if she does. She already has many challenges, and this might make her life even more difficult.

Miriam took on the task of updating Rachel about Sylvia's care. She showed her the new exercises and talked about her fears about their child's health. As usual, Rachel was a calming influence.

"Miriam, I don't think you need to worry so much. The doctor reassured you she's fine. My sister used to have fits, and she's outgrown them."

"Rebecca?"

"No, Rivkah. She's always been the challenge in our family."

"It certainly seems that way," Miriam said as she sat down with Rachel. "Are you still worried about Rivkah and her boyfriend?"

"More than ever. Benjamin comes by every day and they disappear for hours now that the weather is better. I've no idea where they go, but I'm certain they are up to no good. My mother is worried. She often talks with me about how my father would never have tolerated Rivkah's behavior but she's a stubborn girl who doesn't listen when my mother sets limits."

"Rachel, I never talk with you about how difficult it must be that you lost your father and your brother in such a short time."

"My mother still cries a lot. I'm never sure which one she misses the most. Life has been challenging for her, though having this job with your family has given her a sense of purpose."

Dr. Kingsley

"We're so fortunate to have both you and your mother in our lives. You've both become incredibly important to us. And Rebecca too."

"We're both grateful for the jobs you have offered us. Working has given us the opportunity to move out of Denison House into a rooming house."

"I didn't know you moved," Miriam said, embarrassed that she knew so little about these people who were so important to her.

"Yes, last month. Let's get back to the exercises for Sylvia. I want you to show me that last one again."

The focus returned to Sylvia's new calisthenics drills, but Miriam promised herself to ask both Rachel and Mrs. Stern more about their lives.

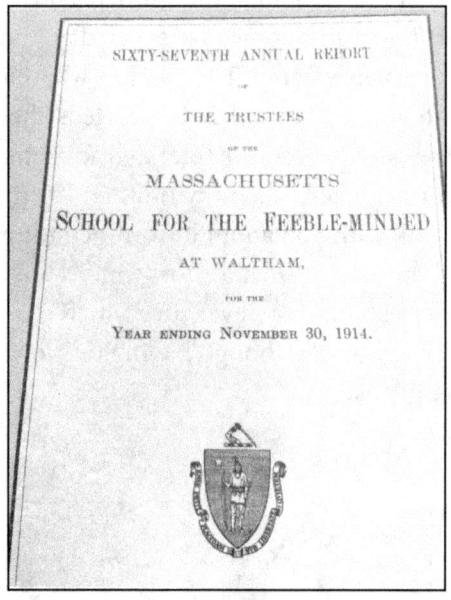

1914 Annual Report

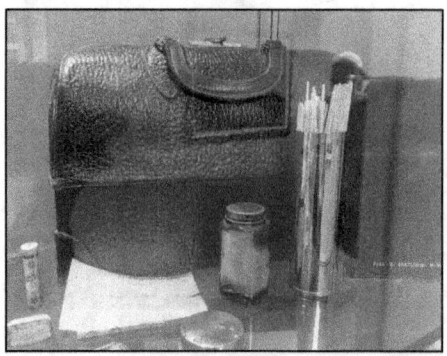

Doctor's bag

CHAPTER 6

Mildred

May 1915

"Mildred, what are you doing here? You look awful," said Deborah, opening the door to find the young girl she had met at Denison House over a year earlier. They'd met after the child's horrible experience after being on an orphan train.

Deborah was glad to be home from work with a slight cold when Mildred arrived.

"It was terrible. I don't want to live on a farm ever again. Things are really bad. Ma is sick and there is no food to eat and Pa can't take care of us. And my friend, who I thought was going to be like a sister, hardly talks with me. I'm so unhappy."

Deborah led her into the parlor. "What's wrong with Ma?"

"I don't know. When she lived at Denison House, she was often sick but now she never leaves her bed. Pa can't work the farm and take care of her at the same time. Sometimes I go whole days with nothing to eat except what I steal from the fields," she said, sobbing.

Deborah wrapped her arms around the ten-year-old child. "Let's get you something to eat and figure out what we can do for you."

Deborah led her into the kitchen, where Mrs. Stern was glad to put out a spread of food. Mildred couldn't eat fast enough. After a short while she leaned over and retched on the floor.

"I'm sorry," said the young girl as she wept.

Deborah brought her to the toilet to clean up, then returned to the kitchen, where the mess had been wiped away.

"How'd you get here?" asked Deborah.

"I rode with Pa into Woburn, so we could buy things. I ran away while he went into the hardware store. He's probably still looking for me. No, he wouldn't care, except I had some of his coins to buy eggs because all our chickens died."

"But the farm where you live is in Chelmsford. That's a long way from Woburn and an even longer way to here."

"We rode the horse and buggy for a long time to get to Woburn, so I figured we must be close to Boston and to Denison House. I walked and walked. When it got dark, I looked for a farm with a hayloft where I could sleep. I found a farm but the only place I could sleep was with the pigs. I must smell awful."

"You do smell pretty ripe. I'll draw you a bath and find something for you to wear."

Deborah filled the tub, and Mildred soaked for a long time. Deborah couldn't find anything to fit Mildred properly, so gave her oversized clothing to cover her while Mrs. Stern washed her filthy clothes.

While Mildred was dressing, Susan and Helen arrived home from work. Deborah sent them to Leah's, a few houses away, to borrow clothes to fit her better while her own dried. Leah was excited to hear there was a girl about her age down the street and sent one of her old dresses and a sweet note inviting Mildred to come to her house to play.

When Miriam arrived home, she found a newly bathed Mildred sitting in the kitchen, wearing a too-small dress from Leah. Miriam recognized Mildred from Denison House and the times Deborah had brought her home while helping her write her story. She looked down at the sallow-skinned young girl and thought she looked unwell.

While she tied Mildred's dark hair in pigtails, Deborah noticed there was no luster to her tresses. She gave Mildred a small portion of food to avoid another stomach upset while Miriam went into the den to get Sylvia, who was crawling on the floor next to Sarah.

"Sylvia has grown up so much," Mildred said when Miriam returned. "May I play with her?"

"She needs to take a nap now. While Miriam puts her to bed, I'll walk you down the street to play with Leah, a young girl who invited you to her house. Would you like that?" Deborah asked.

"Oh yes."

Leah was in her wheelchair by the door when they arrived. Mildred looked at Leah's invalid chair, and Leah looked at her ill-fitting clothing hugging Mildred's body. Both girls shrugged and within three minutes were chatting excitedly. Deborah left them and agreed to come back in half an hour.

At home Deborah and Miriam had a private conversation.

"Why is she here?" asked Miriam. "I thought she was taken in by that nice family from Denison House."

"She was. The mother is very sick and the father needs to attend to her instead of the farm. So poor Mildred wasn't cared for and wasn't fed properly."

Miriam looked shocked. "Do you think they are looking for her?"

"Possibly, though Mildred didn't think the father would care."

"We need to tell the folks at Denison House she's here. We can't just take her in without informing someone."

"Do you think Denison House would take her back?" asked Deborah.

"Yes. I'm certain they will if the family can't keep her." Miriam's tone softened. "Maybe Mildred could stay with us for a while."

"Where would she stay?" said Deborah. "All our beds are taken."

"You forget the small bedrooms on the top floor. Remember? You stayed in one of them when you first came to visit me."

"They're a mess, filled with Sylvia's old clothing and lots of junk."

"It won't take us long to move everything into one of the rooms and give Mildred the other. Is that your only concern about having her here?" asked Miriam.

"I wonder if it will be difficult to send her back to the family or to Denison House once she settles in," Deborah said.

"Would it be so bad to have her here? She's a very sweet little girl."

"Miriam, are you suggesting she join our family?" Deborah asked, shocked and fearful.

Miriam smiled. "No, I'm thinking she could stay here for a little while. We need to ask Susan and Helen, even for merely a short visit. After all, they're part of our household, too."

Miriam stood still, deep in thought. *And it would be good for Deborah to see what it is like with a second child in our home. Maybe this will soften her about the idea of parenting another child.*

Miriam sent a note to Denison House, telling them Mildred was safely with them after running away from the other family. She assumed the workers would be pleased she and Deborah were offering to keep Mildred for a while.

Once Susan and Helen agreed, Miriam headed upstairs to deal with the clutter in the extra bedroom. It was indeed filled. She cleaned it while Deborah went to Leah's house to retrieve Mildred. Deborah found the two little girls happily engaged with Leah's dolls. *Would it be so bad to have another little girl in their family? No. She must not weaken her resolve because before she knew it, Miriam would find them a second child.*

"Life with Mildred is certainly different," said Miriam a few days after the youngster moved up to the third floor. "I didn't expect having responsibility for her would feel like such a strain."

"We've so many things to think about," Deborah said. "She needs clothing and new shoes right away. Then we need to figure out what to do with her while we're at *Shul* this weekend. She won't want to come to synagogue with us since she's not Jewish, but she'll want to go to church, and we can't bring her. Do you think Susan and Helen would let her tag along with them?"

"I bet they would. They both seem to like her."

After a moment, Deborah continued. "And she seems unaccustomed to our food so we need to think about her likes and dislikes. We should discuss this with Mrs. Stern."

"And there's the matter of school. She had no lessons at all while she was living on the farm, so we're going to need to enroll her with younger children until she catches up." Miriam sighed deeply. "And we also need to think about how she's feeling. She lost her parents last year, lived in a terrible situation after the orphan train, and another on the farm where she was overworked and hungry. She now has nowhere to go other than with us. That's a lot for a little girl."

"Slow down. We need to think about her issues one at a time. We can't deal with everything at once."

Miriam nodded. "One problem at a time."

Susan and Helen spent Friday evening and Saturday morning with Mildred while Deborah and Miriam were in synagogue. They took her shopping for new clothes.

"Do you think we should offer to pay for the clothing?" Deborah asked Miriam after they witnessed a fashion show of Mildred's new outfits.

"No, they did this on their own. They might feel insulted, thinking that we're interfering."

"But I think we should offer to buy her something too."

"Deborah, it doesn't have to be even. If they chose to do something for Mildred, we should say it was nice of them."

Susan and Helen took Mildred to church with them on Sunday, and they came home giggling, telling everyone about plans for the three of them to go to the Franklin Park Zoo for the afternoon. By the time the weekend ended, it was obvious they'd bonded quite well with this lost little girl.

In the confines of their bedroom that evening, Miriam asked Deborah, "How did you feel tonight when Mildred sat next to Susan and Helen at dinner and seemed to choose them over us?" Miriam looked at Deborah closely.

"I felt fine and hardly noticed—relieved a bit actually."

Miriam didn't believe her. She wondered if Deborah was a tiny bit jealous. After all, Deborah was the one to bond with Mildred over her orphan train story, and she was the reason this girl came to their home.

"Deborah, are you sure? I would understand if you were feeling a bit left out."

"I really am comfortable with the way it worked out. I would not want to have responsibility for another child."

Miriam sighed.

The next Friday, the Boston Globe newspaper arrived with the dramatic story about the sinking of the Lusitania, the British ocean liner. Helen was the first to see the article, and quickly informed the rest of the household of the disaster. "What a horrible day. Over 1,000 lives were lost at sea yesterday, including over 100 Americans."

"How did it happen?" asked Deborah, impatiently trying to read over Helen's shoulder.

"The Germans fired two torpedoes, striking the ship as it traveled just outside of Ireland."

"Why'd they do that?" asked Mildred, joining the conversation.

The sinking of the Lusitania

The Boston Daily Globe

EXTRA

VOL LXXXVII—NO 128   BOSTON, SATURDAY MORNING, MAY 8, 1915–SIXTEEN PAGES   PRICE TWO CENTS

LUSITANIA TORPEDOED
ABOUT 1500 LIVES LOST

Two German Missiles Sink Big Liner Off Ireland in Half Hour, in Accordance With Embassy's Threat—188 Americans on Board —Only a Few Cabin Passengers Saved, Says Admiralty.

LONDON, May 8—The Germans have made good their warning against Atlantic liners flying the British flag. The big Cunarder Lusitania was torpedoed at 1:50 Friday afternoon off the coast of Ireland, and sank half an hour later, with great loss of life. Passengers landed at Queenstown, Ire, say two torpedoes were exploded against the vessel's side without warning.

The Lusitania, bound from New York to Liverpool, carried 1251 passengers, including 188 Americans, and a crew of 816, a total of 2067 souls. One of the ship's officers stated his belief that all but 500 or 600 were lost, or about 1500 passengers and crew.

WASHINGTON SHOCKED BY LOSS ON LUSITANIA

President Remains Up Late Reading Dispatches, But Gives No Comment.

Feeling Widespread If Americans Were Killed U S Must Act to Protect Citizens.

WASHINGTON, May 7—Destruction of the British liner Lusitania with the loss of many lives shocked the officials of the United States Government and spread profound grief in the National Capital.

Although it was not known how many, if any, of those lost were Americans, the view was general that the most serious situation confronted the American Government since the outbreak of the war in Europe.

The warning of the United States that Germany would be held to a "strict accountability for the loss of American

Continued on the Fifth Page.

LAURIAT OF BOSTON AMONG THE RESCUED

Mrs Henry Adams, of This City, and The Captain Also Saved.

Survivors Landed at Queenstown and Kinsale —Alfred Vanderbilt Reported Among Those to Have Perished.

LATEST LUSITANIA BULLETINS.

LONDON, May 8, 5:28—A statement issued by the British Admiralty says the total number of survivors of the Lusitania is 658. It is believed that only a few first-class passengers were saved, as they thought the ship would remain afloat, and made little effort to escape.

PASSENGERS SAVED.

Word of the safety of Charles E. Lauriat Jr of Boston, a member of the bookdealing firm of Charles E. Lauriat & Company, who was a first cabin passenger on the steamer Lusitania, came

Continued on the Second Page.

LUSITANIA PASSENGERS BOOKED FROM BOSTON

1. HENRY ADAMS, returning to its home in London from visit to Boston, Henry Adams, 209 Beacon st, Newton.
2. OLIVER P. BERNARD, returning to home in London from 26 Winchester st, Brooklyn.
3. CAROLINE B. HEDDRICK, son of Alfred H. Hendrick, of Rosedale st, Newton Highlands; mining engineer, on way to Russia.
4. RICHARD R. FREEMAN JR of 15 Grant View av, Quincy, sailing deckglazer, on way to Siberia.
5. CHARLES E. LAURIAT JR of 15 Lincoln st, Cambridge, book buyer, on business trip to London.
6. MR and MRS STEWART S. MASON, on way to their London home. Mr Mason was Miss Leslie H. Lindsay, daughter of William Lindsay of 225 Bay State road, and was married April 30, in Emmanuel Church.
7. LUCY McCORMICK and MISS ELIZABETH McCORMICK of Princeton, N. B., children of the late Paul W. N. Arrendale, of Cunard Line.
8. SIDNEY TAFT of 252 Hillside av, Needham, machinist, on visit its birthplace in Birmingham, Eng.
9. LEEMUT WITHINGTON, formerly of Newburyport, on way to London from New Haven.
10. J. HARVEY TAGE, vice president of Mark Cross Company, a native Australian, returning from business trip to home in Weiszell, Eng.

Death of George H. Ramsel.
SPRINGFIELD, May 7—George H. Ramsel and family, will in the Star quarters of disabled Swiss Lodge, A. F. M., Mr Ramsel is survived by a wife and several relatives. The Ramsel was more than sixty years old.

TODAY'S GLOBE CONTENTS.

TODAY'S GLOBE CONTENTS.

LUSITANIA PROBABLY UNDER CONVOY AT TIME

Submarine Believed to Have Eluded Accompanying Torpedo Boats.

Confident of Steamer's Speed and Safety, Passengers Were Enjoying Luncheon.

LONDON, May 8—The Cunard Liner Lusitania, which sailed out of New York last Saturday with 2067 souls aboard, lies at the bottom of the ocean off the Irish coast.

She was sunk by a German submarine, which sent two torpedoes crashing into her side while the passengers, seemingly confident that the great, swift vessel could elude the German under-water craft, were having luncheon.

How many of the Lusitania's passengers and crew were rescued cannot be told at present, but the official statements from the British Admiralty up to midnight announced the rest more than 300 or 650.

Continued on the Eighth Page.

TODAY'S GLOBE CONTENTS.

TODAY'S GLOBE CONTENTS.

THE CUNARD LINER LUSITANIA.

"War is hard to explain," said Susan. "You know there is a war going on in Europe. Well, this huge boat, called the Lusitania, was traveling in the sea near where the combat was. Even though this ship wasn't part of the war, the Germans were mad it was traveling in the wrong place so they sent a torpedo, which is like a huge bullet from a submarine, to shoot the ship in case it had guns."

"But why would they do that? Did they know they would hurt people?" asked Mildred. "And what's a submarine?"

"A submarine is a ship that travels underwater."

"And were they right? Did it have guns?"

"No one knows yet, but everyone is upset that the Germans destroyed this boat and so many innocent people who weren't soldiers were hurt or killed."

"I think war is stupid," said Mildred.

Susan agreed and hugged the little girl. Mildred asked what started this war and Susan tried to explain. "An Austrian leader was killed by a Serbian. Then Russia, who was friendly with Serbia, got involved. Then France, who was on the side of Russia and Britain, got really mad and declared war on Germany. And now there were a lot of countries at war with one another."

Helen said, "Your explanation, while quite basic, is still beyond Mildred's comprehension."

"I understand," said Mildred, though it was probable she did not.

Susan nodded.

Susan and Helen were impressed with this girl's interest, and Deborah and Miriam were equally impressed with Susan and Helen's guidance and willingness to educate Mildred.

"Nice job explaining the situation, Susan," Deborah said as she read the newspaper coverage herself.

After reading the article, Deborah was visibly upset. She said, "So many civilians were killed. War has so many unintended victims." The discussion went on for a long time while Mildred turned her attention to her doll, not understanding the full gravity of war.

Over the next week, Susan and Helen continued to take responsibility for Mildred, arranging for her schooling and decorating her room. They brought her down the street to play with Leah several times until they realized Mildred could take herself to visit her new friend. It was becoming clear to everyone that Mildred wouldn't be going back to Denison House in the near future.

After Sylvia and Mildred went to sleep one night, Susan started a conversation about Mildred. The four friends sat in the parlor, with a slight bit of wariness and unaccustomed formality to this delicate topic.

Susan, the more vocal of the pair, spoke directly. "We want to know how you feel about our connection with Mildred. We hadn't planned to take over dealing with her schooling, or clothes, or anything else. It seemed to happen naturally."

"I noticed," said Deborah, a bit coldly.

"Deborah," Miriam said harshly.

"What?" Deborah responded.

Miriam spoke. "I feel wonderful the three of you seem to be getting along so well. That little girl needs people to care about her. Your attention has been well received, and I'm really pleased for Mildred."

"I'm concerned about your feelings, Deborah," Susan interjected. "You were the one to write her story and she came here, rather than to Denison House, when she ran away from that family. We didn't mean to interfere. It just happened."

"Thank you for asking about Deborah's feelings," Miriam said.

"I can speak for myself," said Deborah. "I admit that initially I felt a little left out. I invited her to stay here because I think she's a sweet girl in a horrible situation. The reality is we're already exhausted with Sylvia and the business. It makes more sense for you two to take responsibility for her."

"It's not only about what makes sense. I'm also concerned about your reactions, Deborah," said Helen.

"I agree," Susan said.

Deborah's shoulders relaxed and she sighed, slumping into the chair. "I didn't realize I was feeling anything until we started discussing this just now. However, now that we're talking, it's much better. Although I like Mildred very much, caring for another child would be too much for us. Having you two take more of the responsibility is best for everyone. You have my blessings."

"That's wonderful to hear, Deborah, since we like Mildred very much. We'd be happy to have her stay with us rather than go back to Denison House if you're both all right with that. We've grown very fond of her in a short amount of time," Susan admitted.

"I don't think you should rush into anything," Miriam said cautiously. "You could invite Mildred to stay here for the time being and see how it goes."

"We don't plan to make anything official," interjected Helen. "What if we invite her to stay here for the next three months, assuming the family from

Chelmsford doesn't ask her to return? After that time we can all talk again, inviting Mildred into part of the discussion."

"That's an excellent idea. Thank you all for paying attention to my feelings, as well as to Mildred's," Deborah said with a smile.

"It's wonderful to have you as our friends," Miriam said. "It's important to me that you're open about discussing things of importance."

"Thank you," Susan and Helen said simultaneously.

Helen added, "We feel the same way."

One day Miriam overheard Susan and Helen sharing their values with Mildred. The controversial film *Birth of a Nation* had opened in April at the Tremont Theater, sparking protests. The colored people of Boston rallied, declaring that the kind of prejudice portrayed in the movie would never be tolerated about any other race.

Susan quietly explained to Mildred how the film portrayed black south-erners as unintelligent and violent. It also showed Southern whites forming the Ku Klux Klan, supposedly to defend themselves against the negroes. Helen shared Susan's disgust. Mildred seemed a bit confused since she was used to living with people of all colors, nationalities, and faiths at Denison House and knew nothing of prejudice.

Miriam interrupted their conversation, saying, "As a Jew, a people who have been persecuted for centuries, I believe I should be tolerant of everyone." The three adults shook their heads in agreement. Then Miriam let Susan and Helen continue with this important lesson.

It wasn't long before Susan mentioned this film was in relation to the case of Leo Frank.

"I know about Leo Frank," Miriam interrupted. "Mr. Levine, Deborah's father, told us all about him. Mr. Levine claimed antisemitism was the reason for Mr. Frank's conviction."

The discussion continued for a few minutes, but it wasn't until after Mildred was in bed that Susan talked further with Deborah and Miriam about this horrible case. She had read that Mr. Frank was to be executed soon. Deborah called home that evening, learning from her father that his execution was set for late August. Deborah feared this upsetting news would disrupt her sleep so she sat down to write in her journal to calm herself before heading to bed.

Deborah's Journal, May 31, 1915

I'm so pleased for Susan and Helen. I think they were always a bit envious of our role as parents, but now they too have a child to dote upon. They seem especially pleased since the Chelmsford family relinquished her care to them. Mildred's been especially easy, grateful for everything they do for her. She's cooperative, picks up after herself, cleans plates off the table, and does dishes without being asked. She even keeps her room tidy. I wonder if it was her mother who taught her these habits, or maybe she learned them when forced into servitude with those two families. It's a pleasure to have her here, though it's a relief Susan and Helen are caring for her and I'm not having to fight with Miriam about whether we could keep her. Since Mildred's arrival we seem to be more of a family unit than ever. Everything seems so natural, as if this was meant to be.

*I've been assigned another child at Denison House with a story
to tell—my first boy. I met George this week and I was touched by his
story about losing his father on the Lusitania. As he and Mildred both
noted, the victims of war include those at home, not just those on the
battlefields.*

*I look forward to writing George's story, and if it comes out well,
I will send it to Dr. Hubbard. Though we never discussed warfare as
a topic, I'm certain it would be a popular subject these days for many
magazines. Women may want to hear stories about how war affects those
left at home.*

(SEE ADDENDUM "GEORGE: UNINTENDED VICTIM OF WAR")

Miriam approached Mrs. Stern to discuss how the addition of Mildred to
their household was affecting her.

"It's fine," Mrs. Stern said. "Mildred is a nice little girl."

"But I've noticed you are making some special food for her, things we
would not normally eat."

"Everything I make her is kosher, so don't worry."

"I'm not at all worried. I know how careful you are to keep to our dietary
needs. I was only concerned that it's extra work for you. You never complain,
but I know Mildred loves the cornbread you make, and you've baked the
molasses cookies she likes quite often."

"I'm pleased to make these things for her. My son used to like those
cookies."

"I never ask you about your boy. It must be so painful to have lost a child
so young."

"Yes. He was fourteen, just beginning to grow up. It was sad that G-d took
him so young."

"And this was about the same time your husband died."

Miriam noticed Mrs. Stern's eyes had become damp.

"Yes. That was a very difficult time for us. But we were fortunate that we
were able to move to Denison House."

"Rachel told me that you've now moved into a boarding house."

"Yes, I'm very glad we are on our own. Denison House was a good place,
but I want to provide for my family. That has always been important to us…
I mean to me."

"You lived on a farm before moving to Denison House, didn't you? Rachel has mentioned that you had horses."

"Yes. When we first came to the United States from Russia, we had nowhere to go. We had some cousins who had come here, so we followed them. They had a farm in Natick, and we stayed with them and worked with them for several months. Then my husband heard of a family needing a farmhand and they offered us a small house in exchange for running their farm. It was a very good life, and he was glad to be less of a burden on his cousins."

"Why did you move from there?"

"The husband we worked for died and the wife needed to sell the farm. My husband had been a tailor in Russia so he was able to find work at a garment factory in Boston. Rivkah was a sickly child, and I needed to stay home with her. We moved the whole family into a small place in the city. We weren't there very long when Rachel left for her job at the Lowell Mills. And then after my husband became ill, my son got dysentery and died. I think my husband's death was from a broken heart. He loved our boy as much as any father could love a child."

Miriam put her arm on Mrs. Stern's shoulder as she noticed a tear drip onto her apron.

"I need to get back to work. Otherwise, everyone will be hungry and there will be no dinner. I have finished the batter for cornbread, and I need to get it into the oven."

"I'm certain Mildred will be pleased. Actually, I think we've all become fond of that wonderful treat. Thank you for everything you do for us."

"My pleasure."

Doll with bisque face

CHAPTER 7

Fannie

June 1915

$\mathcal{A}$s Mildred settled into the household, Deborah and Miriam wondered whether this sweet girl would remain delightful. Their family friend, Mrs. Berkowitz, the woman who had supported them during their most difficult times, seeded their doubts about adolescence. They'd known the Berkowitz family, their neighbors in New York and also in Western Massachusetts, since their older girls were six and nine, and the twins were just four years old. In a reversal of roles, Mrs. B. wrote several letters to Deborah and Miriam regarding her concerns about their oldest, their thirteen-year-old daughter, Fannie.

"Miriam, Fannie has become a serious challenge, and Mrs. B. seems unsure how to handle her," Deborah said while folding laundry.

"I agree. Her letters are usually full of cheer, but now they're all about Fannie and her troublesome behavior. It seems things are even worse since the family's returned to Lenox for the summer."

"Being a parent came naturally to Mrs. B. until now. Having a difficult adolescent seems beyond her skills," Deborah said.

"Previously, her soft, easy manner with her children created harmonious relationships in her family. She and her husband work well together, and she told me they rarely disagree on ways to manage the children."

"Now that I think about it, I have never seen her discipline any of the children. The girls always listen to her guidance. I'm sorry she's struggling."

Another letter arrived.

June 2, 1915

Dear Deborah and Miriam,

I feel like we have a stranger living with us, a disagreeable, stubborn girl with a mind of her own. None of my previous modes of coping work

when trying to steer Fannie. "Fannie, it's time for dinner," might be met
with defiance as she runs into her room during mealtime. A simple
question such as, "How was your day at school?" might bring a scowl
and indelicate words of sarcasm.

And Fannie is no longer a loving big sister. Ethel came to me this
afternoon, asking why her sister teased her. I had no answers for her.
The twins, at eight, are too busy with their own activities to notice most
of the time, though sometimes they question me about Fannie's new
behavior. I don't know what to say ....

With Love,
Mrs. Berkowitz

Soon after Mrs. B.'s latest letter, things got worse in the Berkowitz home.
Ethel came into the parlor with tears running down her face. "Mother, why
is Fannie being so mean to me? She said I'm stupid. And she said none of my
friends could possibly like me because I'm dumb."

"Oh, Ethel, you're not stupid and you have wonderful friends who care a
great deal about you. You mustn't let Fannie's words hurt you."

"I don't like Fannie anymore," Ethel said as her tears turned to sobs.

Mrs. B. held her young daughter until she calmed.

"It's difficult to explain Fannie's behavior these days. I'm sad to say she's
behaving like this with all of us."

"Can you make her stop?"

"Honey, I wish I could."

Just then, the twins came running into the room, breathless. "Fannie took
our dolls and threw them out the window," said Minnie with a quivering lip.

"She says we're being babies and we're too old to play with dolls,"
Maggie added.

Mrs. B. released Ethel and encircled both twins. "You're definitely the
right age to play with dolls. I know you treat them like they're your own little
children. Go outside and find the dolls. Bring them back, and we will wash
them and see if they need any repairs."

Within minutes the three girls and Mrs. B. were lined up in the kitchen,
with the cook moving all her pots and pans out of the sink so they could
wash the doll clothes. Luckily the bisque doll faces had not shattered. As
they scrubbed, Mrs. B. said, "I'm sorry girls. Fannie isn't treating you very
well these days."

"What's wrong with her?" asked Minnie.

"I think she's having a troublesome time growing up. She's no longer a little girl like you, but she's not a grownup yet, or even a teenager. She feels a little lost."

"Will we be like that when we're thirteen?" asked Maggie.

"I hope not!" exclaimed Mrs. B., with the sudden thought life could be a whole lot worse if her other three went through this same terrible stage. "I hope Fannie won't be like this for long."

"I don't want to be her sister anymore," said Minnie with tightened lips.

"I'll punch her if she says mean things to me," said the other twin.

"No, girls. That's not a good way to behave. I want you to continue to be my sweet girls. I couldn't stand it if you were all mean." She then took a deep breath and regretted saying that. "I didn't mean to imply Fannie's mean."

"But she is," Ethel said as she looked directly at her mother, pounding her fists on her legs.

"She's going through a hard time. We must remember she's not feeling very good about herself if she's saying those things to you. I hope she'll return to her sweet self very soon."

"I don't think she will," Ethel said, leaving the room.

After the twins scampered off, Mrs. B. stood still, wondering what she was going to do. If she were to approach Fannie, she was certain she'd absorb the brunt of her anger, but she had to confront her. She went upstairs to Fannie's room and knocked on the door.

"Go away."

"No, Fannie. We must talk."

"I don't want to talk."

"I'm afraid you don't have a choice." Mrs. B. entered the room, finding Fannie sprawled on her bed. She quickly decided this wasn't the right time to note that she was wrinkling her dress by lying on it. She sat quietly on the edge of the bed for a few moments.

"You seem very unsettled these days," Mrs. B. said quietly to her daughter.

"What does that mean?"

"Everything seems to be irritating you."

"Like my stupid little sisters?"

"Yes, like them. Though I'd never call them that, nor would you just a few short months ago."

"Well, they are."

"And you think your father and I have become stupid too."

No response.

"I want to find a way to help you. You're troubled much of the time, and I hate to see you so upset. Is there anything I can do for you?"

"No."

Mrs. B. looked at Fannie, who turned her head away. Mrs. B. got off the bed and walked around to look into Fannie's face. There were tears dripping down her cheeks. Without a word, Mrs. B. reached down and gathered Fannie into her arms. Fannie clung to her mother as her tears flowed.

"I don't know what's wrong with me," Fannie said, gulping air.

"Nothing's wrong with you, sweetheart. You're growing up, and that's not always easy."

"I don't want to grow up if it's this hard."

"It will be hard like this for a little while. After you get used to all the changes in your life, you'll love being a young lady. You just need to get through this tough phase."

"It's horrible. I hate this."

Mrs. B. held her daughter for several minutes, sharing her own experiences when she went through this same stage. She knew this wouldn't be the end to Fannie's poor behavior and tomorrow she was just as likely to be mean-spirited. But for now, they shared a bit of love.

The next day, Mrs. B. wrote another letter.

June 5, 1915

Dear Deborah and Miriam;

> *I hope all is well with you and Sylvia. How's she doing with her new exercises?*

> *My husband and I are excited about the Jewish lawyer who was just appointed to the Supreme Court. Can you imagine President Wilson, who was considered an antisemite, appointed the first Jew to sit on the high court? Had you heard of Louis Brandeis before, since he's from Boston?*

> *On a more personal note, unfortunately, we won't be able to visit as you requested. Fannie refuses to join us, and I dare not leave her with Bridget, our governess.*

> *Fannie continues to be very difficult, even when I treat her the same as always. She defies us at every opportunity, talking back to us and challenging our suggestions. She seems to care more about her friends*

than her family, though I worry they're not a good influence on her. She's taken up with a group of adolescents who are defiant and seem to have poor scruples. There has been at least one day when she skipped school and joined these youngsters at the park. One of our neighbors saw them and reported this to me.

I worry about my other girls, when they ask why Fannie is behaving so strangely. They always looked up to her, but lately she has little interest in them. They miss the sister who always watched out for their best interests. Also, I worry they'll learn bad traits from their older sister. I'm at a loss.

Missing you.

With Love,
Mrs. B.

"I'm glad to hear the Berkowitzes are excited about the appointment of Supreme Court Justice Brandeis," said Miriam as she sat in the parlor with Deborah. "It's marvelous to have a Jew on the highest court in the land. My mother and father would have been so pleased. It's times like this when I miss them the most. I'd love to hear their excitement, learning a Jewish man has been rewarded with such an honor." Miriam stared, lost in thought.

"I know how much you miss them," Deborah said, putting an arm around Miriam's shoulder. She waited a minute before she reflected on the rest of the letter. "I'm sad to hear how obstinate Fannie has become."

"Yes," Miriam said as she shook herself out of her reverie. "What an unfortunate turn of events. Mrs. B. seems at a loss about what to do when kindness no longer works. She knows no other way. But maybe we can finally repay Mrs. B. for all the compassion she's offered to us. Do you think we can help her with Fannie?" asked Miriam.

"What do you have in mind?" asked Deborah who was cuddling Sylvia.

Supreme Court Justice Louis Brandeis

"You know me so well. Yes, I've an idea. What if we invite Fannie to spend some time with us this summer? It would give Mrs. B. a break, and maybe Fannie will open up to us. We are, after all, closer to her age."

"She's thirteen, and we're twenty-one and twenty-two, which isn't close at all."

"I know, but her mother is thirty and her father thirty-two, which is a lot older. Maybe Fannie will relate to us better."

Deborah took a minute before responding. "I'd be happy to invite Fannie here, but where will we put her?"

"We have that extra room on the third floor, across from where Mildred is living. I know it's filled, but most of the things we've stored there are unnecessary."

"Like Sylvia's first pair of shoes?"

"Yes. Like those."

After a great deal of discussion between themselves and Susan and Helen, they agreed to invite Fannie to spend time with them. Mrs. B. was very touched by this offer, and to everyone's surprise Fannie agreed without hesitation. They had expected Fannie to refuse this offer since this would mean she'd be separated from her friends. They wondered what she thought Boston would offer her.

June 9, 1915

Dear Deborah and Miriam,

    Thank you so much for the invitation to stay with you. I am really excited to come to Boston. I want to spend lots of time with Sylvia.

Fannie

Once it was decided when Fannie would arrive, Deborah and Miriam planned in earnest. First, they cleaned out the room where she would stay. More importantly, they discussed rules for Fannie, including times she needed to come home, restrictions on the places she could go without supervision, and a requirement they approve of any adolescents with whom she wanted to spend time.

They also listed activities for Fannie, which they hoped would keep her out of trouble. Because they'd be at work, they needed to find constructive endeavors for her during the daytime. They decided to give her options and let her choose. The first choice was to work with them, giving her a chance to earn a small amount of money for tasks she completed at the shop. Another option was to stay home with Rachel to help care for Sylvia and Sarah, again for a few pennies per day. Evenings she'd be expected to stay home with them. They sent Fannie a letter, outlining their expectations and anticipating that she'd push back. Instead, she approved all their ideas and suggested she work with them three days and stay home to help Rachel the other two workdays. Maybe this was going to be easier than expected.

Fannie arrived, as planned, the next Wednesday. As Deborah and Miriam picked her up at South Station, they both noted she looked older and more beautiful than the last time they saw her.

"It was wonderful to take the train. I never got to travel by myself before. I can hardly believe my stupid parents let me," said Fannie.

"Welcome to Boston, Fannie. But no talking of your parents that way," said Deborah, walking Fannie the short distance to the car. Wanting to start by setting a positive environment, Deborah handed Fannie one of her suitcases to carry. She was met with a nasty expression.

Deborah responded firmly. "No grimaces. You get to carry a suitcase, just like we do. We're a house of strong females, and you get to be one of us."

"I'm glad you're here, Fannie. We're going to have a wonderful time together," Miriam said softly.

Fannie wiped the disgusted look off her face and withheld other disparaging remarks.

After giving Fannie a quick tour of Boston on their way through several neighborhoods, they arrived at Homestead Street, Roxbury. Fannie started to run inside, saying, "I can't wait to see Sylvia."

Miriam called her back. "Fannie, you forgot your suitcase." There was no grimace this time as Fannie grabbed one of the heavier valises. Miriam watched her struggle, but thought this show of strength was a good step in the right direction.

When they walked in the house, Fannie dropped the suitcase and ran to find Sylvia, completely ignoring Mildred, who had been waiting anxiously to meet her. Deborah turned to Miriam and whispered, "I think we should let this go. Too many instructions may turn her against us before she's even moved in."

"I'll take care of this one," Miriam replied.

Miriam followed the path Fannie had taken and found her cuddling Sylvia. "I'm so glad you're excited to see Sylvia. Has she grown a lot since you last saw her?"

"Yes, she looks big," said Fannie. "How come she doesn't talk?"

"She's starting to say some words," said Miriam a bit defensively. Regaining her equilibrium, she continued, "You can take her into the parlor so we can introduce you to Mildred. She's been waiting to meet you. I think her feelings were hurt a bit when you ignored her and headed straight to Sylvia."

"Sorry."

"No need for apologies. I think a nice greeting will set things straight."

As Fannie greeted Mildred, Miriam turned to Deborah and whispered, "I changed my mind already. I think this is going to be as challenging as we expected. Supervising a thirteen-year-old might be harder than caring for a baby."

"Agreed. So far I think we're doing okay. At least I hope so."

Both Deborah and Miriam shrugged as they sat in the parlor, feeling old beyond their years.

The first week went much like the first day, with Fannie pushing limits. She complained one evening when she was refused cornbread with dinner, acting resentful when told it contained dairy so couldn't be served with a meat meal. Deborah and Miriam worked well together, setting clear boundaries in a firm but gentle manner. After repeatedly being told grimaces weren't acceptable, Fannie followed the guidance. She was excited to spend time with Sylvia, and she surprised them all by connecting with Mildred. Though she'd been dismissive of her sisters, Mildred was her only option for social interaction with someone close to her age, so Fannie accepted her even though Mildred was three years younger. The two of them played games during the evening when the adults were involved in their own games. Deborah and Miriam heard the two girls giggling on the third floor long after bedtime. They never admitted to overhearing this joyful infringement of the rules, deciding the bonding between the youngsters was more important.

To everyone's delight, Fannie's favorite part of the week was her time at the shop. They found many small projects to keep her busy so she was never underfoot. Marjorie took a liking to her and was pleased Fannie was good with numbers. Marjorie taught Fannie some basic accounting, which assisted Marjorie in her overwhelming job.

At the end of the week, Fannie asked, "Could I come to work four days and stay with Rachel and the babies one day next week? I could help Marjorie with the books on my extra day."

Deborah and Miriam had a small conference with William and Hannah to decide if this would be possible. Her salary was tiny, and Marjorie found her quite helpful so they decided to offer her the job for an additional day. They were all getting used to having someone do all the menial tasks, and they discussed whether they needed to hire someone to do this job once Fannie left.

After settling in, Fannie confided to Miriam about her frustrations in Western Massachusetts and why she'd chosen to come to Boston, rather than spending time in Lenox with the rest of her family.

"I had a fight with this girl who lives near me in Lenox. She said I was annoying, and I told her she was, too. Some girls took her side and I was left out of the group."

"Now I understand why you wanted to get away," said Miriam gently. "What do you think you could do to make things better when you return?"

"Nothing," she said with an unattractive snort.

"What if you apologize for your behavior?"

Fannie raised her voice. "She was being annoying. Why should I apologize?"

"Because you want to fit in with the others. Do you think there was anything you did that was bothering her?"

"No. Well, maybe. I guess I teased her a bit because she's so short."

"That's not something she can change. Maybe an apology is in order."

"Maybe. But she was wrong too."

"You can only take responsibility for your actions, not hers. I think an apology might help," Miriam said.

That evening, when Miriam told Deborah of their conversation, Deborah responded, "You handled that nicely. I hope Fannie will be willing to apologize. You're wonderful, my dear."

"Thank you. I feel like I'm practicing for having an adolescent, though I wonder if Sylvia will ever have these issues."

"We don't even know if she'll have much language. She still just grunts when she wants things, even though she's now three years old," Deborah sighed.

"Hopefully she'll learn to talk," said Miriam wistfully. "At least she calls people by their names, or by the names she's assigned to them. I like when she calls Rachel "Ray" and William "Yum.""

"I want to change the subject back to Fannie. Things are going so well with Fannie that I was going to suggest she stay longer. But given your conversation with her today, I think it would be better for her to return to Lenox to work things out with the other girls."

"I agree. I'd love to have her stay, but I think our discussion today will help her back home."

"What if we tell her we'd like her to come back for a whole month next summer? That way she'll feel appreciated by us, and she'll get to deal with her problems at home," said Deborah.

"Agreed. I'm looking forward to talking more with Fannie about the things that are troubling her. Maybe I can bring up the way she treats her parents and her siblings."

"Mrs. B. would certainly appreciate that."

"That's my goal, to help Mrs. B., because she has helped us so many times," said Miriam.

Before they talked to Fannie about going back to Lenox, Deborah had an idea. "My parents have already returned to nearby Great Barrington for the summer, and I'd love to visit them at Stonegate. What if we take a vacation and travel on the train with Fannie?"

"Deborah, I think you should go. I really want to stay here. Although I've fully recovered from diphtheria, I feel like I'm still behind on work. And now, with Mildred here and Sylvia's calisthenics program working so well, it would be better if I stay behind."

"I'd like to vacation with you. I traveled to see my family in January without you, when I spoke to Dr. Hubbard's class, and I think it would be good for us to go together."

"I really think you should go on your own. Maybe we can find another time to travel together."

"I can skip this trip," Deborah said hesitantly.

"No, I insist you go."

They decided Deborah would make a quick trip to visit her family, and they'd find a date to travel together in August. That would give Rachel some time off from watching Sylvia, and the rest of the group at work could prepare for their absence. Mrs. Stern would have fewer mouths to feed while they were gone, giving her a bit of a break too.

Deborah's Journal, June 29, 1915

Fannie was a surprisingly delightful addition to our household. After all the problems she caused for her parents, I expected we'd have significant trouble with her yet she caused minimal difficulty. She got along well with Mildred and she didn't connect with any problematic girls.

Being responsible for an adolescent has been satisfying. Thinking of ways to say things that wouldn't ruffle her was challenging, yet interesting. I like the forethought required to make things run smoothly. I suspect those skills will rarely be needed with Sylvia.

Fannie is a typical adolescent, sweet some of the time and a terror on occasion. It takes a great deal of vigilance to keep her in line. She's strong willed, sometimes standing firm in her belief, even when she's wrong. I suspect she was more accepting of our directions than her parents. No wonder Mrs. B. is exhausted dealing with her.

Having Fannie around reminds me of my own childhood. I remember being obstinate and disagreeable as she has been. My discontent was because I never fit in and I couldn't share my feelings about liking girls with anyone. I wonder what Fannie's reasons are.

I'm looking forward to my train ride with Fannie since I've never had much time with her alone. I hope she'll be open with me the way she's been with Miriam.

I thought for a minute Miriam was going to suggest I stop to see Ruth when I get to Great Barrington, but I was greatly relieved when she didn't. The birthday gift that Ruth sent Sylvia may have changed her position in our lives, but I don't want to spend any of my short weekend with her.

On the train trip home Fannie was angry because she didn't get to travel alone. During the first hour she gave Deborah the silent treatment, though she eventually got bored and began talking.

"I wonder what my family is doing today," Fannie said.

"I bet your sisters have missed you," Deborah said.

"I bet they haven't. They're babies, and I don't want to play their childish games anymore," said Fannie.

"They're entertaining, and I enjoy listening to their ridiculous jokes."

"They're silly. I used to laugh a lot when they made up one of their funny songs."

"It's good to laugh."

"Pretty good," Fannie admitted.

"I bet they learn a lot from you because you're older. They must listen to every word you say."

Fannie was quiet, mulling this over.

Deborah continued. "I bet you could teach them some of the songs Mildred taught you. I'm certain you remember every tune and every word."

"I remember. I have a good memory."

"You could have a music school for them."

"I could teach them the tunes, and I could write down the words."

"What if you made copies of the words for each of them?"

"What if I wrote down the words one time and they copied them for themselves. They must write carefully or they won't be able to read their own writing."

"It could be like a music school where you teach penmanship."

"And I could also give art lessons. They could each decorate their songs."

"You have such clever ideas, Fannie."

Fannie liked the idea of being their teacher and soon was devising rules for her school. Deborah hoped this would work even if for a short time.

Fannie's family picked them up at the Great Barrington train station, and she greeted them warmly. Deborah hugged Mrs. B. and whispered, "We had a wonderful visit with Fannie."

Mrs. B. returned the hug tightly, watching Fannie greet her sisters as if really glad to see them. "I can't thank you enough," said Mrs. B., looking rested after her break from Fannie. She seemed to have questions on her lips, but it was time to pack Deborah into their car for the short ride to Stonegate.

Mrs. Levine had lemonade and cookies awaiting their arrival, and the two families spent a short while together. The four sisters ran up and down the large expanse of lawn. For a few minutes, Fannie was a child again.

"You worked a miracle," said Mrs. B. "I've not seen Fannie this relaxed in a very long time."

"I hope she continues this way," said Deborah. "She really is caught halfway between childhood and adolescence."

Deborah's visit with her family, while short, was delightful. They took a ride in the countryside on Saturday, something they would not have done on Shabbos if Miriam was with them. On their way home Mrs. Levine insisted she show off the French Renaissance Building in downtown Great Barrington, which housed the Mahaiwe Theater.

Mrs. Levine explained, "This theater was rebuilt in 1905 after a devastating fire. It was named for the original Mahican settlers of the Berkshires and refers to 'the place downstream' from the Housatonic River. The theater has been a significant addition to the arts culture in the region."

"Can we go inside?" asked Anna.

The Levines agreed to take them all to see a vaudeville show that evening, a first for everyone, but especially exciting for Deborah's exuberant sister.

"I loved all the costumes," Anna said as they left the theater. "And the dancers and the magician. He was incredible. And I could hardly believe the tricks the acrobats did. I love this place. I saw the poster for the silent film *Mr. Barnes of New York*. Can we come back to see it?"

"Yes, my dear," said Mr. Levine, knowing he'd be asked daily until he finally gave in. He loved her enthusiasm.

Deborah noticed how Anna always got what she wanted when she asked her father. Deborah noted to be firm and not be so easily swayed to meet Sylvia's every need.

Mahaiwe Theater, Great Barrington, MA

Mahaiwe Theater interior

CHAPTER 8

Marjorie

July 1915

Soon after Deborah returned from her weekend in Great Barrington, the weather in Boston turned uncomfortably warm. "Did you read the paper today?" Miriam asked anyone who was listening.

Susan responded. "Yes. I read several people drowned while on vacation over the July Fourth holiday."

"Yes," responded Miriam, "but I was talking about the weather. No wonder I'm dripping wet. The paper said the temperature on Boston Common reached 105 degrees on July 3."

"I'm certain it's still that hot," said Deborah, as she wiped the moisture from her face.

"The paper said it's an official heat wave," Miriam said.

"I don't need to read the paper to know that. I don't remember it ever being this hot for four days."

Deborah and Miriam were distracted from thoughts of the weather when the mail arrived with two letters.

July 1, 1915

Dear Deborah and Miriam,

Thank you for a wonderful time in Boston. I really enjoyed my work. I might want to try bookkeeping. Please thank Marjorie for teaching me.

I want you to know things are much better with my friends in Lenox. I did what you said and I apologized to the girl and she apologized back. Now we are friends again. Everyone else has been kinder to me too.

I look forward to coming back next summer to work with you again.

Fannie

July 7, 1915

Deborah and Miriam;

What did you do to our daughter? She's been a different person since returning. She's been cooperative, is spending time with her sisters, and she has been much more civil with us. Now she talks endlessly about her skills in bookkeeping. We're so grateful for everything.

I hope you're surviving this heat wave without any difficulties. I assume it's even hotter in the city.

Love,
Mrs. B.

"We must share Fannie's and Mrs. B.'s letters with Marjorie. Her work with Fannie made a huge difference," said Miriam.

"I think we made a difference, too," Deborah said. "Fannie was responsive when we set limits with her. I look forward to having her back."

"Me too. But I think Marjorie deserves some of the credit for Fannie's accomplishments. Marjorie is such a good friend and a tremendous asset at the shop. Not only does she keep the books, something which none of the rest of us has the inclination for, but her cheery disposition lightens our loads and our attitudes."

"I agree. Maybe we should give her a raise," said Deborah.

"That's a great idea, though I don't think money is what motivates her. I think much of Marjorie's joy, of late, is due to her relationship with Micah. He's a fine young man who brings out the best in her. I think things will change for them now that he has finished college."

"You mean like marriage?"

Miriam nodded. "Since he is moving to New York City to teach at the Yeshiva and beginning his graduate studies at Columbia College, he'll soon be able to support a wife."

"The Yeshiva?"

"Yes, the newly created Rabbinical College of America."

"That's impressive. If they marry and she moves to New York, I'd be sad."

"I'd miss her terribly, but we must think about what's best for Marjorie," Miriam said. "Micah is responsible and has gentle qualities, which mesh perfectly with hers. I'm happy to say I think she's found her match."

Shortly thereafter, while sitting in Marjorie's parlor with her whole family, Micah announced, "I've decided to postpone my job at the Yeshiva. Today I signed up for Summer Boot Camp. They began the camps in Pennsylvania and California, and this year there will be four sites. I'll be training at Fort Ethan Allen, Vermont, on Lake Champlain."

"When do you leave?" said Marjorie, in an unsteady voice, wondering why he'd not discussed this with her before taking such a major step.

"August 11."

"Tell us more," she said in a whisper.

"They call this program the Plattsburgh Idea. They trained more than 160 college men in 1913, more last year, and 1,200 men will train this year. Now, we have to pay our own way, so the trainees will be an elite group. They will teach us the skills important to protect our country in this impending war, creating a military reserve. Since the Great War began last year, Europe has become fully engulfed in the conflict. It's become clear our country won't be able to stay out of the war for long, so they're training many more of us this summer. A large proportion of commissioned officers will be pulled from those completing this training, and I wish to be one."

"I respect your desire to serve our country. There hasn't been a war as huge as this could be and there will be many casualties. I worry about your safety," Marjorie said.

"I'll do my best to be careful," said Micah as he put his arm around her.

Marjorie solemnly walked Micah outside. "I'm really hurt you took such a huge step without talking with me."

"I knew you would be upset," he said with a shrug.

"That's no reason to avoid talking with me. If we're going to be a couple, you need to start acting like we are."

"I need to make my own decisions, and I don't want you making decisions for me," Micah said, shocked by Marjorie's firm reprimand.

"I want us to make important decisions together. I want you to think for yourself, but I need to be included. If you make choices independently, we're not a couple. Likewise, I expect to make my own decisions, but I plan to talk with you about my thoughts and feelings."

"I'm truly sorry. I guess I'm not used to thinking like part of a pair. I've never had a girlfriend before. I always make my own decisions."

"I understand. However, I deserve to know what you're thinking and to be offered some input. I was hurt you announced this in front of my whole family before telling me."

"I'm sorry," Micah repeated. "I've a lot to learn about being a boyfriend. Please forgive me and teach me how to work together."

Marjorie's face softened. She was proud she'd clearly and firmly stated her needs and was satisfied with how Micah responded.

"Was this our first fight?" asked Micah meekly.

"I think it was."

"We survived it pretty well, and I think I learned some valuable things that will make me a better boyfriend," Micah said.

"I hope so. I also hope you're safe on this adventure of yours, and the Yeshiva will let you start your job after you return."

"I already talked to them and they said it was fine."

Micah realized he'd also approached them before telling Marjorie. He took a breath, wrinkled his nose, and said, "Next time, I'll talk with you first."

"Thank you. You're learning."

Marjorie asked Miriam to eat lunch with her the next day. As soon as they sat down, Marjorie exploded with the story of Micah's announcement and how she'd demanded he include her in major decisions.

"You managed that nicely," said Miriam. "I'm impressed you spoke your piece. How do you feel about this training?"

"I'm proud he wants to serve his country and, should there be a war, this sounds like the right place to learn the skills he'll need."

"Are you worried?" Miriam asked.

"Sure. I'm worried about him getting hurt, and I'm certainly scared about him going to war should that happen. Everyone is talking as if this war is just around the corner. It's frightening he could be sent overseas since the requirement for service abroad is age nineteen and he's twenty-two."

"When will he start his service?"

"Because he's going to boot camp to be trained as an officer, he assumes he cannot hold off his military service until he finishes his graduate work. He'll be in school for many more years since studies to be a doctor take a long time."

"It's wonderful he's chosen a career in medicine, caring for children like Sylvia. It's marvelous she stimulated his desire to help," said Miriam.

"Maybe someday he can be Sylvia's doctor. In the meantime, I'll miss him when he's gone. But I'll continue to make money at the publishing shop while he begins his job and continues his learning," Marjorie said.

"I hope while he's gone you can work full time. We certainly need you." Miriam said nothing about her thoughts that Micah might ask Marjorie to be his wife and move with him to New York.

"I'm happy to work more while he's in New York. But getting back to the topic of boot camp … who else do you think will be going? It sounds like many well-to-do young men will select to be trained. Do you think others we know will join?"

They discussed the young men from Boston, New York, and the Berkshires they knew who'd be eligible. Mr. Berkowitz was thirty-two, beyond the age limit for the draft. Ruth's father, Mr. Gold, at fifty, was also too old, but his son, David, eighteen, might be interested. They wondered if Ruth's husband, Michael, planned to join. The girls worried what it would be like with all the men gone. They began to think ahead as to what would happen if all the young males went off to war. How would anything get done?

Micah invited Marjorie for a walk after services on Shabbos. They went to the same park where they first kissed.

"It's so nice you suggested we come here. It's such a special place to me," said Marjorie.

"There is a special reason why I suggested this place. Our conversation yesterday made me think about how I want to be the best partner I can possibly be." Micah moved to bended knee. "I'd like you to become my bride. You're the most wonderful person I've ever met. Will you marry me, Marjorie?"

Marjorie's eyes widened and her mouth curled into a huge grin. "I love you, Micah, and certainly I'll marry you." Then she hesitated. "Well, if my father gives his consent."

"I spoke with him this morning at the synagogue, and he gave us his blessing. You have just made me the happiest man in the world!"

After a wonderful kiss, Micah said, "Can we get married before I leave for boot camp? I know that's very soon …."

Marjorie said, "I'm happy to marry you tomorrow if that's what you want, but I don't want to be a war widow. You need to do everything you can to remain safe."

The young couple sat, hands clasped together, making rushed wedding plans. They wanted the rabbi to wed them quickly so they could have some time together before he departed. Neither wanted a large ceremony. Marjorie suggested they spend a couple of nights in Niagara Falls, the most popular spot for honeymoons and Micah was pleased with the idea. They were certain Marjorie's family would allow them to move into her room together since it made no sense to get their own place for such a short time. Once Micah returned from boot camp, they'd find their own apartment in New York City.

A few days later, Miriam shed tears of joy when Marjorie and Micah were wed in a sweet ceremony at the synagogue. Only thirty people were present, so the sanctuary was quite empty. Marjorie wore her mother's white lace wedding dress with a high collar, long sleeves, cinched waist, and flowing skirt. Deborah and Miriam both sniffled, watching Marjorie and Micah stand under the *huppah,* which Miriam had decorated with fresh pink flowers. They said their vows and broke the glass, which signified the fragility of relationships. The reception afterward was a simple affair, with homemade Jewish foods and modest decorations. For a gift, Deborah and Miriam gave Marjorie a week off from work with full pay and a night at the downtown Hotel Touraine for their wedding night. The hotel with well-appointed furnishings was a great treat for the newlyweds, who giggled as they registered for their honeymoon room.

Soon after the wedding, Micah departed for boot camp. Miriam spent many hours comforting her friend, who feared for her new husband's welfare.

"Remember, this is merely training, so try not to worry," Miriam insisted.

"But I've such a bad feeling about this. You know I'm not usually a worrier, but I've had many dreams of Micah being wounded," Marjorie said, with stress showing on her wrinkled forehead.

"You need to have pleasant thoughts, remembering you're married to a very sweet young man."

On August 17, Deborah received a call from her father, which changed her joyous mood.

"I've very disturbing news to share."

"What's wrong?"

"Do you remember my telling you of the Jewish man who was convicted of murdering a young girl in Georgia?"

"Yes, Leo Frank."

"Well, his execution was set for later this month. Because of all the assistance he got from Jewish groups and a campaign led by his wife, Lucille, just days before his execution date, the governor of Georgia commuted his sentence to life in prison."

"That sounds like good news. Why are you so upset?'

"Yesterday, a group of angry white men took him from jail and publicly lynched him, hanging him from an oak tree!"

"How horrible," said Deborah.

"And the most frightening part was the lynching squad, who called themselves The Knights of Mary Phagen. They lit a cross, claiming their right to provide justice on their own terms."

"Is that the same group we heard about in the movie *Birth of a Nation*?"

"Yes, I think so. Leo Frank's case sparked the film. These vigilantes took the law into their own hands. The larger group has called itself the Ku Klux Klan."

Deborah wept.

✿❦✿

Unfortunately, Marjorie's dreams were accurate. After just 12 days of boot camp, Marjorie received the following telegram.

WESTERN UNION TELEGRAM

Form 1201

NEWCOMB CARLTON, PRESIDENT   GEORGE W. E. ATKINS, FIRST VICE-PRESIDENT

RECEIVED AT BOSTON, MASSACHUSETTS
15G R 35 GOVT
WASHINGTON DC 4:42 PM AUGUST 23, 1915

MARJORIE KAPLAN
PLATTSBURGH, PENNSYLVANIA

REGRET TO INFORM YOU THAT PRIVATE MICAH
KAPLAN HAS RECEIVED SIGNIFICANT INJURIES.
AT MERCY HOSPITAL PITTSBURGH.

HARRIS, THE ADJUNCT GENERAL   5:45PM

"Miriam," Marjorie screamed as she flung open the door at the Cohen home. She fell into Miriam's arms. "Micah's been hurt. I was right."

"I'm so sorry. How bad is it?"

"I'm not certain, but the telegram makes it sound horrible. Take a look. What do I do?"

"You go to him. I'll go with you."

"But how will they manage at the shop without either of us?"

"They'll manage. You need me, so let's plan to leave right away."

Marjorie and Miriam arrived in Pittsburgh the next day, after transferring in New York for a fourteen-hour trip on the Pennsylvania Railroad. When they got off the train, the exhausted girls stared in awe for a moment at the magnificent ten-year-old Union Station, even more ornate than Boston's South Station. They found the Liberty Street exit, where they easily caught a taxicab to Mercy Hospital.

The hospital was run by the Sisters of Mercy, an Irish Catholic order ministering to the sick and destitute. Marjorie and Miriam tried not to show their discomfort as they surveyed the crosses and religious statues along every wall in the entry. But they were here to see Micah, so none of that mattered as it might any other day.

Two courteous nuns walked them down the halls in the men's section. They explained that the army sent all the infirmed from all the boot camps on the East Coast to this hospital, so they'd see many gentlemen with devastating wounds or crippling illnesses.

Both girls looked straight ahead, avoiding glimpses into the wards. The nuns turned into an area lined with men, some moaning or screaming in pain, and they made their way to the back of the vast room.

"There he is," said the nun, pointing to a pile of sheets. Micah's right leg was dangling from cloths suspended from a wooden contraption above his bed, and his face was pale and taut. Marjorie approached him quietly, and he managed a weak smile when he saw her. They talked softly as she held his hand. Miriam stepped back so Marjorie could have a private reunion with her new husband.

Miriam tried to ignore the sounds of the other suffering men and avoided glancing anywhere except at her own feet. One of the nuns tapped Miriam on the shoulder and guided her into a quiet side room to wait.

It was almost an hour before Marjorie joined her. Tears were streaming down her face as she sat on a chair next to Miriam. They joined hands and Marjorie quietly explained what she'd learned. "It's very bad. His femur on his right side is shattered. He's in a huge amount of pain and the doctors are worried about whether they can save the leg. They hope to fix his fractures without surgery, to reduce the risk of infection. If they must operate, they'll use screws and pegs, yet those usually cause infection. Either way, he'll be in the hospital for a while."

"That's terrible. How'd this happen?" Miriam asked.

"They were on a fifteen-mile hike, each carrying a thirty-pound pack. From the best of Micah's memory, he tripped when he heard an unexpected shot nearby. Even though they were using blank cartridges, he startled at the loud bang and fell into a small ravine, shattering his leg. The training halted while the other soldiers carried him to medical treatment."

The girls talked for a short while before Marjorie left to see Micah again. Miriam approached one of the nuns who helped them find Micah, asking her where they could get a room for the night. She was surprised when the nun offered them a free room at the convent. Miriam was in a quandary, not knowing whether the nun would rescind the offer if she knew the girls were Jewish. Miriam wondered how she'd feel sleeping in a bed if it had a cross overhead, but she didn't want to reject this kind offer.

When Marjorie was ready to leave Micah's side, they walked with two nuns to a large brick building on the hospital grounds. The antiseptic smell assaulted them as they walked in. They were brought into a large dining hall, offered a simple meal of meat, potatoes and corn scraped off the cob, and then shown to their room. The space was white and stark, with two beds with perfectly tucked sheets and a small, functional nightstand. There were no cracks in the pure white walls, and everything was scrubbed clean. It appeared as if no one had ever set foot in this space. The entire building was uncomfortably hot, but they dared not complain. They were shown to a bathroom down two long corridors.

Miriam whispered to Marjorie, "I hope I don't need to use the toilet during the night. I might get lost." Neither girl giggled as they might have done in any other situation.

Both were exhausted, so after changing into their nightclothes, they talked for just a short while. Despite the uncomfortable beds and the oppressive heat, they both fell into a deep sleep.

Very early in the morning bells chimed, which they later learned was a call to prayer. They dressed, walked down a long hall, and took a turn, which fortunately led to the toilet. Upon returning to their room, they waited for a sister to retrieve them. They were brought to breakfast and then to the hospital. This day was a repeat of their first evening, with Miriam sitting alone on an uncomfortable chair in the small room with blank walls, except for one religious painting, while Marjorie sat by Micah's side.

Miriam read some, glad she had thought to pack a book, but mostly she sat. She thought of home, of Deborah, of Sylvia.

As supper time approached, the nuns walked them back to the convent for another simple meal. That evening Marjorie insisted Miriam return to Boston in the morning. Miriam consented. She suspected Marjorie would be living in Pittsburgh for quite a while.

Back at home Miriam worried about Micah's healing. She wasn't concerned about Marjorie's welfare because she trusted the nuns would care for her. They managed without Marjorie at the office, but it was becoming more difficult after she was gone for three weeks. Miriam was greatly relieved to receive a telegram announcing Marjorie and Micah would be returning to Boston in a few days. She wondered whether Marjorie would be free to come back to work or whether she'd be needed at Micah's bedside for an extended period.

The problems Micah faced were much greater than anything Deborah or Miriam, or even Marjorie, imagined. The doctors in Pittsburgh were deeply concerned about Micah's recovery, knowing 80 percent of people with femur fractures died, mostly due to infections. A military commander was called to the hospital for a meeting and was encouraged to send Micah to Boston for his recovery. Massachusetts General Hospital was at the forefront of orthopedics, being pioneers in bone grafts and physical therapy. If he survived the train trip, he'd be better served by this top-ranking hospital than by Mercy. The commander said Micah would be discharged from his military service once he reached Boston.

Micah was placed on a stretcher and given sedation for the long trip, but even in his drugged haze he whimpered with every bump and turn. From the train depot, he was driven straight to the hospital in a military transport vehicle, and once there they immediately operated to relieve the pressure on his leg and to clean out a developing infection. For the first few days after his operation, it was unclear whether they could save the leg. Or save him.

Miriam visited the hospital, finding Marjorie steadfastly by Micah's side throughout the ordeal. "Thank you for coming, Miriam. I've been starved for conversation since you left. The nuns were very nice to me, as you saw, but none of them talked much. I was alone with Micah all day, and he was in too much pain to discuss anything. Happily, he improved a bit, which is why we were finally free to leave Pittsburgh. His parents have been visiting quite often, but I'm not yet comfortable with them. They give me a few minutes of relief from sitting at his bedside, though they're not much companionship for me."

On Miriam's third trip, Marjorie expressed hope for the first time, saying Micah was doing better than expected, with no further infection. They hoped they'd saved his leg, though he'd have a long recovery ahead with continued pain. After another two weeks, they discharged him home to Marjorie. Although he would need to go back to the hospital regularly, it looked as if he was going to live—at least for now.

Soon after Micah was discharged, Miriam went to Marjorie's home to check on the welfare of her two friends. She found Micah sleeping on a bed in the parlor, with piles of pillows under his leg and Marjorie by his side. Marjorie signaled they should go into the kitchen to talk.

"How much has his condition improved? Has he regained the use of his leg at all?" asked Miriam.

"The doctors think it's unlikely he'll ever walk again. The pain should subside gradually, but the damage was quite extensive and the leg may never heal. We're going to get him a rolling chair, so he can get around."

"I'm sorry to hear that. I hoped over time he'd make a full recovery."

"They weren't encouraging and he remains at risk of complications. The doctors said we need to be patient before making any decisions," Marjorie said with a grimace. She didn't say out-loud that the doctors told her almost everyone with a femur fracture has infections and eventually loses the leg.

"What will he do with himself if he's stuck at home all the time? It sounds like he won't be able to work at the Yeshiva or go to school as planned," Miriam said.

"Certainly not now."

"How awful for both of you."

Marjorie looked Miriam in the eyes. "I'm quite overwhelmed with this whole situation. Micah's parents cry a lot so I sometimes I wish they wouldn't stop by. They thank me for taking such wonderful care of him, but I think they're mostly relieved they aren't responsible for him on a daily basis. It's sad he has no siblings to help out. Some other relatives and friends have stopped by, but no one has been able to lighten his mood. Thus far, no one has returned for a second visit. I feel very alone."

"I'll always be there for you, Marjorie."

"Oh, Miriam. You've been the one person who is always there for me. I didn't mean to belittle your caring. I know you're doing the best you can, but you have Deborah and Sylvia and the business on your mind."

"But you're my oldest friend, and I'd do anything I can for you during this horrible ordeal."

"I'm afraid things will be terrible for a very long time. It's hard sitting by Micah's side every day."

"How can I be of assistance?" Miriam asked her friend.

"Actually, maybe there is something you can do for me. Do you think there is any possibility I could do some work while at home? It would help distract me."

Miriam didn't hesitate a second. "Definitely. Your work has piled up at the office. If you'd be willing to do some of it from here, it would help us greatly."

"I can't get into the office to pick it up," Marjorie said.

"I'll stop by every day with some work for you to do. And we'll be happy to pay your whole salary, even if you can't work full-time."

"I can probably work more than full-time since there's nothing else for me to do here. It would be wonderful to have a useful distraction."

"I've no experience with boredom," said Miriam with a smile. The girls both felt better as they parted for the evening.

Miriam was quite distressed by the situation yet thrilled to aid Marjorie in working from home.

"I'm pleased Marjorie is working again. It's a terrible situation, with Micah in so much pain and Marjorie worried and bored," Miriam said to Deborah, while folding laundry. "I hope having something to do will help a bit."

"It certainly does sound horrible. I'd be miserable in Micah's situation, or Marjorie's for that matter."

"It's a little more labor for us to prepare Marjorie's work to take to her, but it's a relief to have her keeping the books again. I know you did your best to keep up, but this wasn't your priority," said Miriam sheepishly, hoping not to offend Deborah.

"Nor my greatest skill. I'm glad to turn it back to Marjorie."

"How do you think they'll manage? What a difficult way to begin a marriage," said Miriam, handing one end of the sheet to Deborah. They moved in a practiced, synchronized manner, bringing the corners together with ease.

"I don't know how they can get through this unscathed. Our cheerful friend Marjorie is challenged by being a nursemaid instead of a bride."

Deborah's Journal, July 28, 1915

What a bad situation for the newlyweds. If I were Micah, I'd think it is not worth living, being a burden to everyone. If I were Marjorie, I'd be thinking my life had been ruined.

I'm reminded to be grateful for everything I have: my health, Miriam, Sylvia, my family, the business. I need to remember these treasures when I'm upset with something minor.

Their experience has taught me more about the tragedy of war. Not only are young men killed, but those who are maimed and those who love them are affected for their entire lives. I'll write another piece about the effects of war, a topic Dr. Hubbard agrees is of great interest to women's magazines these days. Lots of women are worrying.

WARFARE

When I learned about war in school, I never understood the impact it would have on the entire country. I learned the facts about who was fighting, where, and in what year, but I never imagined the actual people affected. Each of those soldiers had a mother, a wife, a sister, or others who worried about them. And each of them had his own fears. Why was I taught information about the battles, rather than the human side of the conflicts?

As I watch the impact of one solder's injuries, I realize the millions scarred on both sides of each battle. War affects so many, from the people who care for the sheep to produce wool to make the uniforms, to those who build rifles in factories, to the nurses who care for the wounded on the battlegrounds. War touches an entire nation.

What happens to women during wartime? When the young men are called to fight, women are left to run everything. What will happen to us if this war takes our men? Will we all be called into factories? Into hospitals? To run the country? I can only imagine what America would be like if women were to manage everything. Maybe it would be a gentler country, with less strife and less warfare....

After she finished writing, Deborah showed her article to Miriam, who was still awake. Miriam said, "I am impressed with the ideas you put into this article. I've not thought ahead as much as you. It would be a different world if women were in positions of power. Do you think women have the right temperament to run this county?"

"I certainly do. It might take some time for women to prove themselves, but I hope it takes less than 100 years for this to happen."

"It just might. But voting is the first step in this process."

"I will forever dream of women in charge because we think with our heads and our hearts, and with a conscience, which men seem to lack."

"I'd vote for you if you ever ran for a public office," Miriam said, smiling.

"Someday I might hold you to that statement."

Deborah and Miriam hugged tenderly, and then Miriam began stroking Deborah's breasts, signaling her interest in more intimacy.

"You aren't too tired?"

"Not at all. I'm so in love with you, the woman who may be president one day."

"Maybe just vice president."

They moved into a familiar position and demonstrated their love for one another.

CHAPTER 9

Micah

August 1915

Micah's accident at Boot Camp was life-changing. He was in pain much of the time and his movement was severely limited. His mood was usually depressed, and on days when his pain was most severe his attitude was foul. He required frequent visits to doctors, and each trip required significant planning and terrible pain in getting him in and out of the car. He needed a very sturdy man to transfer him, despite his diminutive size. His bed in the parlor of Marjorie's home offered little privacy to the newly married young couple, and his lack of mobility erased all dignity with bodily functions.

Marjorie was grateful for anything that took her attention away from her ill-tempered husband. On one of his good days, she said, "I think it's time I return to work at the office."

Micah looked shocked. "And leave me alone all day?"

"No, only for a few hours. After all, my mother is here most of the day to help you with anything you need."

"She can't help me with my bathroom needs. Please don't leave me."

"Micah, I think it would be good for both of us. I need to get out of this house, and it would be a kindness if you could manage without me for a few hours."

"You're tired of taking care of me. You want to leave me." Tears glistened in his sorrowful eyes.

"Yes, of course I'm tired. I'm not going to leave you, except for a few hours each day. I'll go to work in the morning and come home at lunchtime. Maybe your mother can visit during the mornings when I'm gone. If you don't want her help, you can wait to relieve yourself until I'm home."

Micah had no choice but to relent, though he wondered if this was the first step in her leaving him for good.

Marjorie arranged for a ride home with William at noon when he visited his baby. Getting out of the house for a half-day was a great relief, because she desperately needed to be around other people. Someone from his family came by occasionally, but his disgruntled attitude made their visits short. Marjorie's mother tried to help him, but Micah usually refused anything she offered.

Micah greeted Marjorie each day with the accustomed. She knew her presence made a difference in Micah's otherwise exhausting and boring day, but she needed to do this for herself.

Marjorie regularly leaned on Miriam for support. One day she asked, "Can you help me think of something I can do to bring a little joy into Micah's life? It's his birthday next week, and I'd like to do something to make the day feel special. He has minimal companionship and little activity other than doctor appointments."

"That's a huge question. What did he like to do during his free time before the accident?"

"He was a student so he studied a great deal, and he spent much of his available free time with me."

"Did he like to read? Miriam asked.

"He read a great deal and he loved the Yiddish Theater. He often read the same Yiddish books your Bubbie read. He was appreciative of the books you passed on to him after her death."

Miriam stood up suddenly. "I have an idea," she said.

"What is it?" asked Marjorie.

"What if he were to help us with Yiddish translation at the shop? I've told you about William's idea of separating the publishing and printing parts of the business. Well, one of the problems we're facing in our planning is how to edit the Yiddish books and newsletters. Hannah has been doing most of it, but she's needed on the printing side of the business. What if Micah helps with the Yiddish editing?"

"What a wonderful idea. Right now, it's hard to get him interested in anything, and he'll find problems with whatever I mention to him. I can tell him the problem you're having, and he might be willing to help you if he comes up with the solution."

"Hold on. We can't do anything until I've discussed this with Deborah, William, and Hannah. We work as a team, making all decisions together. The next time we meet I'll bring it up. Actually, I may mention it to Deborah ahead of time as she can often be the one to question new ideas. If I get her approval before approaching the others, the plan might have a better chance."

"We should both work on this gently so no one will feel we pushed this on them. You and I should check back with each other regarding any progress we make. And maybe for his birthday I'll get Micah an English/Yiddish dictionary. He won't need to know it would be of help with translation at the shop." Marjorie's eyes bulged as she said this.

Following this discussion, Miriam suggested to Deborah that Micah could help with translation of a new book project they'd just received. She explained this would free Hannah to focus on her primary duties. As expected, Deborah got worked up about the problem, concerned they'd not solved this in their business planning. Still, to Miriam's delight, Deborah liked the idea of approaching Micah, so they ran the idea by Hannah and William, who approved immediately.

Marjorie followed her plan, talking with Micah about the problem they were having at the shop with translating a book into Yiddish. Micah didn't suggest his involvement, no matter how many openings Marjorie left for him. He wasn't feeling competent in any area of his life lately and never considered he had something to offer. Finally, Marjorie decided to ask him directly.

"Micah, you know the book Hannah has been translating? It's taking lots of her time. Do you think you could help her?"

Marjorie waited a minute as Micah thought about her question. He finally answered. "I've done lots of translating from Yiddish to English. Much of it was verbal, but I could probably help."

"Thank you so much, Micah. It would be a great relief to everyone if Hannah could focus on her regular work."

Thus began the gradual use of Micah's skills to do translations of English to Yiddish and Yiddish to English, something they needed whether they separated the business into two parts or not.

Each day Marjorie came home at lunchtime to find Micah deeply engaged with the manuscript. Marjorie noticed that his focus on his pain and his frustrated attitude shifted when he had something constructive to fill his days. Perhaps the pain would have lessened anyway or perhaps the shift in his attention from his aching leg to the book made things better. Marjorie didn't care which it was; she was relieved he was feeling better. She hoped another book needing translation would suddenly appear when this project ended.

Fortunately, before Micah had finished working on the first book, another manuscript was dropped off at the office, this time Yiddish to English. It was a natural transition to having Micah as a regular staff member. His involvement lightened the load on Hannah significantly and seemed the final missing piece of their plan to separate the publishing from the printing.

Marjorie's other major concern about her husband was how isolated he'd become. Though his family was around him for short periods, and his friends came to visit on occasion, he was lonely. Being stuck in the house all day and night was wearing on him. He was desperate for Marjorie's attention, so she was housebound when she wasn't at work. Then one day Marjorie had another idea.

Marjorie approached William with her notion, knowing he'd be the one person to help her. They talked each day, finding a quiet corner for their meetings. Their sudden connection didn't go unnoticed, though they didn't disclose the content of their discussions with anyone, despite repeated inquiries. Even Hannah had no idea what Marjorie and William were planning.

After some time, William announced at their weekly meeting that he'd like to invite Marjorie to join them for a few minutes. Everyone hoped they'd finally be privy to information about the secretive discussions these two had been having.

Marjorie approached the meeting in a formal manner, unlike her normal chatty way. William stood at her side with a large folder. Everyone's eyes were riveted on the packet in his hands. "Thank you for letting me join you for today. As you probably noticed, William and I have been working very hard on a plan," Marjorie said.

"Okay; tell us what it is. The suspense is too much," Deborah blurted out.

Marjorie continued, still formal in her manner. "I know you all appreciate Micah's contribution to this business. He has greatly enjoyed his role in helping with the Yiddish translation. I think he could be of even more help to you."

"Marjorie," Deborah said loudly, "get to the point."

"I think Micah should come to the office to do his work."

Deborah, Miriam, and Hannah all looked from Marjorie to William, wondering what the two of them had concocted. After all, Micah was stuck at home in bed.

"The first thing Micah will need is an invalid chair to make him more mobile." Marjorie said. We've already ordered one from Sears, Roebuck, and Company so that part of the problem will soon be solved."

William then shared part of the contents of the packet he was clutching. In the folder were drawings he'd obviously enticed Helen to draw; he certainly couldn't draw that well. Deborah and Miriam now understood where Helen had gone after work on several occasions, making her late for dinner.

William laid some papers on the desk for everyone to see. On the first and second pages were pictures of two ramps, one each for Marjorie's family's home and the other for the office. "That way Micah can get out of his house and into the office," explained William.

After everyone gawked at the drawings, Miriam asked, "How would he get from one place to another? It's too far to roll the whole way to the office in an invalid chair."

William patiently brought out another series of drawings from his folder and laid them on the table. Everyone gathered around to see detailed sketches of a cart pulled behind a car. The wooden cart had a short ramp and a wooden platform with side panels on hinges to create a box-like apparatus. There were straps to hold the wheelchair in place as it was driven through the streets. They marveled at this contraption, aware of the hard work that William, Marjorie, and Helen had put into this project.

"Perfect," said Deborah with no hesitation. "This is brilliant. I vote to invite Micah to come here to work with us if this cart functions."

With great excitement, they all agreed to the idea. When Marjorie arrived home to tell Micah of this project, he burst into tears. He and Marjorie wept with joy, knowing life would be very different for the two of them if he could leave the house.

Building the ramps would be the first step, and constructing the cart would be next. Who had the expertise, and how would they afford the project? Miriam offered to approach the Brotherhood at the synagogue, where her father had been a longtime member, for their assistance. The men of this group offered to take on the whole project in her father's memory, including funding it. Some of the men offered to build the ramps, and others would construct the cart once the wheelchair arrived, enabling them to build it to the correct measurements.

The Brotherhood men were excited about doing this *mitzvah*. They arranged to travel as a group to Micah's house to look over the site of the proposed ramp. Once they saw Micah's living situation, they decided to take the project a step further. They offered to convert the back porch of Marjorie's family home into a private bedroom for the young couple, which caused Micah and Marjorie to shed tears.

Above: *Micah's leg in traction*
Left: *Micah's wheelchair and transport cart*

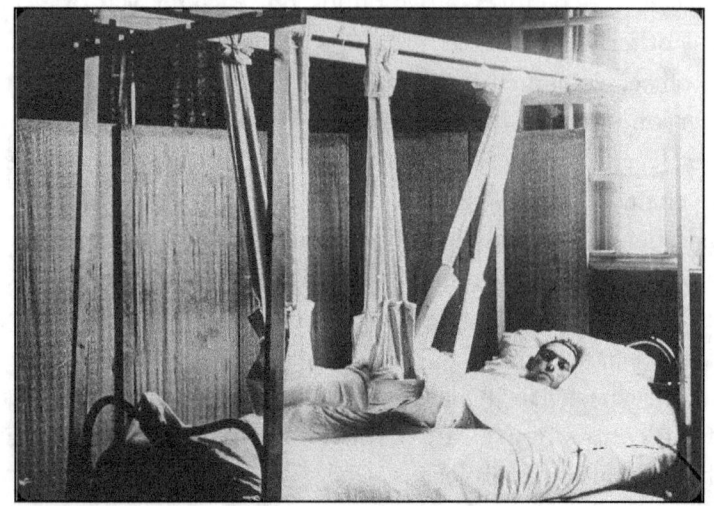

Micah with his injured leg in traction

Micah's invalid chair and the cart built to transport it

(SEE ADDENDUM "INVALID CHAIRS")

There was one more change from this project. When the Brotherhood men went to the office to evaluate where they could put the second ramp, they found challenges. The front door led directly onto the sidewalk, so this wouldn't be a possible solution. Behind the back door was a large tree, which would make ramp building very difficult. As the group from the Brotherhood surveyed the situation, a man exited the attached building and came to ask what the problem was. When they explained, he offered an answer. His office next door on Newspaper Row was too large for his book-binding business, and he was thinking about renting out some space. Would the publishing shop be interested in renting an additional room? Access to the building would be simple, and the car with the cart holding the wheelchair could be pulled up to their door. And working with a book-binding company was an added benefit.

The Brotherhood men told William about this solution, feeling most comfortable dealing with the male owner of the business rather than the three females. William immediately gathered the others to discuss this.

Deborah spoke first. "Renting this space would be an additional expense."

"Yes," interjected Miriam, "but this new plan will bring in more business and more money. I think we can afford the extra cost."

"With the addition of new staff, an extra space would be advantageous," Hannah added.

"And we could actually separate the two parts of the business," Deborah said. "The publishing shop would have separate quarters from the printing shop. We could keep the noise level down in the area where we're meeting with clients as we're editing their books and newsletters."

Their enthusiasm was evident in the loud chatter every day. As soon as the renovations of the new space and the addition of the ramps were complete, Micah could begin working with them in the attached yet separate publishing shop.

Within a month after the invalid chair arrived, Micah was able to attend the grand opening of Mordechai S. Cohen Publishing Company, named after Miriam and Hannah's father, the man who had founded the business. Prior to their guests arriving, everyone who'd be working in this new shop stood around the back door to attach the *mezuzah* on the right side of the door. Marjorie quietly asked to place it lower than typical, so Micah could reach it from his chair; they were pleased to accommodate him. They said the prayer in unison, taking a moment to reflect on this important moment. As each of them entered, they touched it, as was the custom, as a way of showing respect to G-d in a simpler fashion than saying the prayer. They repeated this ritual as they tacked a *mezuzah* on each new doorpost. They then opened the doors for their friends and neighbors to come inside to wish them blessings on their new venture.

(SEE ADDENDUM "MEZUZAH")

Deborah spoke softly as she and Miriam were putting Sylvia to sleep that night. "I was pleased how many of our regular customers showed up and was thrilled to meet new people."

"I have a really good feeling about this. It will be hard to work separately from you, but I think this new situation will allow the business to grow," Miriam said.

"And having Micah there with us today made it really special."

"It was the first time I've seen him smile since his accident."

"I hope that will happen regularly now. Marjorie deserves to have a happy husband."

Miriam's Diary, August 30, 1915

What an exciting day! The opening of the new business was thrilling for all of us. Deborah will run the publishing business, and William, Hannah, and I will run the printing business. Susan and Micah will assist with publishing and Helen with printing. Marjorie will split her time between the two shops for now and when it seems necessary, she'll train someone to work under her. Aaron, her brother, has begun to work with William full-time as an apprentice. With Rachel's sister Rebecca also apprenticing, our dreams of an expanded business are coming true.

The best part of this change was not the success of the now separate publishing and printing shops, it was the joy on Micah and Marjorie's faces.

Deborah's Journal, August 30, 1915

What a wonderful day! Today is the beginning of my own business, Mordechai S. Cohen Publishing. I'm having trouble believing my good fortune. I have a wonderful team to work with in Susan and Micah. I'm certain this business will be successful.

A short while ago none of us imagined a day like today. The shop was struggling, we weren't able to keep up with the work, and Micah was horribly depressed sitting at home day after day, finding no joy in life. Now, thanks to William's ingenuity, I'm certain we will have two successful shops.

I wonder how many other problems can be solved with a new vision. Rather than complaining about things that don't work, I hope to remember today and imagine solutions rather than problems. William's ideas have added tremendously to our business. It was wonderful to see the pride on Hannah's face when her husband was acknowledged as the person who figured out how to accomplish Marjorie's idea. We're a happy group today and a hard-working group tomorrow!

I think Miriam has forgotten entirely about her promise to take a vacation with me. July and August have been overwhelming, with Micah's accident and the opening of the new business. There was no time to visit with my family so I'm very glad I took the trip in June. I wonder if Miriam would be willing to go to Great Barrington with me this weekend before my parents leave for the season and before the High Holidays. I'll ask her.

Deborah, Miriam, and Sylvia went to the Berkshires for the Labor Day weekend, pleasing the Levines greatly. One surprising part of the visit was when Ruth, who was visiting her parents, invited the three of them next door for tea. While there, Ruth fussed about Sylvia, something she'd never done before. This change in her behavior made Deborah even more curious about the conversation between Miriam and Ruth during her visit to Boston. Miriam remained silent about it, but it looked to Deborah like Ruth was becoming part of Sylvia's life in a small way.

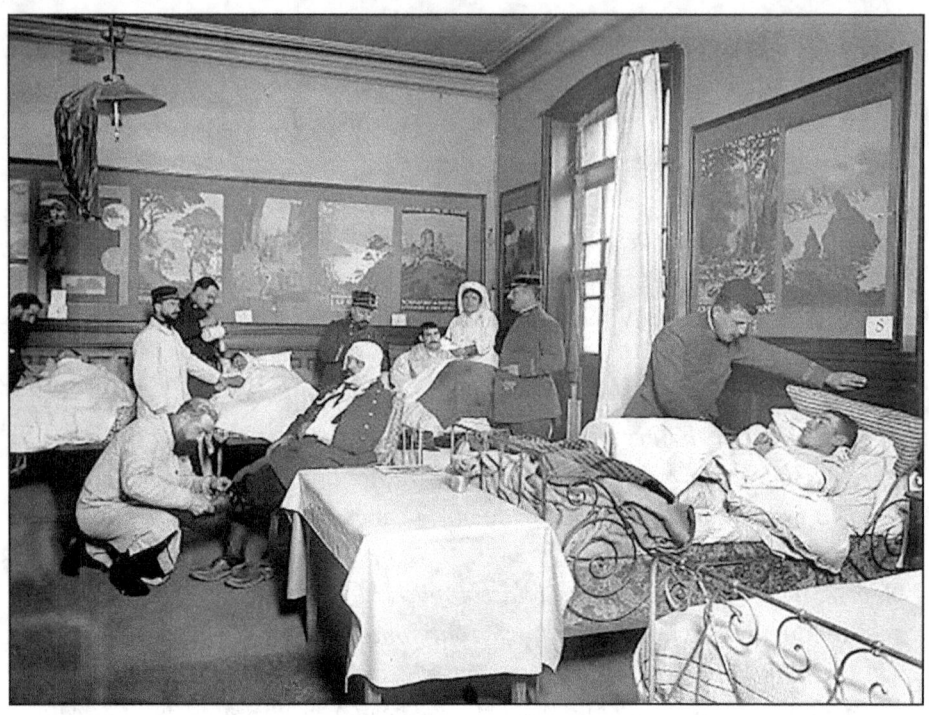

World War I infirmary

Mess hall at Plattsburgh

CHAPTER 10

Rachel

September 1915

$\mathcal{A}$s Rosh Hashana approached, Miriam thought about how Marjorie's family would celebrate this holiday. She and Marjorie had always gone to temple together, and since her mother and Bubbie died, the two families had spent the holidays together. But this year would be different for Marjorie's family with their house rearranged to accommodate Micah's invalid chair. Miriam knew they would need to celebrate on their own.

Rachel was the one to mention the upcoming holiday first. "My mother and I have been discussing the High Holidays, and we wondered what you will be doing this year to celebrate."

"We aren't going to Marjorie's house this year, so I guess we'll just have a quiet dinner at home. Oh, that was unkind of me. I should have talked this over with your mother. We would not expect her to cook us a holiday meal."

"She told me she would like to. We've not done much to celebrate the holidays since my father and brother died. She mentioned that it would be nice to cook you a traditional, festive meal."

"How very sweet of her and how insensitive of me to not think about how you would be celebrating."

"It doesn't matter to us as it does to you," Rachel said quietly.

"I have an idea. Why don't you all join us for dinner? We can participate in preparing the meal, and then you and your mother and sisters can celebrate with us."

"I'm not certain how my mother would feel about that. You know that she never likes to interfere with your family meals."

"Nonsense. It is decided. You will come to dinner with us."

Mrs. Stern had different ideas. She loved the idea of cooking the full holiday meal, including all the traditional foods for the seder plate, but she was not comfortable sitting at the table with the family. Deborah insisted they stay for dinner, but Mrs. Stern would not concede. Instead, she agreed that she would prepare the meal and take some of each item home to eat with her own family.

"Why is your mother being so stubborn?" Deborah asked Rachel as the holiday neared.

"I think it is a matter of pride," Rachel said. "I also think that holidays are difficult for her. Since my father died, she has let go of the traditions, which my father, as head of the household, made important. I think it would be kind to let her do this her own way."

"You would be welcome to join us for dinner even if your mother will not," Miriam said.

Rachel declined, explaining that she needed to be with her own family for the holiday. "It is very kind of you, but we need to follow our own practices, no matter how simplified they are."

Miriam felt bad. Although they probably would not have a full service before eating, she agreed to respect Mrs. Stern's decision.

Rachel, with her mill and Denison House experiences behind her, had turned into a sweet young woman. She took wonderful care of Sylvia and Sarah while their parents were at work. Deborah and Miriam often spoke of it being a fortunate decision to offer her the governess job for the two children. Luckily, because she was equally competent with infants and older children this arrangement could last a long time.

Rachel had a full figure and didn't fuss with her appearance yet she was a natural beauty. She handled the little ones' needs with ease—feeding, changing, and playing with them as effortlessly as any mother would have done. At eighteen, Rachel was the same age as many new mothers, though life had not yet provided her with a family.

When Hannah came to pick up her child after work one day, she asked, "How do you know how to entertain Sarah?"

"I've had a lot of experience with infants, caring for my little sisters, brother, and cousins. And Sarah is an easy baby," Rachel answered.

"You have such a gift. Sarah is thrilled to see you each day."

"Why thank you, Hannah. I'm glad you like the way I care for your child."

The next day Miriam also sang Rachel's praises. "You're so competent with Sylvia, following the instructions we received from Dr. Kingsley from the Experimental School so effectively. You arrive with plans each day, including physical exercises and lessons you created. I doubt Deborah and I could have done as well, were we the ones caring for her all day."

"Today, Sylvia's project is matching things. I'll have her pick out all the oranges from a pile of fruit and if she succeeds, I'll have her put the apples together too," Rachel explained, embarrassed by the accolades.

"You come up with such interesting games," said Deborah.

"Some days Sylvia is able to do these tasks. Other days she's more interested in tasting the orange or apple," laughed Rachel.

As was their pattern, Deborah wanted to push Sylvia to do everything she possibly could, and Miriam wanted to protect her from frustration. Rachel was aware of their differing opinions and was skilled at avoiding their conflicts.

Afternoons were Rachel's favorite part of the day. After lunch she'd take Sylvia and Sarah down the street to visit Leah. After several tumbles, it became a game to get Sylvia back onto her feet and keep her upright. Rachel always timed their arrival to get there long before Leah left for work at the printing shop.

Rachel often greeted Leah and her mother with a finger on her lips, signaling quiet as Sarah was close to sleep on her shoulder.

As soon as Sarah was settled in for an afternoon nap, Leah engaged Sylvia. She typically had prepared something to entertain her, such as stacking pots and pans. After some rigorous play, Sylvia was ready for her nap.

"Now it's time for your lessons," Rachel said quietly as she walked Leah into the dining room, where she laid out arithmetic materials.

"Thank you, Rachel. I love it when you're my teacher."

Leah already knew how to read, but her mother, her regular teacher, was never good at mathematics. Rachel taught her number skills, and Leah proved to be a natural to her mother's amazement.

When Sylvia and Sarah woke, Leah's mother provided a snack, appreciative these lessons had been accomplished by someone else.

When they arrived back home, Rachel took the girls into the back parlor to play until everyone got home from work. Sylvia and Sarah were always engaged in fun when their parents arrived. They both squealed when they saw the familiar faces peeking in the doorway. Sylvia headed directly to Deborah and Miriam, varying whom she saw first. Sarah was excited to see Hannah and William, snuggling happily in whichever arms reached down first to pick her up. Rachel watched this daily reunion with pleasure, though she often thought of how wonderful it would be to have her own child to *kvell* over with pride.

Catching up everyone on the day and commenting on the children's health, activities, sleep, and diaper changes, Rachel excused herself. She headed into the kitchen where her mother was putting the final touches on dinner for everyone.

"Mother, you look so tired," was what Rachel usually said as she glanced at her mother, who arrived a few hours before breakfast to make the family their first meal.

Mrs. Stern, a small woman with a head full of unruly ringlets that spilled out of her bun, made lunches for those working, making her early mornings extremely busy. She made simple lunches for Rachel, Sylvia, Sarah, and herself, so she could put the rest of her energy into creating a wonderful dinner. Each day Rachel and her mother ate dinner at the girl's insistence, but only after they'd served and cleaned up from everyone else's meal. Although Miriam tried to persuade them to eat with the family, Mrs. Stern insisted they eat separately, saying she was not fresh after being in the hot kitchen all day.

"Fridays are always so difficult for you, Mother. After you prepare a large Shabbos meal, you make food for everyone for Saturday."

"It's my pleasure," said Mrs. Stern, grateful Rachel helped out while the babies napped on Fridays, the one day they didn't go to Leah's. Rachel put herself in charge of baking fresh challah from the dough her mother made during the morning and preparing a pie for dessert for Shabbos dinner.

"I think the pie I'm making for tonight will be the best ever," Rachel said to Miriam, who came into the kitchen to check on dinner preparations and to thank Rachel for another wonderful week with her daughter.

"Why will this pie be better than the one you made last week? They're always wonderful."

"This will be my first pie with that new special glass pan you bought, the Pieflex pan."

"It's called 'Pyrex.'"

"Why is it called that?"

"When I bought the pan, I heard how they created the name," said Miriam, sitting at the table as she watched Rachel cut the apples for the pie. "They wanted to call it 'Pie Ex,' but it sounded funny, so they added the 'r,' hence Pyrex."

"We will see if it really makes a special pie. Some time, when we're not having a meat meal, I'll make a Boston cream pie, like the famous dessert at the Parker House Hotel downtown."

"That sounds wonderful," said Miriam, licking an invisible bite off her lips. "I've never been to the Parker House. Maybe someday you and I could go there for a piece of pie."

Rachel blushed, unused to thinking of doing something with Miriam outside the house. It was a pleasant thought.

On Saturdays Rachel or her mother returned to serve lunch. It was against Jewish practice for them to work on the Sabbath, but neither of them cared. Miriam, whose parents would never have allowed a Jew to heat and serve the food, turned a blind eye to this rule.

Rachel enjoyed her work with the babies, but when she got home, there was not much awaiting her. She rationalized she was too tired to do anything; in reality, she had few friends other than her younger sisters, Rebecca and Rivkah. Rebecca worked at the print shop during the daytime and had a busy life in the evenings. When Rivkah was not with her boyfriend, Benjamin, she spent time with some girls who were her age, who also stopped attending school. Rachel worried about her youngest sister, hoping she would be smart enough to stay out of serious trouble.

Rachel wondered why her life didn't include others her own age. She had friends when young; schoolgirls invited her to their homes. Later, she got along with the other girls at the Lowell Mills boarding house. Now, she no longer waited for invitations, resolving to be alone.

"Why do you stay in all the time?" her sister Rebecca often asked her.

"I need to plan activities for the children."

This seemed to satisfy her sister though Rachel knew that after finishing her planning, there was extra time before bedtime. She read book after book and crocheted baby bonnets to donate to the hospital. On the weekends, it was more of the same. She was glad when it was her turn to serve lunch for Deborah and Miriam's families so she'd have something to do. She offered to do it weekly, but her mother insisted they share this responsibility.

One Saturday, after Rachel served lunch, Miriam asked her to sit in the parlor. "What are you doing this weekend?" Miriam asked, innocently.

"Nothing much."

"I see you practically every day, and I really don't know much about your life. Do you have a boyfriend? You must have exciting activities for the weekend."

Rachel blanched. She didn't want to admit how empty her life was, but she couldn't lie to this wonderful person who had enriched her in so many ways.

"I don't have any plans," said Rachel with down-turned eyes.

"I don't understand. You're clever and sweet—and also very pretty. What's a girl like you doing sitting at home?"

Rachel tried to hide her feelings, but Miriam noticed she seemed upset.

"Oh, I didn't mean to make you feel bad. You've been so wonderful to us, and we both like you so much."

When tears started streaming down her face, Rachel realized she couldn't keep her feelings inside any longer. Miriam sat on the divan and put her arm around Rachel. They were only three years apart in age, but they seemed worlds apart right now.

Miriam thought about how Mrs. B. had guided her when things weren't right. Keeping in mind what Mrs. B. would do, she came up with an idea. "Would you like to go to the synagogue with us next Saturday? I'd be glad to introduce you to some of the other young people. Maybe you could join them if they've planned something fun for after Shabbos ends."

Rachel didn't know what to say. She might meet nice girls and boys, but she still wasn't sure how to turn acquaintances into friends. She was embarrassed to admit this to Miriam or to anyone. Miriam was being kind, so Rachel felt she had to accept her offer.

The next Saturday was her mother's turn to fix lunch so Rachel dressed in her nicest dress and headed to *shul* with Deborah, Miriam, and Sylvia. It wasn't her custom to go to synagogue, and she was embarrassed when she didn't know the prayers. She tried to copy everyone else though it was difficult. She was glad when they got to the "*Shema*," the central prayer of all Jewish services, and she sang out loudly, bringing some unwanted attention to herself. After the familiar part, she mumbled the rest.

When the service ended, Miriam escorted Rachel to where she could meet others. "I'll watch Sylvia for you," Rachel said.

"No, I'll take Sylvia," said Deborah. "I don't get enough time with her during the week and look forward to being with her on the weekends."

Rachel looked to Miriam, hoping she'd disagree, but Miriam grabbed her hand and led her to the gathering spot for the young people. She introduced Rachel to many of the youth and left her to chat.

Miriam kept an eye on her, amazed at Rachel's obvious discomfort with people she didn't know. Rachel stayed by herself, and Miriam realized she needed to intervene. She went back into the crowd and held Rachel's hand again. She walked her toward Aaron, Marjorie's brother, the young man who was now an apprentice at the shop. As Aaron was a bit shy, it might be more comfortable for Rachel to talk with him rather than the other chatty youth.

Miriam had to work hard to engage these two young people, trying several conversation starters that fell flat. But then she asked what Rachel was reading these days. "I just finished *The Scarecrow of Oz* by L. Frank Baum," Rachel answered.

Aaron's eyes sparkled. The two of them became animated, discussing this ninth book in the series that began with *The Wonderful Wizard of Oz.* Both of them had read every book, including this newest one, which had been published in July.

Miriam slipped away unnoticed as these two young people chatted on and on about a wizard and somewhere called Emerald City. She was pleased to have sparked this potential new friendship. Mrs. B. would have been proud of her.

By the end of the second week after this introduction, Miriam asked Deborah, "Do you think Aaron is a friend, or do you think our shy Rachel has a boyfriend?"

"I think they're smitten with one another. How did you manage to introduce them? You're quite the *yente*, a real matchmaker," said Deborah while making the bed.

"I actually had to work hard at it. Neither of them was much of a talker, and most of the topics I brought up between them fell short. I asked Rachel what she read. She has so few interests I didn't have many choices for topics, and I was greatly relieved when that one set the stage."

Deborah smiled. "Well, you did a wonderful job. Rachel seems to have a new bounce, starting and ending each day with as much glee as she shows with the babies."

"I think the two of them are seeing each other quite often. Have you noticed she didn't serve us lunch on Saturday? I think her mother was glad to take over this task in favor of her daughter's new relationship."

"Even her mother seems more enthusiastic these days. I think she's probably been worried about Rachel for a long time," Deborah said, handing the pillowcases to Miriam.

"I bet you're right."

Deborah's Journal, September 30, 1915

I'm so proud of Miriam. She has done something wonderful for Rachel. I never would have figured out how lonely Rachel was. Miriam has a gift with others, though I can barely manage to figure out what my Miriam needs.

Rachel is a very sweet girl, yet she seems shy. Although she has many admirable traits, Miriam says she has no skill at small talk, and she was desperately awkward when trying to talk with her peers.

Rachel is quite a miracle with Sylvia. I noticed how much Sylvia has changed with Rachel's constant attention to her development, especially with language. Sylvia is hard to understand, yet Rachel seems to know what she's saying more often than I do. Sometimes I wonder if Sylvia understands everything and is too stubborn to do what she doesn't want to do. Rachel doesn't seem concerned so I should probably relax.

Rachel has also helped Leah. I didn't realize her mother was not skilled in mathematics. Rachel saw more than I did. This is another example of how I need to hone my observation skills.

I'm glad she's spending her free time with Aaron. They're adorable together.

Israel Press and Photo Agency (https://commons.wikimedia.org, Dan Hadani collection 990044437980205171)

Simchat Torah

CHAPTER 11

Rivkah

October 1915

$\mathcal{A}$fter the High Holidays, Deborah and Miriam's focus turned to *Simchat Torah,* which occurred on the first of October this year. This holiday, which marks the conclusion of the annual cycle of Torah readings and the beginning of a new cycle, is the one time the Torah scrolls are taken out of the synagogue's ark and read at night.

They attended shul with Sylvia, Hannah, and William. As was the custom, the scrolls were removed from the holy ark, the *aron kodesh,* and a parade of men, with their sons and daughters, joyously circled the sanctuary seven times with the Torah. Deborah and Miriam, carrying Sylvia, joined William and the men. As they completed the last round, Leah's father approached them. "It's lovely to see you both," he said. "I'm pleased you girls feel comfortable to participate in this ritual."

"Thank you for saying that," said Deborah. "We were a bit worried the men would be upset with us joining them, but we really want Sylvia to experience this."

"I think it's brave of you, and you seemed to get a positive reception. Everyone knows Sylvia has no father and you girls are doing your best for this child."

"Thank you. I appreciate your support," said Miriam. "How is this holiday for you? You always came with Leah when she was small enough to carry around."

"I miss having her with me, but she's grown too much for me to lift her. And it would be too difficult to get her invalid chair here."

"She's maturing into quite a lovely young lady," Miriam responded.

"Thank you."

Everyone gathered for spirited dancing and singing. The women and men celebrated in separate circles, as had been done for centuries in their old countries.

Miriam looked around the room, eying the large families enjoying this celebration. She was a bit envious of the mothers encircled by groups of youngsters, though she dared not mention anything to Deborah. She knew Deborah would never have that same reaction.

After two hours, Miriam said to Deborah and Hannah, "I'm too weary to continue enjoying the festivities. How would you feel about leaving soon?"

"I am thrilled you said that," said Hannah, yawning. They soon returned home, finding Sarah snug in the bed in Sylvia's room and Susan and Helen, her minders, also sleeping.

As Miriam opened the door the next morning, she was shocked by Rachel's tear-stained face. While holding her breath, Miriam asked, "What's wrong, Rachel? You look horrible this morning. Are you ill?"

"I'm not sick, but thank you for asking. I received very difficult news last night."

"Is your mother ill? Or did someone die?"

"No, not Mother and no one died. But do you remember my sister Rivkah, who you tutored at Denison House? We talked of her working with us and decided she was too unruly."

"Certainly I remember her. She's very bright and learned quickly. It didn't take long for her to catch up on lessons she missed when she wasn't able to go to school. What's wrong with her?"

"She isn't bright enough to keep herself from getting into trouble."

"What kind of trouble is she in?" Miriam asked.

"The baby kind."

"I'm sorry. Is she going to marry the father of her child?"

"No! She's fourteen years old and looks about ten. She's not old enough to be a mother."

"There are girls her age who are married and have children," Miriam said.

Rachel shook her head. "Not Rivkah. She's still a child."

"What will she do with the baby?"

"I suspect when she tells our mother tonight, Mother will be very angry. It's likely she'll insist Rivkah give away the baby."

"That's very sad news."

"I know. I'm really worried for her. She must deal with Mother's wrath, and she'll have little say about what's to happen. I better put my personal problems aside to focus on Sylvia and Sarah today, and you need to get ready for work."

"Yes, I do. Let me know if you need any time off to be with your sister."

As soon as they got into the car, heading to work, Miriam told Deborah, "Rivkah is going to have a baby."

"Who's Rivkah?" Deborah asked.

"Rachel and Rebecca's sister. Remember? I used to tutor her."

"I forgot her name, but I do remember Rachel talking of her younger sister. I didn't know she was married."

"She's not married and she's only fourteen."

"How sad. She's very young to have a baby on her own. Is she going to keep it?"

"I don't think so." Miriam took a deep breath and let it out slowly.

Both girls became very quiet, thinking of this unfortunate infant who'd have no home.

The next couple of days brought more information. Rachel's mother, Mrs. Stern, was extremely distraught and embarrassed to have an illegitimate grandchild. She berated Rivkah for her illicit behavior, and, as Rachel had predicted, their mother demanded Rivkah give away the baby.

Rivkah spent her days alternating between crying and vomiting. She was extremely upset about giving her child to strangers, but there was no way her family could afford another child.

Miriam arrived at her volunteer job at Denison House on Wednesday evening to find Rivkah waiting for her.

"May I speak with you, Miriam?"

Miriam's heart beat quickly as she found a quiet place to talk with this young girl.

Rivkah took a deep breath and spoke softly. "My sister told you my problem. Did she tell you my mother wants me to give my baby to strangers?"

"Yes, Rivkah. I'm very sorry for your situation."

"You can help."

"How can I help?" asked Miriam as the probable solution spun around in her head.

"I want you to take my baby," Rivkah said in a firm voice.

Miriam was silent as she took in these words. She stared straight ahead, deep in thought, her heart beating wildly. Eventually she said, "I'll consider it."

"Thank you."

Miriam went through the evening at Denison House in a daze. She admitted to herself she had thought about taking this baby before Rivkah brought up the idea. She longed for another child, and now this one was offered to her. She had many questions in her mind: *How could she care for a second child? What if Rivkah changed her mind? And most importantly what would Deborah say?*

"Another child?" asked Deborah loudly when Miriam told her about Rivkah's request. "I told you I don't want a second baby. And besides, how could we manage? We're already busy with Sylvia and the business. Splitting the shop has challenged all of us of late. How could we possibly find enough time to care for a new infant?"

"I don't know how we'd manage," said Miriam. "I know it would be foolish of us to raise another child. However, when I think of Rivkah giving this child to perfect strangers, I'm very sad. And I'm certain the child wouldn't go to a Jewish home." Miriam thought, but didn't say out loud, *And, I really want another baby!*

"It's not wise of us to take this on."

Miriam's eyes turned downward as she said, "You're right," walking away.

Deborah saw the sadness on Miriam's face and, in a moment of weakness, she called out, "I'll think about this. Give me a few days."

Miriam's Diary, October 13, 1915

I'm overwhelmed. Thoughts of a new baby have taken over my mind. I'm upset, thinking this probably won't happen. Deborah has told me before she wouldn't consider another child, yet she said she'd think about it. How will I feel if she refuses to take this infant?

There are so many thoughts running through my head. How would Sylvia be with another baby? Would she be enriched by a sibling or be overshadowed by a normal child? Would she be shamed by her limitations when this youngster surpassed her?

And what if this second child has problems? Could we deal with another baby with challenges? Would it take our attention away from our business?

What if it's a boy? Could I love a boy as much as I love Sylvia?
And what about Susan and Helen? How would they feel about having
a third child in our home? There is so much to think about.

Deborah's Journal, October 13, 1915

During this evening, I felt palpitations in my chest while thinking
about the challenges of parenting a second child. I'm happy with our
lives, and I'd hate to disrupt our hard-earned serenity.

I know how much Miriam would like another child, but it makes
no sense for us to take this baby. Another child would add significantly
more stress and expense. Miriam is all emotion in her decision. I must
be wise in my choice because it affects the rest of our lives.

On the other hand, when would we ever have another opportunity
to parent a Jewish child? And, most importantly, will Miriam ever
forgive me if I say no?

A few days later, things changed in a way neither Deborah nor Miriam
could have predicted. As soon as they arrived home from work, Rachel asked
to talk privately with the two of them. The stern expression on her face made
it clear this was to be a serious discussion. Deborah and Miriam asked Hannah
and William to watch the children while the three women settled themselves
into the parlor.

"I've been thinking," began Rachel. "You know about the baby my sister
Rivkah is carrying. Well, I've wondered where the baby will live for the rest
of her life."

Miriam made steady eye contact with Deborah, assuming Rivkah had
shared her request they take the baby.

"I've been really worried about what will happen to this child," she repeated.

Deborah began to say something about how they were still considering
Rivkah's offer when Miriam grabbed her hand tightly, squelching the words
she was about to emit. Deborah took the hint and sat back.

"I've been thinking of raising the child myself," said Rachel.

Miriam took in a huge gulp of air, and Deborah tightened her grip on
Miriam's hand.

"You two would need to accept that I'd have another baby with me while
I care for Sylvia and Sarah. I wouldn't do it if you thought it would distract
from the care I provide to your child. And I'd need to make certain Hannah

is willing, too. And I'd expect you to pay me less since I'd be caring for all three babies."

"Slow down, Rachel," said Deborah. "Apart from the daytime child-minding issue, have you seriously thought about raising this infant by yourself? It's a huge responsibility to take on a child, and it will change the rest of your life."

"I know what a significant undertaking this is. And I don't know what Aaron would say. We're getting along very well, but our relationship is still so new. I'm unsure how he'd feel if I were a parent, especially to a child who wasn't his. I don't even know if he wants children."

"That sounds like an important conversation, Rachel," Miriam said, barely above a whisper.

"Yes, it would be. And I don't know how I'd raise the baby, except with the help of my mother and Rivkah. And I don't know how I could afford this. You know what I make and that isn't enough to have a household of our own."

"Why are you doing this, Rachel?" asked Deborah, trying not to sound judgmental.

"I want to help my sister. She's distraught and worried about what will happen to this child. Anyone could take it. They might not be Jewish. Or they could be bad people. Or people who want another hand to help them with their work. Anyone."

Miriam, trying not to cry, asked, "Has Rivkah talked with you about the options she's considering?"

"No. I don't think she has any. I'd be the only logical choice."

Deborah moved next to Rachel. "Raising a baby is a huge decision. You must think about all the consequences in your life of doing this. You would need to take time off from work if the baby was sick. You would need to pay doctor's bills. And you might be alone again if Aaron doesn't like the idea."

"Deborah, stop with all the concerns," Miriam said. "Rachel isn't asking us for our opinions. She's only asking us if she could care for this baby while she's caring for our child. I think our answer to her is 'yes.' It would be okay with us."

"But ...."

"No 'buts,' Deborah. That's the question Rachel has approached us with and that's the only question we should be answering."

Deborah sat back, sighing deeply.

Rachel began to cry, and Miriam comforted her.

"I don't know if I can do this. I don't want to tell Rivkah I will and then not be able to follow my promise."

"It sounds," said Miriam, "like you need to think more about this. Our answer is 'yes,' but there are many issues you need to resolve for yourself. And it sounds like you should talk with Aaron."

"I'll give this a lot more thought, and I'll ask Aaron how he'd feel. I don't want to let his opinion be part of my decision yet I must admit I don't want to ruin my chances with him."

As they ushered her to the front door, Rachel said, "Thank you, Deborah and Miriam."

"Is that you, Rachel?" Mrs. Stern called from the kitchen.

As Rachel headed to her mother, Miriam went upstairs to check on Sylvia, and Deborah sat in the parlor, pretending to read a book. They were both dazed. Deborah couldn't even pull her thoughts together enough to read. And Miriam, well Miriam couldn't think straight. Her dreams of taking this baby may have been squelched even before she heard Deborah's decision.

They were both startled from their thoughts when they heard loud noises from the kitchen. Deborah headed that way, stopping as Mrs. Stern called out, "I don't deserve to have a slut for a daughter."

Rachel ran from the kitchen and threw open the door, sobbing. Miriam started after her, but quickly realized this was their family problem, and she shouldn't get involved. By now Miriam had reached the bottom of the stairwell. Deborah silenced her, pointing up, and they ascended the stairs.

In their room, Deborah turned to Miriam. "That was a shock. I've never heard Mrs. Stern raise her voice before."

"Neither have I. But having a pregnant fourteen-year-old is a good reason for her to be upset. It seems she's taking it out on Rachel as well as Rivkah."

"I think she's so upset she can't control herself. I certainly hope she won't throw Rivkah out of their family," Deborah said.

"I hadn't even considered that," said Miriam. "I know some families do that. I see Mrs. Stern as being loving and accepting."

"She's accepted us, but this is her own flesh and blood."

"It makes things more complicated. I wonder how she'd react if we took the baby." Miriam then became silent, remembering this decision hadn't been made and was still unlikely.

Deborah went downstairs to sit in the parlor, lost in thought. She was glad she hadn't told Rachel that Rivkah asked them to take the baby. It would have made things even more confusing.

The next couple of days were a blur. Although Deborah and Miriam did their jobs effectively, the rest of the time they were both numb. They talked to each other in short sentences, never referring to Rachel or Rivkah or the baby. When Miriam spilled ink onto copies of a newsletter she'd just printed, she got exceedingly upset. When Susan asked Deborah to help her with a suffrage paper she was writing, Deborah declined to help, feigning not feeling well. In their own room, Susan and Helen wondered what was going on with this couple. Obviously, it was something terrible.

Several days later Rachel called them together for another discussion. Deborah and Miriam sat quietly on the sofa.

"I've been doing a lot of thinking about this situation," began Rachel. The air was still as the two young women awaited the decision that might change their lives. After all, Rivkah's sister would certainly have priority over them should she decide to take this baby.

"Being a parent is a huge responsibility and an expensive endeavor. Nevertheless, this baby needs a loving home, and I could help my sister tremendously."

Stillness.

"I gathered my courage and discussed this with Aaron. Although our relationship is still new, I wanted him to be included in this decision. He had very strong feelings."

Rachel paused, and neither Deborah nor Miriam breathed as they waited for her to continue.

"Aaron felt this would be a mistake. If I took on the parenting of a small child, he believed there would be little left for him. He didn't think he could wait for me while I cared for a newborn."

Another pause.

"Although Aaron matters a great deal to me, I know the decision needs to be what's best for me, not for him, and not for Rivkah."

She took a deep breath, then went on.

"So, I made a decision based on my own needs. I can't take this baby. As much as I want to help my sister, I can't give up my future to save her the pain of giving the baby to someone she doesn't know. You know how much I love children, but this isn't the right time for me to become a parent."

Miriam let out a huge sigh and hoped Rachel was too caught up in her own feelings to notice. Deborah had a hard time withholding the smile that was ready to burst. Although she'd not made a decision, she didn't want the option taken away from her.

Rachel went on. "I felt great relief once I decided. I was really glad I didn't tell Rivkah I was considering this. She'd be terribly disappointed."

"I'm pleased you made a decision," said Miriam.

"But that's not all. In thinking about Rivkah's situation, I came up with another idea."

Miriam turned to Deborah, fearful she'd suggest that another family take on this baby.

"I think you two should take the baby," Rachel said. "You're such wonderful parents, and since you can't have one of your own, I think you should take Rivkah's baby."

"That's an interesting idea, Rachel," said Deborah softly, not wanting to give away that they'd already been asked.

Rachel left, and Deborah and Miriam went their separate ways, still not discussing this.

Another day passed, and Rachel was again looking for them at the end of the day. Deborah and Miriam looked at one another as they again sat on the divan in the parlor.

"I want to tell you what happened when I told Aaron my decision," Rachel said.

"What did he say?" Deborah asked.

"I'm really relieved you made the decision. I want us to have our own children."

"I looked him in the eyes and said, 'But we're not even engaged,' and he said, 'Not yet,' and then he smiled. He didn't say anything further, but I think he's about to propose to me!"

"It certainly sounds as if he is," Miriam said with a smile.

"You two will be the first to know. Thank you so much for helping me with this."

"It was your choice alone, Rachel," Deborah said with a slight grin.

"But you helped me a lot."

"I'm glad to hear that."

Miriam said nothing, but Deborah noticed she was teary-eyed as she hugged Rachel.

Upstairs, they were both deep in thought. Deborah sat at the desk to write a letter to her mother. She'd never turned to her mother with such a major decision, but she'd been turning to her father regarding the business, and it felt right to ask her mother about this personal issue. Then she decided to call in the morning, rather than write to her, since it was nearing the time to decide.

Deborah put down the stationery she'd addressed to her mother and picked up another piece. She wrote to Mrs. B. instead.

October 17, 1915

Dear Mrs. B.,

As is too often the case when I write to you, I'm looking for advice. Miriam and I are faced with something enormous.

Rivkah, one of the girls Miriam tutored last year at Denison House, is expecting a baby. She's only fourteen years old and unmarried. You met her sister Rachel the last time you were here. Rachel is the nice girl taking care of Sylvia and Sarah. You actually met their mother too, Mrs. Stern, our cook.

The dilemma we're facing is that Rivkah approached Miriam and asked her to take the baby. It's a huge decision, and I'm unsure what we should do. I saw the disappointment and hurt on Miriam's face when I told her it would make no sense for us to take a second child. I know how badly Miriam would like another baby and here's one being offered to us—and a Jewish child. I've asked for a few days before I make my final decision.

I wish I could say yes. This would bring Miriam great joy, but I must be practical. I'm filled with worry about the responsibility we'd be taking on. The business is overwhelming, and taking care of Sylvia takes a huge amount of time and concern. It would be a strain on us, and I worry we'll be too stressed to be good parents.

This should be an easy decision because I never desired to be a mother. When I listen to my heart instead of my head, I find myself torn. Sylvia has brought us so much joy that the idea of another child is tempting. I must admit, having a child who doesn't have the same problems as Sylvia is appealing although there's no promise this second child will be free of difficulties. Fear of that plays into my decision.

By the time this letter reaches you, I may have hurt Miriam to the core, or we may have a second child on the way. The weight of this choice is tremendous.

> *With Love,*
> *Deborah*

The next day Deborah postponed calling her mother until she was alone in the kitchen. After explaining the situation, she waited while her mother considered her response.

"I understand all the practical reasons you've outlined as to why it makes no sense to take this baby. I also understand you're worried about how Miriam will react if you say no. Now, I want you to think about your own feelings. Would you like to have another child?"

Deborah was jolted by such a direct question. "Well, maybe. If it weren't such an enormous responsibility."

"Talk to me about what it would be like for the two of you to be the parents of another baby."

Suddenly the discussion was not about the financial responsibilities, nor about Miriam and her desires. It concerned her own feelings about being a parent. Deborah's heart softened a bit.

Her mother talked about her own decision whether to have a third child, something that wasn't an automatic choice. They'd never had a discussion like this before. Deborah thought about what her family would be like without Anna. She felt empty. Maybe this was what Miriam was feeling.

After their discussion, before heading to bed, Deborah wrote in her journal.

Deborah's Journal, October 18, 1915

I'm still unsure what to do. There is part of me that is tempted to accept Rivkah's offer, just to please Miriam. It would delight her beyond anything else I could ever do for her. Also, it would prove to her how much I love her.

But I can't just think of Miriam's needs; I need to scrutinize my own feelings, as my mother had me do. Is there room in my heart for another child? I love Sylvia as much as I could ever love another human being, other than Miriam, of course. Would I love this child equally?

Having a child is for a lifetime. It's not the love of an infant, but the love of a child, who will cause challenges for the rest of our lives. Yet she'd provide equal amounts of joy. If we were fortunate enough to have a healthy child ….

I must be practical and honest. We barely have enough time and energy for one baby. How would we manage without Rachel, should she decide to leave or to marry and have her own family? And I never wanted a second child. I must decide. Oy!

Two more days passed. Deborah and Miriam did not talk further about Rivkah's baby; the silence between them was loud. Deborah knew there was limited time before Rivkah made arrangements for her unborn infant.

Once Sylvia was settled into her bed for the night, Deborah took a deep breath. "I'd like to talk with you. Please come into our bedroom."

Miriam said nothing, but her heart raced as she walked into their room.

"We need to talk about Rivkah's baby. As I told you, though I never thought it wise for us to take this child, I've needed to reconsider. You've looked horrible. I haven't seen you smile, even when you're with Sylvia. Are you angry with me?"

"Oh, Deborah. It's so hard to put words to my feelings. I'm not angry with you because everything you said made perfect sense. It's not reasonable for us to raise another child. We're already stretched tight, and we have both a household and a business to run. I know you never wanted a second child."

"Finally, everything seems to be fitting together so well for us," Deborah said. "We have friends who are like us, as we always wanted, and Susan and Helen are a wonderful addition to our lives. Besides Sylvia, we have Mildred living with us, little Sarah coming here every day, and the children you work with at Denison House. Our lives are already filled with children."

"Yes, you're right." Miriam said without expression.

Deborah looked at her and said softly, "But you really want this baby."

"Yes. I told you I always wanted several children. My heart has an empty space. Also, I worry Sylvia doesn't have any siblings. You and I both grew up with sisters, and you have a brother too. What would our lives have been like if they weren't part of our childhood? And now that they're grown up, they're just as important to us."

"Do you think Sarah and Mildred can fill that empty spot?"

"It's not the same."

Deborah paused and said, "What else is on your mind?"

"I worry the baby won't be brought up Jewish if we don't take it, which matters to me."

Deborah sighed. "I think it also matters a great deal to Mrs. Stern, though she hasn't said anything about it. She doesn't go to *shul* regularly, like we do, but she's very aware of every holiday and she has special recipes to match each one. I think being Jewish matters to her a great deal."

"Okay."

"What else?" asked Deborah with the tilt of her head.

"Nothing, I guess."

"Well, I worry about one very important other issue. I wonder if you'll always resent me if I say no. Will you always think it's my fault that our family isn't complete?"

Miriam looked directly into Deborah's eyes. "I wish I had a clear answer for you. I hope not. I know you're being reasonable and not saying 'no' as a way to hurt me. I know you want me to be happy. I wouldn't want you to take on something as huge as another child just for my sake. It would need to be something you wanted just as much."

"I never had a desire for children, as you know," said Deborah. "But I love Sylvia more than anyone in the world other than you and my family. Not for one single moment have I questioned our decision to parent her. It was the best choice we ever made together."

"Is there even a little part of you who wants another baby? No, that's not a fair question."

Deborah inhaled. "Anything is fair in this conversation. I want us to talk openly, and, yes, part of me wants to take in this child rather than have her go to strangers."

Miriam sat up straighter and said, "But …?"

"The practical part of me is screaming that this isn't a good choice. Our lives are so wonderful right now, and I'm not as disagreeable as last year."

"Yes, you're right. That's one of the reasons I think this could work. I trust we'll be together forever. I love you, Deborah, and I want to respect your decision. I don't want you to take this baby because I want it."

"It needs to be a choice we both make."

There was a silence, with both of them deep in thought. After a couple of minutes, Deborah said, "Can you give me one more day to think about this before we give Rivkah our final answer?"

"Yes. And thank you, Deborah, for taking this decision so seriously."

They embraced in a long, tight hug before heading downstairs to spend time with Susan and Helen before going to bed.

Marjorie noticed Miriam was distracted at work and asked her about it. Miriam tried not to disclose the issue, but Marjorie was relentless. She sensed her friend was overwhelmed by something.

Miriam fretted, but words came pouring out. "I know Deborah is giving the issue of taking Rivkah's baby full consideration. I trust any decision she makes is the right choice for her. But will the decision be healthy for our relationship? I can't make her want it. And I wouldn't want to have a child unless it was loved equally by both parents. I am pretty sure she's going to say 'no.'"

Marjorie noticed Miriam's eyes were moist. She asked, "How will you feel if Deborah decides not to take this baby?"

Miriam began to weep. "I'm not certain. I want this baby so badly. She's definitely paying attention to my feelings, so I hope I can accept whatever she decides."

"I hope she decides on motherhood. Still, if she doesn't, you must accept her decision without resentment."

"I'll try my best."

Miriam's Diary, October 24, 1915

Why do I need this baby so badly? My mother would say I was born with a desire to be a parent. She always teased me, saying I cherished my dolls more than any other little girl she ever met. She assumed I'd be a mother, and I know that was on her mind when I chose to be with Deborah instead of a boy. We never discussed it, but she knew parenthood was in my heart. She was thrilled for me when we took in Sylvia.

I wonder if I want this child so badly because of Sylvia. Having a Mongoloid child is fine but having a healthy little girl would be thrilling. I could sing with her, cook with her, and teach her my values. I would delight when she learns to read and be proud one day when she walks down the aisle with the boy of her choice.

It would be wonderful for Sylvia to have a little brother or sister. Although she'd probably not be like a typical older sister, it would be fulfilling for her. Sylvia would have someone to love her for her whole life.

It was decision time. The next evening, Deborah asked Miriam to come into their bedroom right after they got home from work. As she had no expression on her face, Miriam had no idea what the final answer would be. They both knew the next step in their lives together was about to be decided.

"I'm certain you know why I asked you to come talk with me," said Deborah.

Fearing Deborah's answer, Miriam could barely get out a response. She finally squeaked out, "Yes," and then bit her lips.

"I've given this issue a huge amount of thought. You know I went into this decision process with a strong probability of a negative answer. I thought about all the practical issues first, which clearly led me to say 'no.' Next I thought about what this would mean for you, which led me to another clear answer, 'yes.' The final decision had to be in my heart. Could I love another child? Would I be a wonderful, accepting mother, no matter what child came into our lives? I asked my mother, who was very helpful. I sent a note to Mrs. B., though I've yet to hear her response. Just the process of writing down my thoughts helped me to think this through. I've come to a decision. I hope it won't affect our lives in any way that will hurt us."

"Deborah, I can't wait another minute. My heart is beating wildly. I'll love you no matter what you have decided. I'm prepared to move on with our lives when you tell me 'no.'"

"My answer is 'Yes!'"

Miriam didn't move a muscle. She stared at Deborah with a look of disbelief.

Deborah repeated, "I said, 'Yes.' I want us to welcome another child to our family."

Miriam burst into tears and ran into Deborah's arms. She sobbed loudly enough that Susan and Helen came to their door, knocking and asking if everything was okay. Miriam threw open the door and said, "We're going to have another baby." They all cried.

Deborah and Miriam invited Rivkah to their house to discuss their decision. Rivkah cried when they told her they wanted to raise her child. She hugged the girls so tightly they could barely breathe. Miriam's focus was on the bump in Rivkah's belly throughout their embrace. When Deborah and Miriam told Rachel of their decision to take Rivkah's child, she was elated. They never told Rachel the idea was Rivkah's, long before it was hers.

Not long after this conversation, Rachel arrived at work very excited. "Aaron proposed. I know our romance is new, but our relationship was intense from the first moment we met. I can't thank you enough, Miriam, for introducing us."

"I'm so happy I did. Is your mother excited?"

"I'm certain she's concerned we're young and haven't known each other long, but our family needed some good news to balance the upset Rivkah's pregnancy caused. The news that you will take the baby may be as exciting to her as my engagement."

Miriam asked Rachel to go to the Parker House Hotel downtown to celebrate her engagement with Boston cream pie. Rachel was touched that Miriam remembered her offer of several months earlier. The two of them walked into the most elegant establishment Rachel had ever seen, with chandeliers hanging from decorative ceilings, tall arched windows, starched white tablecloths, and impressive cream-colored plates with gray trim and the hotel's special insignia stamped directly into the center. They spent a delightful Sunday afternoon together.

Rachel talked briefly of Aaron—of meeting his family and her hopes for their future together. Miriam asked questions, but Rachel rarely had answers, which led Miriam to wonder what these two shy folks would have to talk with each other about once the initial intrigue had worn off. She hoped they would find other book series to read together, or they would find other hobbies to share.

Miriam asked about her mother. She found Rachel knew little about Mrs. Stern's life in Russia. Once that conversation fell short, they shifted to a lively discussion of their shared love of horses followed by talk of Sylvia and the new baby.

Parker House dining room, Boston

CHAPTER 12

Susan

November 1915

What excitement there was in the Cohen/Levine household! The thought of another child was the focus of practically every conversation. Miriam was overwhelmed with anticipation, and Deborah felt at ease with her decision. Susan and Helen supported their friends, and Mildred asked question after question about this unborn child until they wondered if they should have waited to tell her the news.

With the business officially split and the increased staff, things improved for everyone at work. Susan and Helen, as well as the four owners, no longer had conflicting tasks filling their days, and all were satisfied with their more significant roles. Susan adjusted well to the Mordechai S. Cohen Publishing Company, appreciating her role working closely with Deborah and Micah. She felt valued for her organizational skills, and she was proud Deborah shared the editing responsibilities with her.

One day, when one of the printing presses suddenly shut down, everyone from both shops gathered around the large, silent machine, wondering what to do. Susan figured out the small adjustment needed to get the machine humming again; everyone praised her talents.

Susan was extremely happy living with Helen and in the role of parenting Mildred. She was also content living with Deborah, Miriam, and Sylvia, feeling more like family than friend. She enjoyed the large number of visitors to their household, especially appreciating Hannah for her intelligence and William for his sincerity and quirkiness. Yet Helen sensed Susan was troubled.

Helen assumed Susan's distress was due to the recent frustrations in the suffrage movement, a cause dear to her heart. The House of Representatives had voted down the federal woman suffrage amendment, a disappointing defeat. Each week Susan came home from their suffrage meeting dejected.

One evening, as Susan and Helen sat in the parlor with Deborah and Miriam, drinking tea and chatting amiably, Helen introduced a different topic. "I read about the Suffrage Envoy, which left San Francisco in September and is due in Washington next month."

"I haven't heard about Suffrage Envoys. Tell me more," said Miriam, interested, even though she'd not been going to meetings.

Helen explained. "These envoys are groups of women traveling across the country to stir up enthusiasm for women's votes. The first one was three women who went to Dayton, Ohio, to personally ask the mayor for his support for women's right to vote. He flatly turned them down, but the idea of women's rights envoys had been born. Last year 5,000 women traveled to the steps of the Capitol, and this year they hope to have an even bigger crowd. President Wilson will have to listen."

"I don't think he will," said Susan, solemnly. "He hasn't been a supporter of women voting."

Then, sharing more suffrage news, Helen said, "I also learned New York held the largest parade to date."

"I wonder if it did any good," Susan said, snorting. "The voters in New York, Massachusetts, Pennsylvania, and New Jersey continue to vote down suffrage for women,"

"I hope it swayed some voters," said Miriam, always the optimist.

Helen offered more information. "I read that the parade organized by the Massachusetts Woman's Suffrage Association had over 15,000 marchers. The parade route began at the corner of Massachusetts Avenue and Beacon Street, passing the Public Garden, Boston Common, and the State House."

"I'm extremely sad I wasn't able to attend the Boston parade," Susan said. "I was busy with work and with Mildred, and I let those things be more important than my work for women. I'm also bitterly disappointed I couldn't be one of the 40,000 women who marched along Fifth Avenue last month."

"Sometimes we must let others stand for the causes we believe in," Helen said.

"We're fighting a losing battle," said Susan. "I'm afraid our efforts are wasted."

"No, we're making progress. Thirteen states have already enfranchised women, and New York seems on the verge of changing. And maybe, just maybe, Massachusetts will vote in favor of women's suffrage," Helen said firmly.

"I'm not convinced it will happen, but I feel badly I've not done my share."

On November 3 there was more bad news regarding suffrage, but this time it was more personal. When Miriam arrived home from Denison House, she found Deborah, Susan, and Helen sitting in the dining room, sipping tea. She announced, "I heard some horrible news. Deborah, do you remember the girl, Elizabeth, you wrote about for the newsletter? She's the one whose mother was a suffragette."

"Certainly I remember her. She was in a terrible situation. Her father threw the four of them—Elizabeth, her mother, and her two sisters—out of their home. And, just to clarify, I wrote the story with her, not for her. What happened to her?"

"It's not Elizabeth who is in trouble, but her mother. Yesterday was the vote on suffrage by the men of Massachusetts. There was quite a ruckus from the women in attendance, and Elizabeth's mother was arrested."

"Oh, no," said Susan, who seemed extremely distressed, more than was fitting for a family she didn't know. "That poor woman."

Helen put her arm lovingly on Susan's back, glad to delay telling Susan the outcome of what they'd hoped to be a monumental decision in favor of suffrage. But the delay was short. Susan asked, "How'd the vote go? Did you hear anything, Miriam?"

"The bill failed," was all Miriam said, sad to share the news she'd just heard.

Susan began to weep. Helen put her arms around her, but through her tears Susan said, "Is there no justice for women? Men don't understand that our votes can help them to create a more righteous world. And it's unfair women like Elizabeth's mother are jailed for standing for their beliefs."

"I know," said Deborah. "I've heard horrible tales about the suffragettes in jail in England. They've been treated terribly."

"I hope she'll not be mistreated here in the United States," said Miriam, trying to steer the conversation from a discussion about the abuse of incarcerated women. She looked at Deborah sternly, hoping she understood this line of thinking would do nothing to raise Susan's spirit.

"How close was the vote?" Susan asked, ignoring Deborah.

Miriam admitted that two-thirds of the men voted down universal suffrage.

"Why are these men so stubborn?" asked Susan becoming pale and clutching at her stomach.

"Are you okay?" Helen asked.

"It's all unfair and unjust. I feel bad for Elizabeth's family. With her mother in jail, the children will be on their own." Susan burst into tears and gagged as she ran towards the toilet.

(SEE ADDENDUM "ELIZABETH'S MOTHER'S ARREST")

Back in their room, after comforting Susan, Helen asked her, "Why are you so despondent? You didn't even know the woman in jail or her children."

"I'm feeling overwhelmed these days. I'm upset about the failure of Massachusetts and New York to accept suffrage. It's not only Elizabeth's mother getting arrested that has upset me." Susan paused while deep in thought, then added, "I think I'm so unnerved because her family was separated. The situation triggered my own concerns."

"Concerns about what?"

"As I predicted before I accepted this job, I miss my family. I've never been apart from them for so long. Since moving to Boston a year and a half ago, I've gone home once, for Christmas last year. Now Christmas is coming again, and I want to be with them. I wonder whether I should have taken this job."

"Oh, Susan, I need you here."

"It's hard to be away from my family. Everyone—my aunts, uncles, and cousins—all get together over the holidays, and I'll not be with them."

The next day, Helen came upstairs to find Susan crying once again.

"So much is upsetting me these days. I'm missing my family and also New York."

"I know you are."

"If I were living in New York, I'd get involved in something meaningful. Not that working at the printing shop isn't important," said Susan.

"I understand what you're saying. You've always had a desire to help others, and printing Yiddish books doesn't fit your expectations."

"No, it doesn't, but I know we're helping our dear friends and I want to be with you."

"What would you do if you were in New York?" asked Helen, trying to be understanding.

"There is a call for assistance with *The Woman Rebel*, the monthly magazine by the woman who is fighting for women's reproductive rights."

"Margaret Sanger? I thought she escaped to England to avoid jail time for distributing information about birth control."

"Yes, that's her. She recently returned to the United States and opened a birth control clinic in Brooklyn. I would work for her if I were living there."

"I bet she'd appreciate your work for the cause," said Helen, trying to be supportive of her girlfriend's dreams of valuable employment, while knowing her own heart would break should Susan decide to do this.

When Susan continued to weep the next morning, Helen said, "You need to visit your family. It's tearing you apart to be away from them. You need to ask for time off from work."

With tears streaming down her face, Susan blurted out, "I think I need to move home."

"No," Helen said, more forcefully than she wished. "Go visit them and come back to me after the holidays. I think you need to be with them and then go on with your adult life."

"You think I'm being foolish and childish?"

"That's not what I mean. I think you need to reconnect with your family and then return to the life you and I are creating together. Even if I were a man and you were married to me, it would be important for you to make a new life for yourself."

"But you're not a man and we're not married. It would be different if I could bring you home with me and my family would welcome you with open arms, but that can't happen. I'm living a life they know nothing about."

"Let's not mix up issues. The issue at hand is that you miss them and need to spend time with them. Let's deal with that first; then we can talk more about your feeling isolated from them because you're not married."

"It's all tied together, Helen. Maybe I'm not cut out to be with a woman. I love you very much, but I can't deal with the separation of my life with you and my life with my family. Maybe I should move back home and let you find someone who can totally commit to you."

With a rush of tears, Helen swept Susan into her arms. "No, that can't be. We'll find a way to work things out. I love you and want you in my life forever. Please don't leave me."

"I don't want to, but you won't want to live with me if I'm unhappy all the time." With tears running down her face, Helen said, "And what about Mildred? She adores you, and you've made a commitment to her."

"I can't help how I feel. You'd do a great job with her. You don't need me to raise her. I'm certain she'd be happy to stay with you."

This was the first of many conversations between the two of them. Night after night Susan wept and Helen tried to persuade her to stay. Each evening, Susan talked of not being strong enough to be a lesbian and her fears of being rejected by her family. She also talked of how she no longer had time to be involved with the suffrage movement, which had been such an important part of her life since college.

Susan cried as she repeated her sadness about not being able to walk in the New York Suffrage parade. "It was the largest suffrage parade ever and I missed it."

Helen didn't point out that she probably wouldn't have been able to attend while living at her parents' home.

Helen was distraught, watching her girlfriend so upset. She tried repeatedly to persuade Susan to ask for some time off over the holidays, but Susan felt that wouldn't be enough. She'd always been close to her family, and she'd never kept secrets from them. Helen would need to remain a secret, and she couldn't choose Helen over her family.

In mid-November, Deborah approached Susan and Helen, suggesting they both take a few weeks off over the Christmas season. Susan burst into tears. Her worries flooded out all at once. She told Deborah how wonderful her offer was, but she wasn't sure it would be enough. She was seriously thinking of leaving. Helen, with tears dripping down her face, said they'd been talking about this for several weeks and she was fearful Susan might move back to New York.

Deborah put her arms around her friend and said she'd figure out something. "I value you as an employee and as a friend. I'm distraught you're so unhappy, and I want you to stay. Let me think about this, and maybe we can come up with a plan that will work for you."

The next few days were a whirlwind of conversations between Deborah and Miriam and with their two friends. Deborah, as she was prone to do of late in times of trouble, turned to her father, who came up with an idea she hoped would work. After she and Miriam put it in writing, they approached William and Hannah, who were supportive of the idea. They all agreed with Deborah's well-thought-out proposal; they didn't want to lose Susan either.

Deborah went to Susan and Helen's room. Before she knocked on the door, she could hear the sound of crying. She hoped the new plan she devised would be enough to keep Susan in Boston.

When Deborah entered the room, she noticed Susan's bloodshot eyes. "Susan, we have a suggestion. I hope you'll listen thoroughly. We're all in favor of solving this dilemma. I think this can work."

"But …."

"No 'buts.' Please listen."

Deborah explained a solution that gave Susan a significant amount of time with her family. She handed her a piece of paper outlining her plan.

Susan's scheduled time off:
One week during February
One week during Easter/Passover (which usually overlap)
One week in July (when business is slower)
Ten days between the holidays of Rosh Hashana and Yom Kippur
Christmas Eve to New Year's Day

In order to be fair to Helen, Deborah handed her a paper, which offered her time off as well, though not as much.

Their friends were very touched by the generous offer, and Helen immediately accepted.

For Susan, the time off was more than she could have hoped for. It resolved the issue of not being with her folks enough, though it did nothing to resolve her continued angst about not being able to be open with them. She and Helen talked about this issue at length.

"Honestly, I feel bad you need your family more than me," Helen bravely admitted.

"I need you too, but I miss them. They've been part of my life since my birth, and you've only been in my life for the past few years."

"There's nothing I can do about that," said Helen with hurt written across her face. "That's not easy for me to hear."

"You always ask for the truth."

"I know I do, but you're making me feel helpless about situations I can't do anything about." Helen looked away, afraid to look Susan in the eyes.

"It's the way I grew up, assuming I'd be close to them as they aged and through the rest of my life. It pains me to keep secrets from them."

"We don't always get whatever we want. Life is full of compromises," Helen said.

"You know I've sacrificed a great deal to come here to live with you. You don't sound very appreciative." Susan's eyes burned as she said this.

"I'm grateful for everything you offer me. No one has ever loved me like you have, but it hurts deeply to know I'm making you miserable."

"It's not you who is making me miserable. It's the situation," said Susan. "Do you have any of these same feelings? Or are you immune to feeling deep love for your family?"

Helen took a deep breath, wondering how Susan could imagine she didn't feel terrible she couldn't tell her parents of their love. She started to walk away, ready to head downstairs to hide in the playroom for the night. She didn't want to be hurt any more by Susan's words.

"No, don't leave. I'm sorry for making you angry," Susan said.

"How could you think I don't struggle with being unable to be honest with the people I love the most—my family?"

"Oh, Helen, I'm not being sensitive to your feelings. Certainly, you feel the same way; obviously you manage your emotions better than I do. Please don't be mad at me."

"I'm hurt and feel as if I don't matter to you."

"Oh, but you do. I'm so sorry. Please trust that I love you deeply."

They reached out to one another for a tearful embrace. Susan moved into their bed and Helen followed. Rather than continuing this argument, they told each other repeatedly how much their relationship meant to each of them. For now, they just wanted to focus on the goodness of what they had.

After many discussions, Susan agreed to try the plan and accepted Deborah and Miriam's generous offer, grateful they wanted her to stay at her job. Helen was relieved and hopeful Susan wouldn't renege on her decision.

"I'm so relieved Susan accepted your proposal. What would we have done if she hadn't?" Miriam said to Deborah, once Sylvia was settled in bed for the evening.

"And what would Helen have done?" said Deborah, frowning. I'd be devastated if your family was more important to you than me."

"I'd never choose them over you, Miriam. I love you too much to ever leave you."

"You forget so quickly. Think back to last year when you thought I'd taken up with Sadie. Were you considering leaving me then?"

"Yes, I guess I was, but that was for infidelity."

"I wasn't actually unfaithful. It was one kiss."

"Don't remind me. That was the worst time in my life," Deborah said.

"I'm so glad we've moved on from that horrible experience."

They were both lost in thought, remembering that time of terrible angst in their relationship. After a few minutes of sad memories, Miriam came back to the issue at hand.

"How would Mildred manage if Susan left her, after all her previous losses?"

"I'd hate to think of her facing that. I certainly hope Susan and Helen can manage to stay together for Mildred, as well as for each other."

"And we will stay together for the sake of our child," Miriam said.

"And soon to be children, and for each other. I love you," Deborah said as she reached over to kiss Miriam.

"I love you, too."

Deborah moved close and kissed Miriam with a mouth full of love and desire. Miriam reciprocated and soon they were engaged in tender loving.

Deborah snuggled in Miriam's breasts, licking them until Miriam was writhing in expectation. She reached down to Miriam's sweet spot and found it wet. It was only a minute before Miriam's breathing became ragged. She gasped quietly before her whole body relaxed. Deborah feared Miriam would fall into a deep sleep, though she was too excited to want that. She gently pulled Miriam's hand toward her own wetness, signaling her interest in continued play. Miriam obligingly rubbed Deborah's tender spot until she too was satisfied.

Miriam immediately crawled into a comfortable sleeping position and within moments was purring rhythmically. Deborah was disappointed since she anticipated more. She reached down and with her own fingers expertly brought herself back to the brink of explosion. She rubbed, then stopped, and repeated the process, eking out every bit of pleasure she could. Finally, she could wait no longer and rubbed faster and harder. She didn't want to awaken Miriam, but she couldn't stop the increased volume of her breath. She stroked some more, enjoying the moisture beneath her fingers as they slid the length of her private areas. As she felt almost ready, she increased the speed and pressure, and her final burst of satisfaction came with a small shriek. Miriam rolled toward her, lightly sleeping but drawn to the excitement at her side. Deborah moved into Miriam's embrace, and while still lost in dream, Miriam rubbed Deborah's wet spot vigorously, as if she'd been the one creating all the pleasure Deborah had enjoyed. Without fully waking, Miriam moved right back to the loving and they moaned together as they submitted to another apex of release.

In the morning, Miriam wrote in her journal about Susan.

Miriam's Diary, November 30, 1915

What a horrible fright we had. Having Susan leave us would be devastating to the business and equally disastrous for Helen. It would also be a terrible loss to Deborah and me; she's become part of our family.

I can understand her being desperately lonely for her family. I miss my parents and my Bubbie every day. If I had a chance to spend more time with them, I, too, might have chosen that over work. I doubt I'd have chosen them over Deborah. I was fortunate I never had to decide.

And then there is the complication of Mildred. Both girls clearly love her, but how would Mildred have coped with losing one more parent? She seems so secure these days that she'd be devastated if Susan were to move away. I'm relieved for her, too.

I'm happy to have this settled before we light the first Chanukah candle tomorrow evening. Though it is a minor holiday, it would have been difficult to feel grateful had Susan gone home.

As I look forward to this holiday, I find myself thinking of this being one of the last holidays we will have as a family of three. My dreams are about to come true, with another baby on the way. I'd like to invite Rivkah to celebrate the holiday with us, though I wonder how her mother or sister might react. I'd better check with Deborah first, then Mrs. Stern, before offering an invitation.

WOMAN'S JOURNAL
AND SUFFRAGE NEWS

VOL. XLIV. NO. 10   SATURDAY, MARCH 8, 1913   FIVE CENTS

PARADE STRUGGLES TO VICTORY DESPITE DISGRACEFUL SCENES

Nation Aroused by Open Insults to Women—Cause Wins Popular Sympathy—Congress Orders Investigation—Striking Object Lesson

AMENDMENT WINS IN NEW JERSEY

Easy Victory in Assembly 46 to 9—Equal Suffrage Enthusiasm Runs High

MICHIGAN AGAIN CAMPAIGN STATE

Senate Passes Suffrage Amendment 26 to 5 and Battle Is Now On

General Rosalie Jones in Pilgrim Costume; Miss Inez Milholland on White Steed Leading the Parade. One of the Scores of Imposing Floats; One View of the Procession

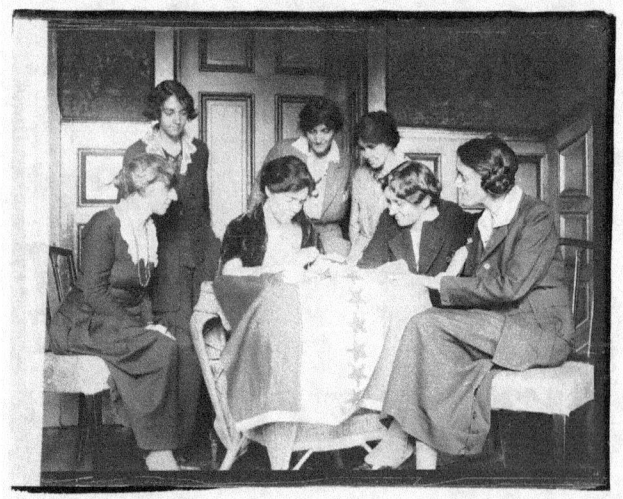

CHAPTER 13

Chava

December 1915

Deborah believed it was inappropriate to invite Rivkah for holidays, but Miriam asked Mrs. Stern. When Mrs. Stern asked why they would celebrate an unwanted pregnancy, Miriam wished she had listened to Deborah. Miriam decided to acknowledge the holiday with a gift for Rivkah instead of Chanukah *gelt*. She asked Leah's mother, a fine seamstress, to make a large dress that would fit Rivkah throughout her time. It was unlikely she would fit into her own clothing much longer, and there was certainly no spare money for bigger clothes. Miriam dropped off the gift at Rivkah's, not waiting for a response. The young girl did not write a thank you note as Miriam had been taught to do, but she did thank her when Miriam next saw her.

Hannah and William stayed each night for candle lighting and their only other guest was Deborah's friend, Chava, on the third night of the holiday. After they lit the candles, Hannah and William went home to put on their Shabbos clothes.

As the others sat in the parlor, Chava handed beautifully wrapped packages to Miriam and Sylvia. Miriam peeled the floral paper carefully off Sylvia's present first, revealing hand-knit light blue mittens. After putting them on her, Sylvia took them off; it was too warm to wear mittens inside. Miriam opened her package, finding a matching pair. Then Chava reached into her satchel and came out with a large gift for Deborah.

"You've gone too far, Chava," said Deborah. "We don't usually exchange gifts for this holiday. But it just so happens, I've recently purchased something to celebrate your graduation from the nursing program at Massachusetts General Hospital. It wasn't a holiday gift, but since you've introduced gift-giving, I'll get it for you."

"There's no reason for you to reciprocate. You don't need to give me anything, though I appreciate you acknowledging my graduation. It was a grueling program and I'm glad to have finished."

"I'm proud of you, my friend. Please wait while I run upstairs."

Upon her return, Deborah hid something behind her back. "These are unwrapped, but I hope you like them." She handed Chava two newly published books of poetry, *Tender Buttons* by Gertrude Stein, and *A Tear and a Smile* by Kahlil Gibran.

"I love both of them. Thank you so much. I'll read some of the Gertrude Stein poems as soon as I get home. Now open your gift."

They all stared at the large present, wondering what it could be. Chava was a skilled knitter, and Deborah was impressed with the magnificent shawl in her package. It was cream-colored mohair in a lacy pattern with large decorative tassels.

Chava, a pretty girl, with a slim figure, dark eyes, and soft waves of dark hair she piled on the top of her head, was pleased with their friendship. Until she met Deborah and Miriam at *shul*, she'd not found other girls like herself. As she and Deborah got to know each other, they found they could talk personally.

Chava desperately wanted a special relationship. She'd admired a girl when she was in school, but since then no one had intrigued her. Well, there was a new girl at synagogue Chava found very appealing. How would she know if this stranger liked girls in the same way she did?

⚜

A few days later, when Deborah was visiting Chava at her home after work, Chava asked, "Have you ever noticed the new girl who has been coming to *shul* lately? I think she's new in town because I haven't seen her until recently."

"I noticed her, too. Why do you ask?"

"I think she's really attractive. Did you ever see her with other girls? Or boys?" Chava asked with a shrug.

"No. She arrives with her family and stays with them the whole time she's at services."

"Maybe I'll try to befriend her. Do you think there is any chance she is like us?"

"No way to know." Deborah said as she got up from her chair. "I'll invite her to our house Sunday afternoon. That way you can get to know her better and figure it out."

"That's sweet of you. Help me decide what to wear. I want to make a good impression."

On Friday night, right after services, Deborah suggested Miriam go alone to meet the other girls at their regular spot so she could approach this girl.

"*Shabbat Shalom.* I've noticed you here, but we haven't been introduced. I'm Deborah Levine."

"I'm Maya Greenbaum. My family moved to this neighborhood recently. I really don't know anyone."

"That's why I wanted to introduce myself. If you'd like to meet some other girls, you can join us Sunday afternoon for tea."

"I'd like that very much."

Deborah stayed with Maya long enough to give her the address and set the gathering for 2:00 p.m. Then she headed to their meeting spot to inform Chava and Miriam of their plans, and once at home she told Susan and Helen. After *Havdalah* on Saturday, they headed to Marilyn and Julie's house to invite them too.

On Sunday, the seven of them gathered at the house, awaiting Maya's visit. Chava greeted her at the door. Maya, a striking brunette with huge eyes and a glowing smile, seemed a bit nervous.

Chava helped her with her heavy woolen coat and large-brimmed hat. "Hello, I'm Chava Rosen. Come in and I'll introduce you to the others. You met Deborah Levine at *shul* and this is Miriam Cohen. Susan and Helen also live here and this is Marilyn and Julie, who live in the West End."

The knitted shawl

Maya

Maya glanced around at all the young women, trying to track who was who. They sat around the dining room table with the couples taking their places next to one another and Chava sitting next to Maya. They chatted comfortably about what it was like in the neighborhood. Susan and Helen explained they too were new to the area, and Marilyn and Julie said they'd moved to the West End recently. Chava proudly discussed her recent graduation from nursing school and her job as a nurse at Mass. General Hospital. She hoped this would impress Maya.

Just then there was a noise from upstairs as Sylvia awoke from her nap. Deborah went to retrieve her. When she returned a few minutes later, Deborah handed her to Miriam, who asked, "How's my little girl this afternoon?"

Maya looked puzzled. She turned to Miriam and said, "I didn't know you have a child."

"Yes, she turned three in April," Deborah answered.

Maya looked more confused. "Is she your child, Miriam, or is she Deborah's?"

Deborah and Miriam looked at each other, and Miriam was the first to respond. "We're sharing the care of this baby. Our friend wasn't able to parent her, and we wanted to keep her out of the institution."

"How nice," was what Maya said, but she seemed distracted by her thoughts. She looked at the child to figure out what type of institution they were saving her from and looked back and forth from Deborah to Miriam.

The conversation continued with Susan and Helen talking about how they'd moved to Boston from different parts of New York. Maya said little, seeming confounded by the things she was hearing.

Miriam proudly brought out a tray of *munn* cookies she had made that morning. They looked similar to Bubbie's poppy seed delights, though darker. They were a decent attempt at replicating everyone's favorite treat. As she put them on the table, everyone except Maya began to talk about Bubbie and how much she was missed. When tears came to Miriam's eyes, Deborah quietly put a hand on Miriam's shoulder for comfort. Maya's eyes were riveted to this.

Suddenly, Maya stood up. All eyes turned to her as the flush across her face became noticeable. She stammered as she said, "Thank you for inviting me today, but I, I, I think I need to go home. I don't belong here."

"Please stay," Chava said innocently.

"No, I really need to leave," Maya said as she awkwardly moved away from the table.

"What's wrong? Are you okay?" asked Chava.

"No. I finally figured out why I'm ill at ease. You all say 'we' rather than 'I.' I'm not used to girls like you. I think I should leave."

"I'm sorry you're not comfortable," said Miriam.

"I really need to go. Thank you for your hospitality. It was kind of you to invite me."

Chava got Maya's coat and hat for her. Maya didn't even wait to put them on but rushed out the door clutching them, even though it was quite chilly outside.

As soon as Maya was down the steps, Deborah turned to Chava and said, "Sorry, my friend. I guess you got your answer about whether Maya is like us."

"I certainly did. It's too bad we upset her."

Although Chava was disappointed in the way things turned out with Maya, she'd not made Maya's acquaintance until that afternoon, so there were no deep feelings to get over. She admitted she was concerned about the general state of being single, fearing there would never be someone special in her life. She had no idea where she'd ever meet anyone with similar notions.

As Deborah and Miriam sat in the wing chairs in their room that evening, they discussed Chava's dilemma.

"I think we should include Chava in a gathering of the girls from Denison House, where there are always many lesbians," suggested Miriam.

"Good idea," Deborah said. Over time, Deborah was less concerned about going to events where Sadie might show up. They actually attended a few gatherings where Sadie was present. Sadie stayed away after a quick hello, and Deborah was surprisingly relaxed in her presence. She wondered how Miriam felt, seeing her old "friend," though she never asked Miriam to describe her emotions.

The next Denison House event was a holiday party at the home of a couple they didn't know well. Luckily, it occurred before Susan and Helen left town to celebrate Christmas with their families, so they could watch Sylvia. With Miriam's and the hostesses' consent, Deborah invited Chava to join them. Deborah and Miriam were uncomfortable about going to what they assumed would be a Christmas party, but they went for Chava's sake. Miriam wouldn't have gone had her father still been alive.

They picked up Chava en route to the house in the North End together.

"This is Chava Rosen, our friend. Thank you for including her," Miriam said to the two young women who greeted them at the door.

"Very nice to meet you, Chava," said one of the women. "Let me introduce you to some of the others." Grasping Chava's arm, she led her to the back parlor.

As they searched for Marilyn and Julie, Deborah and Miriam noticed a Christmas tree in the corner of the parlor. Though uncomfortable, they were also fascinated. Neither had ever seen a decorated tree in someone's house. It sparkled with silver threads and was adorned with strings of popcorn. Without saying a word to each other, they found themselves stopping in front of the tree.

They were riveted to this spot until they spotted Marilyn and Julie across the room. Following hugs and greetings, Miriam said, "I'm pleased we don't need to chaperone Chava all evening. She was escorted to where the single girls have gathered, so we're free to enjoy ourselves."

Miriam was still focused on the Christmas decorations. "Why do they have tree limbs on the mantle? It looks pretty, but I've never before seen greenery like that brought into a home for decoration."

Marilyn smiled at Miriam's wide-eyed fascination of common Christmas items and answered several questions about the holiday decorations, including the wooden soldier nutcracker. Although Jewish, she'd learned about Christian holidays from her next-door neighbors growing up.

While Miriam was engrossed in the holiday decor, a woman approached Deborah. Deborah immediately guessed why. This friendly staff person had been the one to request Deborah's help every time there was someone who needed assistance to tell their story for the Denison House newsletter. After many compliments about how Deborah had helped so many residents, she mentioned the newest child needing assistance. As usual, Deborah was fascinated by the story and unable to refuse. This story was to be about a mail-order child.

(SEE ADDENDUM "SALLY: THE MAIL-ORDER GIRL")

Deborah was glad when this woman left, and she was able to return her attention to Miriam. Miriam was still busy asking questions about the Christmas holidays, though once Deborah was back, they focused on one another.

"I was asked to write another article for the Denison House newsletter," Deborah said hesitantly, knowing this might anger Miriam.

"What is this child's story?"

"She was a mail-order child. I have no idea what that is, but the woman from Denison House assured me it is not the same as a mail-order bride."

"It sounds intriguing," Miriam said sincerely.

"It does. Are you upset I'm doing this?"

"No. You get a lot from meeting the children. We would never have met Rachel or that sweet girl Mildred if you had not written their stories, so this project of yours has enriched our lives. I'm not going to be complaining any more."

"That's very generous of you. I know writing with each of these children takes time away from you and Sylvia, but it's important to me."

"Deborah, I have tutoring and you need something that is yours. I understand your motivation."

"I appreciate your support. I told her I couldn't start this story until after the new year."

"That was sweet of you. But now we'll have to wait a long time to find out what a mail-order child is," Miriam said with a smile.

"Miriam, now you are complaining I'm not doing it right away? There is no winning with you."

They held hands as they went into the next room, searching out some of their friends. They forgot about Chava as they spent time chatting in the dining room, remembering about her suddenly when people began to leave the party. Susan had offered to put Sylvia to bed so they weren't rushed, but they were getting tired. They felt quite old, now used to retiring early.

Soon after Deborah and Miriam went in search of Chava, they spotted her, sitting in the parlor, deeply involved in a conversation with another women. As they moved, they both stopped short when they saw whom Chava was talking with. It was Sadie. Neither of them wanted to approach, so they stood at the edge of the room and looked at one another, frozen in place.

At that moment someone walked by who recognized them and called out, "Deborah and Miriam, I've not seen you all evening."

Chava and Sadie turned around at the sound of Deborah and Miriam's names, and stood up. Chava excused herself and approached them, asking if they were ready to leave. They nodded, unable to speak, and Chava went back to bid farewell to Sadie.

The three of them walked out to the car silently, but as soon as they got in, Chava began speaking excitedly, "I had a wonderful time. Thank you so much for inviting me. I met so many interesting girls and there was one girl I especially enjoyed."

"How nice," was all Miriam could say. Deborah said nothing.

Chava went on with enthusiasm. "Her name is Esther. She had to leave early, but we arranged to see each other tomorrow. I can hardly wait. We're going to see the new Charlie Chaplin film, *A Burlesque on Carmen*."

Deborah and Miriam chuckled in relief when Chava mentioned the name Esther. They didn't hear another word Chava uttered, relieved it was not Sadie who had captured her fancy.

After dropping Chava at her house, they headed directly upstairs to Sylvia's room to check on her, finding her cozy in bed. Susan and Helen were probably asleep, so they talked quietly when they reached their room.

"Please sit with me for a few minutes before we head to bed. I want to talk about the evening," Deborah said.

"Certainly," Miriam said as she snuggled under the afghan, which typically sat on the back of the wing chair. "It was a nice party."

"How'd you feel about seeing Sadie?" asked Deborah as she looked directly into Miriam's eyes.

"It was nice to see her I guess." After a moment's hesitation, Miriam said, "Actually, it wasn't nice."

"Tell me more."

"I'm angry with her for messing up our lives, yet part of me feels sad we never got to continue our friendship."

"Do you want to be her friend now?" asked Deborah with no visible emotion.

"No! She caused so much friction in our lives I'm happier without her."

"I'm relieved to hear that, though part of me feels badly you couldn't have a friendship with someone you liked so much."

"I thought I liked her, but I love you so much it's not worth having a friendship that hurts you," said Miriam as she rose to put her arms around Deborah.

Deborah rose and turned to embrace Miriam. After a long, passionate kiss Deborah asked, "Are you awake enough to show me how much you like me?"

"Definitely. I love you, Deborah."

They headed to bed.

They lay down, naked, holding their bodies tightly against one another until they warmed, despite the cold night air. Slowly, as they stroked one another tenderly, the heat in their bodies increased. Miriam reached down between Deborah's legs, and found everything cool and dry. But she knew how to touch the special parts, to massage gently until Deborah became moist. Deborah omitted cooing sounds, clearly enjoying the intimate caress. Miriam continued until Deborah's breath became ragged and she could feel her own parts responding with excitement. She moved deep under the covers, turning her body around so her mouth could find Deborah's sweet spot. She positioned herself so Deborah could reciprocate. Under the weight of the comforters, they lost themselves in each other's sweetness, licking and sucking. Together they panted as they brought each other great pleasure. Once they exploded with passion, they turned themselves around in the bed and snuggled tightly as they fell asleep.

Miriam's Diary, December 31, 1915

I'm relieved 1915 is coming to an end. These past two years have been fraught with crisis. After losing both my parents and my Bubbie, there has been an emptiness in my life. I'm relieved Deborah and I have reached a wonderful place in our relationship, and I am thrilled we will soon have another child. I will always be grateful to Deborah for making the decision to add Rivkah's baby to our family.

Other areas of our lives are also wonderful. Hannah and William have an adorable baby, and it's lovely to live with Susan and Helen. I'm thrilled for them about Mildred coming into their lives, making them a complete family. Now we have friends like us, something Deborah and I always wanted.

And I have Denison House, where I derive pleasure tutoring young children who appreciate everything I do. And Deborah has her writing. And Marjorie has Micah, who although disabled is now a working man, which gives him great satisfaction. Oh yes, we also have the business. It's hard to believe we've made such a success of my father's shop. He'd be so pleased with what we have done.

My plan for 1916 is to be satisfied with the riches all around me.

Deborah's Journal, December 31, 1915

This has been a wonderful year. Seeing Sadie at the party could have thrown off everything in my life; instead, it made me feel more secure with Miriam. I was quite difficult to live with last year when I feared losing her. Although I still have moments of jealousy and can be cantankerous, I have grown into a less reactive person. Also, Miriam has lost the edge she had when she worried I'd verbally attack her at any moment. And we're both calmer without worries about Mother and Bubbie, may they rest in peace. Miriam and I are doing better together than ever, being deeply in love.

Speaking of love, Chava seems to be smitten with her new girl, Esther. It has only been a few weeks, but this might be a good match. They've seen each other many times, and Chava talks of little else. And Rachel and Aaron, the shy young couple, hold hands whenever together, and no one could be more in love than Hannah and William.

1915 was memorable. Sylvia is gaining skills every day, which pleases us both. She hasn't had any additional fits, which the doctor says is a good sign. Rachel has done a wonderful job of encouraging her development. I'm thrilled to make Miriam happy with my decision to add another child to our family. I was content with our family as it is, but I must admit that I've become very excited at the prospect of parenting another baby.

My concern for my mother seems to have ended; she seems her happy, confident, capable self. And my relationship with my father is surprisingly strong, better than it has ever been. We relate better as adults, sharing a wonderful respect for each other, especially when I turn to him about my business concerns.

The publishing company is one of my great joys. I love the responsibilities I've taken on, and we seem to be off to a wonderful start. Our clients are much happier and the company is thriving since we split the business and added more staff.

The sadness over Micah's injury has affected us all, but I'm glad we've brought some comfort to him and to Marjorie by employing him in the business. He has been a wonderful addition and has allowed us to start our publishing company.

My writing is going well also. Dr. Hubbard has secured another magazine to publish some of my articles. I am so relieved Miriam gave up the idea of my writing a book about Ruth. I'm not sorry I spent all that extra time with Ruth, but I'm happy to have abandoned such a difficult task. If I tackle a project such as writing a book, it needs to be on a different subject.

My life is very happy right now. I hope that my good fortune will continue.

CHAPTER 14

Hannah

January 1916

The secular new year brought happiness to the whole extended family.

"My life feels settled right now," Hannah said, smiling, when Miriam asked her about her obvious joy. "I'm so proud of William's suggestions for our business. I am also thrilled by his support as a husband and tickled by his enjoyment of our baby. I love William more than I ever imagined I could love anyone. He is the sweetest, kindest, and smartest man I ever met. It's true the only men I knew before were Father and the boys from school and synagogue, but for me he is perfect."

"You still seem like a newlywed, even though you've already been married for more than two years."

"I hope I will always feel like a bride, even though I am already twenty-five years old. I never expected to be loved. William loves me the way I am, and now we have Sarah. Our little girl is precious and learns everything so quickly. I am pleased to have a healthy, sweet baby."

"Sarah is really adorable."

"Oh, Miriam. It wasn't kind of me to say those things. You do not have a healthy child, nor one who learns quickly. I feel bad that my words may have been hurtful."

"It's just fine, Hannah. I know you were talking about your feelings for Sarah. I, too, love my child and probably say things that make you feel bad your infant cannot live up to her."

"That is kind of you to say. I hope I can always support you regarding Sylvia. I know she brings you lots of worry, though she's a lovely little girl. And I have great hopes that your new child will bring you more joy than *tsoris*."

"Enough of that talk. Tell me how you're feeling about our new business arrangements. Do you feel comfortable with all the changes?" Miriam asked.

"I will admit to some concern when we first discussed separating the business, but I am really pleased someone else is responsible for the Yiddish translation. I feel free to focus on the printing, rather than being pulled in multiple directions."

Hannah talked on, especially about how she felt valued for her opinions. Everyone's support helped her to feel comfortable speaking up during their meetings.

Miriam noticed a slight change in Hannah's expression. "What's wrong, Hannah?"

Hannah took a deep breath as she brought up something Miriam would never have anticipated. "There is one area of my life that is troublesome. I wish I had friends. Certainly, you will always be my best friend and I could also count Marjorie, though Marjorie is really *your* best friend, not mine."

"And Deborah—and Susan and Helen are also your friends," said Miriam. "And Rachel, too."

"You are right. They are all my friends yet all those friendships feel incomplete."

"Why could that be?" Miriam asked, frowning.

"Each of those people has other friends they consider their best friends. I am only first with William. It should be enough to have him, yet I crave a girlfriend who is my friend."

"Oh, Hannah, you never seemed to care about friendships in the past."

"That is not true. I never talked about the aching in my heart. Other than you and William, I've never had anyone with whom to share my innermost thoughts. I should be satisfied, but recently my old ache has returned."

"Is there anyone you know who you would like to have as a friend?"

"No one. Mine is a good life, and I feel a bit guilty wanting more."

Miriam encouraged Hannah to continue this discussion. Miriam asked if she felt the need more acutely after Mother and Bubbie's deaths. Or maybe it was after Miriam fell in love.

"I don't think so. Recently, I have been aware of all the other girls who come to your house with their best friends."

"I'm sorry you feel this way," Miriam said, not knowing how to comfort her sister.

Then one day Hannah realized it had happened. She'd made a friend and hadn't noticed. And she'd been there all along.

Batya Shapiro, a small girl with unruly hair, was a school chum. They never went to each other's homes, nor did they choose each other as partners for school projects. If anything, there was some tension between them because they were the two smartest girls in their grade. Some years Batya won the spelling bee, and other years Hannah did. Sometimes Hannah's grade on a test was a little higher, and other times it was Batya's turn. They never said anything competitive to each other, though they noticed each other's grades when the scores were posted. When school ended, they parted.

Lately, Batya's and Hannah's paths had crossed again. Batya worked in her father's downtown clothing store, and Hannah saw her every time she went to buy an item. They talked about their children, comparing their accomplishments, reawakening their old competition somewhat, but now both were older, more secure in themselves, and had less need to be the best, the smartest, the quickest. They talked about their school days, finally acknowledging the ways they had tried to outdo each other.

Hannah found herself needing one item after another at Batya's father's store. The amount of time Hannah stayed in the shop became longer and longer. Hannah realized she was really going there to see Batya.

Hannah made the first move. One day when she was shopping in the store for one more baby outfit Sarah didn't need, she approached Batya and asked directly if she would like to get together sometime. The excited look on Batya's face said as much as her words.

"I'd love to get together with you," Batya said. "I always look forward to your visits."

"Then let us plan an afternoon together. Would you be free this Sunday afternoon? Maybe we could take our children to the park."

"Without our husbands? That sounds delightful and a bit scandalous. I'd love to."

Thus began the friendship between these two young mothers. After their first rendezvous, they got together several more times, bringing Batya's son and Hannah's daughter on outings together. They shared their children's accomplishments and milestones and talked of their work. Hannah was enjoying this friendship a great deal when suddenly one day it ended.

Hannah stopped by the store a couple times, but each time Batya seemed to be too busy for her and not able to make plans for another outing. On the third occasion, Hannah pulled Batya aside and demanded to know what was happening.

"Why are you unavailable to see me?" Hannah asked.

"Oh, Hannah," Batya said with sadness in her eyes. "My husband, Moshe, has forbidden me to get together with you and Sarah."

"Why would he do that?" Hannah asked.

"It's difficult to explain. I don't want to hurt your feelings."

"You can tell me."

"It has to do with your sister and her friend. And the other girls who come to their house. Moshe has heard about this being a house of women, and he thinks they are deviants. I never thought that."

"I don't know what to say. My sister and her friends are happy, healthy young women. They choose to be with girls but there is nothing wrong with them."

"I assumed that, but I think he fears they might influence me."

"Does he worry I might be like them, too?" Hannah asked.

"I think he might. But I can't talk about this anymore. He has forbidden me to spend time with you. You'd better leave."

Hannah went home distraught and talked this over with William.

"Why would Batya's husband be so narrow-minded? How can he worry about me influencing her badly? After all, I am a married woman. I do not know what to do."

"I am sorry. I know you were enjoying your new friend," William responded.

Hannah was distracted and upset. She tried to go on without Batya, but it wasn't the same. She frequently glanced across the sanctuary each week on Shabbos, focusing on Batya and Moshe, but neither acknowledged her.

As they left *shul* one day, Miriam asked her sister what was wrong. Hannah replied, "Nothing."

Miriam didn't believe her.

One day Batya unexpectedly came to the printing shop. She went directly to Hannah and hugged her. "I missed you so much. Both you and little Sarah."

Hannah, who was unused to hugging anyone other than William or Miriam, held on tight. Her voice cracked as she said, "I missed you too. What has changed?"

"It was your husband; he's a most wonderful man, just as you said."

"What does William have to do with this change?" Hannah asked.

"He saw how upset you were, and he talked to my husband at *shul*."

"So that is where he went. He wouldn't tell me what he was doing when he left me for a while. What did he say?"

"He spoke privately with my husband, and Moshe had a complete change of heart." Batya smiled.

"I told you how special William is. I am so glad things have changed. Would you like to go to the park on Saturday afternoon before *Havdalah*? Sunset is at 5:40 p.m., so I need to be back before then."

"I'd love to."

When Hannah got home that evening, she asked William how he'd changed Batya's husband's mind. At first, he said, "I do not know." When Hannah challenged him, he explained that he'd had a man-to-man conversation with Batya's husband, something he wasn't usually good at.

"I explained how wonderful you and Miriam are. I talked about Deborah giving up her life in New York to help save the family business and how she'd offered to co-parent their special child. I talked about the volunteer work Miriam does at Denison House and how Deborah has written stories about the children there."

"And that changed his attitude?"

"After my description, Moshe seemed convinced it is not an immoral home. When I started to talk of how fortunate I am being married to you and how special you are, her husband grew tired of my describing your wonderful attributes."

Hannah hugged her husband. "Thank you for being the most wonderful man in the world."

Batya and Hannah were pleased to resume their routine outings.

"I've a story to tell you about William," Miriam said to Deborah as they settled into their bedroom. "Hannah told me how he saved her relationship with her friend Batya."

"How?" asked Deborah.

"He talked with Batya's husband, Moshe. Moshe had forbidden Batya to befriend Hannah because we are a couple. He worried she'd be badly influenced, but William convinced him we're honorable people."

"I've heard concerns like Moshe's before. It sounds like the same apprehensions as the Sisterhood women."

"I know. I was a little afraid to tell you, for fear you'd get upset all over again," Miriam said.

"It's good you told me, my dear. I'm afraid these problems will continue."

"It was wonderful William intervened."

"I'm very happy for Hannah. She must be proud of her husband," Deborah said flatly.

"Yes, she is."

Nevertheless, Deborah's countenance was sad, and she was clearly upset at another example of how they might face discrimination.

Miriam's Diary, January 30, 1916

I'm so happy for Hannah. William was her hero. She's proud of him and thrilled to have Batya back in her life. I hope she never has to face further repercussions based on our way of life.

I wonder if this will make Deborah upset. She's sensitive, and I fear she'll react strongly to another occurrence of people rejecting us. I hope not.

Deborah's Journal, January 30, 1916

I'm saddened there are still people who judge us as immoral. I'm grateful William saved Hannah's friendship with Batya, but I wonder who'll be upset with us next. I fear this will be a lifelong problem. It's unfortunate the discrimination toward us affects other people. Intolerance is a horrible thing and we will always be victims.

William is a fine man, with odd mannerisms and difficulty relating to people until he gets to know them. He's bright, creative, and steadfast. Since meeting Hannah, William's awkwardness is still evident yet he seems less afraid of how others will treat him. His confidence at work has made him a valuable participant in decision-making, and he shines as a husband. I'm pleased he's in our lives.

Batya and her son

CHAPTER 15

Leah

February 1916

Miriam was excited to focus on a celebration for Leah, who was about to turn thirteen, rather than on concerns of prejudice. It was not usually significant for a girl to turn this special age as the right of passage to adulthood was only important for Jewish boys. There would be no *Bar Mitzvah*; girls had no equivalent acknowledgment of their coming of age.

Although this birthday might not be significant for other girls, for someone who spends every day trapped in an invalid chair, this was momentous. She could no longer be picked up and carried into the doctor's office. She couldn't be placated with small pleasures such as a dish of ice cream. No longer satisfied with stories of how others entertained themselves, Leah now desired to be part of the world.

The best thing that happened to Leah this past year was having a friend. When Mildred moved into the Cohen house, just down the street, Leah experienced the first real friendship of her life. Although Mildred wasn't yet eleven years old, she was worldlier than Leah. When together, they spent most of their time chatting enthusiastically. Mildred's experiences surpassed those of most girls her age, and to Leah, who rarely left her home, she seemed exotic and exciting. Every day together included yarns Mildred wove about her adventures. Leah sometimes wondered whether all the incredible stories Mildred told could possibly be true, but it didn't really matter. Even if the tales were fabricated, they took Leah's mind outside of her home into the countryside or into a new city. Leah devoured Mildred's anecdotes, imagining herself traveling alongside her new friend. Both girls delighted in this game, turning problems into high-drama adventures.

One day Mildred arrived at Leah's house with exciting news. With a high-pitched squeal she said, "I started working at the printing shop today. Susan and Helen took me with them this morning, and I got to do fun things for them all day. I moved stacks of paper from one room to another; then I got ink from the supply room. Then they asked me to staple papers they printed. My favorite job was when they asked me to look over a book for mistakes. Sometimes the printing presses make a mess of one page, and they needed me to search every page to spot a problem. When I found a mistake, they told me I have keen eyes."

"I have keen eyes, too. I want to help. Do you think they'd let me work like you?" Leah asked.

"I think you should ask Miriam. It would be really fun if you could," Mildred responded.

"Do you think there will be a problem because I'm not able to walk? They'd have to bring everything to me."

"I think they'd be silly to say no to you. You're smart, and I bet you could do even more things than I can."

Mildred made certain it wasn't long before Miriam visited Leah's family. As soon as Miriam arrived, Mildred left the room so Leah could ask the question about working for them.

"What a great idea, Leah," said Miriam with a cheerful voice. "We can always use extra help. I'll ask the others what they think about this."

Mildred popped into the room. "I told you she'd like your idea."

Miriam asked the others about Leah's suggestion. Because they were always behind, everyone approved as long as Miriam agreed to be the person to coordinate this project and to transport the work back and forth. They sent Miriam home with the first job for Leah that very day.

Leah was overjoyed to do something productive. She took her work seriously. She was a little slower than Mildred because it was sometimes awkward to get the papers into her lap without spilling them.

When Miriam mentioned this at one of their meetings, William said, "I will find a way to solve this problem."

"Mr. Creative is at it again!" said Hannah with a warm smile.

After a few days, William arrived at work with a special board. "This will fit over the arms of Leah's wheelchair, giving her a larger work surface."

Hannah grinned proudly.

Then one day a miraculous thing happened. Mildred and William surprised Leah at home early in the morning and suggested she dress in her winter jacket because it was cold outside. Because Leah rarely left the house, she'd not put on an outdoor coat for quite a while and it no longer fit.

"It must have shrunk from my last visit to the doctor. It was cold that day, too," Leah said.

Leah's mother laughed and said, "No, my sweet daughter. You've grown a great deal lately, and I think you outgrew your old coat. I'll give you one of mine."

"Where am I going? You still haven't told me," said Leah. "And why are you here instead of at school, Mildred?"

"It's a surprise," said Mildred, her eyes gleaming.

They bundled Leah and wheeled her chair to the back door instead of the front door where her father usually picked her up to transfer her to his vehicle. There in front of her was William's car with a strange contraption attached to the back.

"This is how we get Micah to work every day. I am happy to drop him off at the office and then come to get you each day," said William.

"Get me? Every day?" asked Leah with wide eyes.

"Yes. We work every day," William said in a matter-of-fact tone. "I do not know what we will do in the snow, but every day for now."

Leah looked from person to person, confused. "Come to work? What are you talking about? I do my work here."

"Now that we have this cart, you can work at the office," said William, with no thought as to how this news would affect this young girl.

Leah started to cry, and within a minute everyone was crying, even William. Mildred could hardly believe her best friend would finally be able to create adventures of her own, thanks to William's cart.

Getting Leah through the door of the shop for her first day of work was challenging. Her chair was older than Micah's newly purchased invalid chair and a little clumsier to manage.

As they wheeled her through the office, she was wide-eyed. "I've never seen anything like this," Leah said. "It's not like it was in my mind."

"Is it better?" asked Mildred.

"It's bigger and noisier."

"And better?"

"Yes, much better."

They situated Leah in the area they'd prepared for her, with a table built to the right height to fit over her invalid chair. Mildred had a new seat beside her. The two girls were giddy with excitement.

They were given their first task right away, with instructions about how Leah was to collate the pages of a newsletter that had just been printed, and Mildred was to staple the pages together in exactly the same place each time. Their first attempt was messy, with the pages slightly askew. Leah had lined it up perfectly, but it shifted when transferred to Mildred.

William, who was overseeing this project, said, "Not good enough. Our customer is paying for this job so it needs to be perfect. The pages need to be neat and exact."

The girls looked at each other with horror on their faces. Hannah came to their rescue and showed them exactly how to do this.

Hannah whispered to the girls after William walked away. "I will make certain you know how to do things. Sometimes William can be a bit rough in the way he says things because he wants everything just so."

The girls relaxed some with Hannah as their guide. They produced a few more packets before William came by and approved their job. They understood this was real work and were aware they would be paid if they did a good job.

Leah's temperament changed completely, once employed. Joy was written on her face every day, and there was also a serious new attitude. Working gave her a sense of importance, and she became more deliberate in everything she did. At times she became a bit bossy, telling her parents exactly how things should be. They thought this was probably a good change, though it was difficult to be corrected by their thirteen-year-old.

About a week after Leah started, Deborah walked into the printing office and found Miriam hunched over a project. "How's Leah doing? I know she had a rough start with William on her first day, but how's it going now?"

"William's very pleased with her work, and I think he's completely for-gotten his dismissal of her first project," said Miriam. "He's left it up to me to give her assignments, and he's nodded in approval, which is probably the most acknowledgment he can offer. He's much better at criticism than praise."

"I know, but I'm glad he's pleased, and Leah seems much happier."

Miriam smiled. "She certainly is. Her mother reports to me, when I go to their house to bring Sylvia for a visit, that Leah's becoming quite assertive at home. I think her new responsibilities have gone to her head."

"She's blooming as an adolescent, which may have something to do with the change in her. Have you noticed her body is beginning to change? There are little bumps forming in the front of her dress."

"Yes, I've noticed. I hope she doesn't outgrow her friendship with Mildred when she's a full adolescent and Mildred's still a little girl," said Miriam.

"I hope not. Leah's world is still limited, and she has no other friends. Though I fear it will happen the other way around: Mildred will outgrow Leah. Mildred has a lively personality, and she may develop other friendships at school and leave Leah out. That would be so difficult for Leah."

Just then they heard Leah calling frantically from the bathroom they'd outfitted in the new office space to accommodate Micah's and Leah's invalid chairs. When they rushed in, they found Leah in tears, holding out blood-soaked panties. They rushed to her.

With excitement Miriam exclaimed, "Now you're a woman!"

Deborah shushed her, knowing Leah wouldn't want the whole office to know this news. "Congratulations," she said softly.

"I've stained my dress," Leah said through her tears.

"We'll help you clean up," said Miriam, excited to be part of this important moment.

Miriam's Diary, February 13, 1916

It was a scary day for Leah. I don't think she was emotionally ready for this to happen. I wonder if it will be harder for her to take care of her woman's needs from the confines of her chair.

I wonder whether Sylvia will ever experience this rite of passage. Will she grow into adulthood, like other children? Will she be able to take care of herself, or will Deborah and I need to clean her bloody panties each time?

My conversation with Deborah this afternoon about Leah and Mildred concerns me. How will Leah's change today affect their friendship? Will Leah still feel close to her young friend? I remember my mother's warnings that my sister might be different when she became an adolescent. She might not want to be with her little sister anymore.

That didn't happen for me because Hannah never became a typical adolescent. She never had friends who became more important to her than family. We saw this happen with Fannie, though, who dismissed her siblings in favor of her friends.

Special children, like Leah and Sylvia, may have different journeys than others. Leah is the only other child I know with medical problems. Even though they are not at all like Sylvia's problems, I feel like I get to practice creating goodness in Leah's life, as I hope to provide in Sylvia's life. I hope my child has as rich a life as Leah does and I feel grateful for what I have been able to offer her.

I hope that our new child will be regular, a child who'll pass through life's stages at the right time, unlike Leah and Sylvia's destiny. I feel a bit guilty having these dreams, but I don't know if I'm strong enough to face the challenges that another special child would bring to our lives.

Deborah's Journal, February 13, 1916

What an important day this was for little Leah! When I think back to my own transition to adulthood, I remember feeling fear. I was eleven years old, and my mother had not yet warned me about this, thinking there was time before anything changed. Luckily, I was at home when I first bled, so she was able to give me clean panties and explain what was happening.

I was relieved Leah's mother had properly prepared her. Her upset was about her clothing, though I'm certain some of the tears were brought on by the sudden shift from childhood. I hope adulthood brings her happiness. The timing of this job is perfect.

Leah's been a wonderful addition to our staff. She's willing to do anything we ask of her, and she takes her work seriously. Her mother has been great about shifting her school hours to fit with her work schedule, knowing this job is a blessing for this delightful young girl. She takes classes with her mother each morning, works hard with us in the afternoon, and then spends her evenings studying. It's a full life for a child who had so little before.

For Leah, the transition to being part of the larger world has added enormously to her sense of purpose. Leah is no longer merely engaged in her own imagination. She's now among others, watching them intensely. Now she can see options other than those within her own home.

CHAPTER 16

Mrs. Stern

March 1916

Miriam was pleased to have several young girls in her life. In addition to watching Sylvia and Sarah grow and change, she now had her eyes on Leah as she transitioned to young adulthood and Mildred, who was blossoming. And there was Rivkah, several years older than Leah and Mildred, and pregnant, though less mature than the other two.

Miriam began seeing Rivkah regularly, devoting every Monday evening to visiting this needy girl. Deborah was supportive, even though this was a second evening out of the house weekly as Miriam continued her Thursdays at Denison House. Rivkah's life was shrinking each week, with no friends visiting because she wanted to hide her bulging stomach from everyone. There was no longer a boyfriend to add cheer to her days. Miriam's visit became increasingly important, though Rivkah had no idea that Miriam's motivation was partially to oversee the development of her unborn child.

An additional benefit of these visits was Miriam's opportunity to get to know Mrs. Stern better. The family lived in tight quarters at the rooming house. They were recently able to rent a second room for the four of them, thanks to increased wages in the new year for Mrs. Stern, Rachel, and Rebecca. Soon Rachel would be married and leaving, making their space less crowded.

Mrs. Stern arrived home after dinner hour each day, pleased that the rooming house offered meals for her three daughters. She was too exhausted to provide adequate nutrition for them. On Mondays, Mrs. Stern found Miriam engaged with Rivkah, entertaining her as appropriate for a young child, offering sewing or art projects to occupy their time together. Sometimes Miriam brought jigsaw puzzles or playing cards to entice Rivkah into activity, which pleased Mrs. Stern. With Purim arriving on March 18, Miriam engaged Rivkah in creating groggers, the noisemaker cranked every time wicked Haman's name was used during the recitation of the Purim story. Mrs. Stern made hamantaschen to commemorate this holiday.

Miriam asked Mrs. Stern questions about her life in Russia and was met with one-word answers. When Miriam persisted, asking specific questions about the foods she ate as a child, she was finally able to engage her. It became Miriam's challenge to encourage this quiet woman to share her history. Rivkah was fascinated with her mother's stories of "the old country," tales which were new to her.

Over time Miriam learned tales of life for Mrs. Stern as a young girl, working on the family farm in a small rural village near the Romanian border of Russia. The third of seven children, she and her sister were expected to work with their brothers in the fields. They grew rye to feed the animals and the family, and for export. Once the grain was harvested, the two girls were assigned kitchen duties, making loaf after loaf of hearty bread to feed the family and to barter with local farmers who raised potatoes or beets. It was through their exchange with a farm family from a nearby village that she met the man she would later marry. The young Mr. Stern, a beet farmer, would arrive with his father to exchange products, and he would weave tales of the adventures he planned. His vision of finding a ship to carry him away to America sounded like a faraway dream, yet once they married he was true to his word.

Mrs. Stern was pregnant with Rachel by the time they arrived in New York. Thanks to family connections, they were welcomed into a tenement on the East Side, where they lived with extended family members as they learned English and American ways. By the time they had saved up enough money to take their family, which now included Rebecca and their son, to New England, Mrs. Stern was pregnant again. Settling in a farm near Boston, they added a sickly Rivkah to the family, making it impossible for Mrs. Stern to work in the garment industry as did most of the other Russian immigrants. Instead, she made bread and other foods to supply to local stores while her husband found a job in the textile industry. Rebecca made dresses, and Rachel, the child with the most potential, took a liking to the farm horses. There were few opportunities for a Jewish farm girl so Rachel found a job in the textile mills of Lowell, Massachusetts, and left the family for a year of hard labor. Rivkah, still a child, suffered from seizures and displayed little interest in pulling her own weight for this hardworking family.

Mrs. Stern's son, barely fourteen, contracted diphtheria, and perished soon after Rachel's departure to the mills. At the same time, Mr. Stern became ill.

Eventually, he became too weak to carry the bolts of fabric and he lost his job. Mrs. Stern baked from morning until night to make up for her husband's inability to work. She nursed him, though it was not long before he succumbed to his illness, and Mrs. Stern was left with two girls to feed and clothe. Rachel was able to send home small amounts of money while employed at the mills but it was not enough. The family arranged to move into Denison House where they were offered shelter and steady meals. Just as they were about to leave their home, Rachel returned, moving with the family into their new accommodations. It was there where she was asked to write about her experience as a Lowell Mill Girl once she met Deborah.

"Mama, how come you never told me how you met Papa?" Rivkah asked.

"It wasn't important," Mrs. Stern answered.

"It is important to me." Rivkah chastised her mother for this oversight.

"It doesn't matter." She seemed embarrassed she had shared so much, and was reluctant to give more details, though Rivkah tried regularly to extract additional information.

Miriam went home after each visit with a tiny bit more of Mrs. Stern's story. It was hard to fathom that this woman's whole life was reduced to these few, sketchy tales that barely satisfied her daughter's curiosity. As she repeated each week's tiny bit of new information to Deborah, she tried to imagine this woman's whole life, reduced to a very short story.

"A short story. That is what this is," Miriam said.

"What are you talking about?"

"You need to help me write a short story about Mrs. Stern."

"To what purpose?"

"To honor our baby's heritage," Miriam said with excitement.

Thus began the project of writing this story. Deborah and Miriam worked together, crafting a tale that a small child would enjoy. They kept this a secret for the first week, but Miriam then confided in Rivkah, telling her what they were doing. Rivkah was pleased with the project, and each week Miriam arrived to hear Rivkah's latest details about her mother's life. Rivkah pestered her mother with questions, and Mrs. Stern began to open up. Rivkah suggested they craft this into a book.

Rivkah began drawing pictures, giving life to the scenes her mother painted. Though rudimentary, they were startling in their depiction of this simple life. Deborah and Miriam worked to write the story that matched the drawings. Miriam bought a small palate of watercolor paints, offering them to Rivkah, who immediately dabbed them on her drawings.

Miriam thought this project had more significance than merely telling Mrs. Stern's story. It was the story of many immigrants who were taken from their homelands with a few memories of the life they left behind. So busy with making enough money to feed their families, their tales were lost. Mrs. Stern was obviously pleased with her daughter's interest in hearing of her youth, and Rivkah was engaged wholeheartedly in this project, spending hours drawing her mother's tale. In the end, there was a book, which Deborah and Miriam were pleased to produce at their shop, binding into a small volume.

One evening, before Mrs. Stern left for the day, William and Hannah arrived with a carful of guests—Marjorie, Micah, Aaron, Rebecca, and a very large Rivkah. Mildred rolled Leah down the street to join in the surprise. Susan and Helen, Marilyn and Julie, and Chava and Esther all showed up, quietly gathering in the parlor. Miriam, surprised Mrs. Stern had not heard the commotion up front, invited their unsuspecting guest into the front room as she motioned for Rachel and the two children to join them. She was confused by the gathering, never suspecting this party was for her.

Rivkah, surprisingly unashamed of her huge stomach, stood in front of the familiar crowd and told her mother that she wanted to give her something special. She handed the book to her mother amid cheers by everyone. Mrs. Stern, embarrassed by the attention, was struck dumb. She thumbed through the book, spending time looking at each drawing, as Rivkah read the words out loud. There was not a dry eye in the room. Mrs. Stern marveled at the project, amazed at the attention and love bestowed on her.

Deborah and Miriam made copies of this book for Mrs. Stern, Rivkah, and their unborn child. There were additional copies for Mrs. Stern to distribute to others who had similar journeys.

Before long a new business venture had begun. Starting with the story Deborah had written about Rachel as a mill girl, Rivkah began illustrating and the shop produced the story in the format of a small children's book. One by one, Deborah's stories took life, as Rivkah drew pictures to match the tales.

William created a bookshelf for the new baby, who would have a small collection of illustrated books once he or she was born. And all the children whose tales Deborah had woven marveled at their own printed copy of a book. It was clear that Deborah's job of writing stories would continue. Rivkah, who suddenly had a purpose to her days, seemed to have a new spirit, and Mrs. Stern, the loving mother who had given her daughters the best life she could, at the cost of losing herself, now had a new pride in her previously lost child.

CHAPTER 17

Mendel

April 1916

Deborah was so thrilled with this new book project that she went to Denison House to see whether there was another child she could write about. Deborah was surprised when she was asked to meet a ten-year-old negro child; she had not been close to a negro before. It did not take long for her to become comfortable as she learned about what it was like to be a sharecropper in the South and how life was different for a negro who had moved to the north. She thought she might like to meet other negro children if someone else had a story to tell. She'd ask about it.

(SEE ADDENDUM "CLEO: THE SHARECROPPER'S DAUGHTER")

In fact, Deborah became so engaged in writing Cleo's story that she barely noticed Miriam's concern about the upcoming holiday of Passover. One day Miriam broke down in tears, telling Deborah that she assumed Marjorie's family couldn't manage hosting them for the holiday, due to caring for Micah. The thought of another holiday on their own saddened her. Deborah felt bad that her own interests had blinded her to Miriam's worries, and she vowed again to be more conscious of Miriam's needs.

The very next day they were delighted with an invitation for Passover at Marjorie's home.

The only problem during the holiday was that Hannah was not well. She got up twice during the meal with rushed trips to the bathroom. Miriam followed her the second time and returned with a smile, thrilled there was wonderful news. Hannah was pregnant and due in July. Miriam and Hannah marveled that they'd have babies to bring up together.

Following the Passover holiday, Hannah's symptoms increased. She needed to urinate more frequently even when she'd just emptied her bladder. She felt like she was running a fever some of the time. Also, she sometimes had trouble voiding and, on a few occasions, she experienced painful urination. She didn't tell William because she didn't want to worry him. William got worked up easily, especially when Hannah or Sarah wasn't well.

Hannah was not as ill as with her first pregnancy, but enough to disrupt her work schedule. She was extremely tired, which she assumed was a combination of the child inside her and having an energetic daughter who would soon be two years old. It wasn't until she had blood in her urine that Hannah became scared and told William. He called for the doctor immediately.

The doctor diagnosed an infection and recommended a medication, hexamine, and had her rub an herbal cream on her private areas. He also suggested she take it easy, but Hannah was too busy with Sarah to get any rest.

When Hannah ran a high fever and was unable to urinate at all, William got the doctor again. By the time the doctor arrived, her breathing was rapid, and the doctor's face wrinkled with concern. He explained that Hannah was septic, but William had no idea what that meant. When the doctor insisted they send Hannah to the hospital immediately, William hesitated. The doctor scared him, telling him privately that both Hannah and the baby could die if untreated so he relented.

When William dropped Sarah off at Deborah and Miriam's, Miriam insisted she go to the hospital. When Miriam climbed into the car, she found Hannah sweating profusely, anxious, and confused. Miriam was most frightened with how pale Hannah looked.

"My heart is pounding so hard it feels as if it will beat right out of my chest," Hannah said, fear across her face.

"You'll be fine. The doctors will take care of you," Miriam assured Hannah and William, though neither believed her words.

At the hospital, the doctor examined Hannah privately before inviting William into the examining room. When Miriam was included, Hannah was crying uncontrollably. "They are going to take my baby right now even though it is too soon. It's not due for three more months, but they are saying it might die."

William didn't mention the doctor's comment that her life was also at risk. Miriam watched as they wheeled Hannah into the operating room.

"How's your sister?" asked Deborah, when she arrived a while later.

"Not good. They took her to surgery. They're going to take her baby whether it's ready or not. It's the only chance Hannah has." Miriam began to cry. "I'm scared, Deborah. I'm afraid Hannah could lose her life, too. I don't know what I'd do without her."

After more tears, they quietly settled into the hard chairs in the waiting room. William joined them, too nervous to sit down, even though it was several hours before the doctor came to talk with them. "We took Hannah in for surgery, knowing it was a big risk for both her and the baby. We delivered a tiny boy, but he wasn't alive. I'm very sorry."

William, with tears running down his face, asked, "How is my Hannah?"

"She has a better chance now that the baby has been born, but her life is still at risk. We're treating her and hopefully she'll pull through. But I do have some difficult news. When we took the baby, we found the infection had spread throughout her body. The only way we could save Hannah was to take out her child-bearing organs. I'm sorry to tell you she won't be able to have more children."

"Oh, William, I'm so sorry," said Miriam between tears. She hugged her brother-in-law as he cried.

William said, "As long as Hannah is well, we will be all right. We have our wonderful Sarah so our family will be fine."

It was a long night. The three of them sat quietly in the hospital. Each napped in a chair for a short while, though no one had any real sleep. In the morning, the doctor returned.

"I'm pleased to tell you Hannah is doing much better. The treatment seems to be working. Her fever is down, which is an encouraging sign."

"Thank you, Doctor. I could not manage if Hannah did not make it," said William.

Many more tears followed. Finally, Hannah was strong enough for William to see her. From the wails they heard from her hospital room, they knew he'd told her the news.

"My love, I am so relieved you are going to recover," William said tearfully as he reached over to hold Hannah's hand.

"I cannot have any more babies, and we just lost our son, who would have carried on your name."

"We have our wonderful little daughter, and I have you. That's all that matters. *Hashem* makes decisions about who shall live and who shall die, and he has decided you will stay with me."

It was several days until Hannah was released from the hospital. When she was home, she and William planned the funeral for their little boy. Although Jewish funerals are usually a day after the person has died, the rabbi agreed it was important for the mother to be there so they had waited until Hannah was out of the hospital. Before the funeral they named their baby Mendel Avrum, after Hannah and Miriam's father's father of blessed memory.

"What a horrible experience for Hannah," said Miriam after she and Deborah were home from Mendel's funeral.

She and Deborah sat in the parlor with Susan and Helen, who had wanted to go to the funeral, but Hannah had requested no one other than Deborah and Miriam attend. Instead, they'd stayed home to mind Sylvia and Sarah.

"I'm glad Hannah requested no guests. I don't think she could have faced anyone yet. She's weak, both physically and mentally," said Miriam. "I worry about whether she'll ever get over this."

"I don't think it's possible to get over the loss of a child," said Helen. "My mother lost a baby, and she was never the same afterward."

"It's so sad Hannah can't have another child. I know how much she wanted this baby. She talked about the child as if it were already born," Helen said.

Deborah added, "And it's probably hard on her we're about to have a new baby. She'll be reminded daily of the child she never had."

"We must remember to be glad she survived this horrible illness, which might have taken her life."

The four girls talked further until Sylvia needed a diaper change, bringing them back to the present.

Later that evening, Miriam brought up a subject that shocked Deborah. "Do you think we should offer Rivkah's baby to Hannah and William?"

"I had not thought of that," Deborah sighed.

"I know it wouldn't be the same as having their own baby, but this baby needs a home."

"And it would be easier for the baby to grow up in a normal family, with both a mother and father."

"Yes, it would," said Miriam.

They sat quietly, pondering this monumental issue.

"It would be the right thing to do," said Deborah.

It was obvious to Miriam that Deborah was distraught at this notion, but neither felt strong enough to discuss this. Instead, they embraced and sobbed onto each other's shoulders.

They decided to approach Hannah and William the next evening with this offer.

The discussion with Hannah and William was difficult for all. Hannah said quietly, "No. Mendel was our baby, not this child. We must mourn him and not substitute another child for him."

William also spoke up. "That was the kindest offer anyone could ever make, but this new baby is yours. You already love this unborn child in the same way we loved our son. You are wonderful parents, and you deserve this new baby."

More tears and hugs.

Mendel's final resting place

CHAPTER 18

Ida

May 1916

May began with a small wedding for Rachel and Aaron. Neither wanted a fuss to be made, so the gathering was for their immediate families. Held at Marjorie and Aaron's family home, it seemed much like the Passover gatherings Deborah and Miriam had become accustomed to, minus the celebratory meal and Seder and the absence of matzoh. Mrs. Stern baked pastries for the celebration, which was short and pleasant. For a gift, Deborah and Miriam gave the newlyweds a night at the downtown Hotel Torraine, like they had given Marjorie and Micah for their wedding. The following day the young couple planned to move into a small flat on the top floor of a house not far from Marjorie's family.

"Rivkah is extremely moody," Deborah said on their way home.

"As I expect any unmarried fourteen-year-old girl in her condition would be," said Miriam."

"She was quick to argue with us and was very demanding. She complained about being lonely, yet I suspect everyone is staying away from her because she's so difficult."

"Poor Rivkah. Her behavior leads to more isolation and more irritability."

"Miriam, only you would say 'poor Rivkah.' Everyone else blames her for her disagreeable behavior.

"I felt bad for her."

Rachel arrived at work early a couple of days later, looking as upset as the day she'd found out Rivkah was with child. "Miriam, I need your help. I went to visit my family yesterday evening after work. Rivkah's boyfriend, Benjamin, left her, and she has become so despondent that she's scaring me. My mother says she does nothing but sleep and cry. I fear she'll do something rash."

"What can I do to help?"

"Please talk with her. Maybe you can say something that will make a difference. She's talking about wanting to die and to kill her baby."

"That's frightening. I'll go with you right now."

"You need to go to work."

"Some things are more important than work. I'll get Deborah to drive us on her way to the office. Please ask your mother to watch the girls until we return."

They arrived at the boarding house where the Stern family lived, and Rachel showed Miriam to the room she had shared with Rebecca and Rivkah until her marriage. She found a tearful girl lying in bed.

"Rivkah, your sister is worried about you."

"You should both worry about someone else. I'm not worth your concern. I've no friends and a baby I can't keep. My mother is furious with me, and Benjamin thinks I'm fat and worthless and he doesn't like me anymore." Rivkah broke into sobs.

Miriam, thinking about what Mrs. B. would say in this situation, sat by Rivkah's side. She nodded for Rachel to leave, then rubbed Rivkah's back, humming a soft tune. When Rivkah's breathing relaxed and her tears dried, Miriam spoke quietly. "I'm sorry Benjamin has broken up with you. Was he upset you're giving up his baby?"

"He doesn't even know about the baby. He thinks I'm fat and cranky, and he doesn't want to be around me anymore. I'll be alone for the rest of my life. It's not worth living."

"Rivkah, you have a wonderful life ahead of you. And right now you've a very important role to fulfill. You have a life inside you, a tiny baby who needs you."

"She needs you, not me."

"Oh, that's not the case. Right now, she needs you. You must take care of yourself so you can provide a home for her until she's ready to come into the world."

"What if she hates me because I'm giving her away?"

"Rivkah, you're doing the best thing for your baby. She'll always appreciate that you've given her the best life you could. For you that means letting others raise her. And you're giving Deborah and me the greatest gift you could ever give to anyone."

"You aren't taking her to be nice to me?"

"No, my sweet girl. You're giving us a wonderful treasure. We thank you every day for taking care of her while she's still growing in your body."

"Do you think it's a girl?"

"I think it is. She's a precious little bundle. We will care for her and give her as much love as any child could ever receive." Miriam thought to herself, *I don't know if this is a girl, but I must do anything I can to calm Rivkah, so she won't do harm to herself or the baby.*

"It's a girl. I know it is. What will you name her?"

"We've not talked about that since it's Jewish practice for parents to name a child after it's born. We must name her after someone we loved very much who passed away."

"May I name the baby?"

"Certainly. We can discuss this as soon as she's born. And if you want to be part of her life, you can."

"Will she know she was my baby?"

"Rivkah, you get to decide that. We'll respect any choice you make. You can tell her yourself when she gets older if you like."

"No, I don't think I'll tell her, but I want to watch her grow up."

"Then you can be a regular visitor to our home. She can call you *Doda*, aunt, if you like."

"Oh yes, I would like that. I'll be Doda Rivkah, and I'll visit her and teach her things."

"It will be my pleasure for you to be her auntie, and we will love having you be part of our family."

"Thank you, Miriam, that will be wonderful. I want to watch as she gets bigger."

"Then it will be so. And when you're all grown up and have more children, they can be special cousins."

"Yes," said Rivkah, no longer crying.

Miriam and Rivkah sat together for a while, with Miriam continuing to sing soft melodies while she rubbed Rivkah's back. When Rivkah fell asleep, Miriam quietly left the room. She found Deborah and Rachel waiting for her. Miriam was pleased Deborah had waited for her, rather than going to the office. Miriam put her finger to her lips, and the three of them quietly slipped out.

Rivkah stayed home for the rest of her pregnancy. This isolation was difficult for a young adolescent whose friends were important. Miriam assured her that life would return to normal after the birth, though she didn't believe her own words. Giving away an infant must be one of the hardest things any girl could do.

To celebrate Rivkah's birthday, Deborah and Miriam invited Rachel and Aaron to their house for a little party. Susan, Helen, and Mildred, the only others to know about this pregnancy, joined them. They invited Mrs. Stern, who stayed in the kitchen, still distraught by her daughter's indiscretion and the young boy who didn't do right by her. By this time Rivkah had reached her seventh month. Deborah and Miriam watched her, imagining their baby growing inside this child. They encouraged Rivkah to eat well, but the adolescent was only interested in cake and ice cream. They worried she'd gained so much weight that she'd no longer look slender once this baby was born. They thought of Ruth, who never lost all her pregnancy weight.

One day, when Miriam arrived, she found Rivkah in pain.

"What's wrong, dear?" Miriam asked.

"My back. It hurts so much."

"Let me rub it," suggested Miriam.

A few seconds later, the pain subsided.

"Tell me how long you've been having these back pains."

"It feels like for hours, and they're worse every time. The pain stops, then comes again."

"Sweetheart, I think you're in labor."

Rivkah looked at Miriam, confused by this diagnosis. "But my belly isn't hurting."

"Some women begin their labor with back pains," said Miriam, feeling old and wise beyond her years.

"What do we do?" Rivkah asked in panic.

"I'll go downstairs and ask someone to contact the midwife."

"No, don't leave me. I'm so scared. I can't have this baby alone."

"You'll be fine for a few minutes. It's not going to happen so fast."

"I want my mother," said Rivkah as her face crumpled.

"Once the midwife is here, I'll go home and get your mother and make certain she's here with you throughout the rest of your labor."

"She needs to cook for you."

"Nothing is as important right now as birthing this child."

Luckily, the midwife was found and arrived quickly. She agreed to stay with Rivkah so Miriam could head home, where she found Rivkah's mother preparing dinner.

"It's time for Rivkah's baby," Miriam announced as soon as she walked into the kitchen.

"I'm almost done here," said Mrs. Stern. Her daughter needed her so she put aside her own complicated feelings.

"Leave the rest for us. I'll get Deborah to drive you, so you can be with her. Rivkah was asking for you."

"She must be scared," said Mrs. Stern.

"She is, but you'll be there shortly."

Deborah drove Mrs. Stern home. When she returned, Miriam had completed preparing the meal and had packaged portions to take with them. She'd arranged for Susan and Helen to feed Sylvia and put her to bed so they could attend the birth.

"Our girls will be exactly four years apart," noted Deborah.

"We still don't know if it's a girl," whispered Miriam.

"I can hope."

"We'll always celebrate their birthdays together. One party with two cakes."

"Unless she's like me," said Deborah. "I always insisted on my own party, even though my sister Anna's birthday is a week after mine."

"This baby may not be as stubborn as you," Miriam said, smiling.

Soon, they were by Rivkah's side. Her water had broken, and she was in traditional labor. As she writhed in pain with each contraction, they took turns mopping her brow and holding her hand. It was hard to know whether Rivkah was appreciative of their kindness, but her mother was.

After five hours a healthy baby was born. Rivkah was exhausted but recovering well, and, as they all hoped, the baby was a girl!

Miriam stayed by Rivkah's side the whole night, handing her the baby each time she needed to nurse. Deborah went home to get some sleep before she took the next shift. They alternated staying with her for the first two days. Rachel, despite being a newlywed, offered to relieve them after work hours, but they refused to let her stay more than an hour, feeling the need to be there themselves. Mrs. Stern was clearly torn, wanting to be with this precious new baby and her daughter, though her cooking responsibilities took her away for much of the day. Knowing Deborah and Miriam were by Rivkah's side helped her.

Deborah and Miriam discussed their concerns about whether it would be harder on Rivkah to give away the infant after this time together, but Rivkah insisted the baby stay with her. When the day came to bring the baby to her new home, Rivkah wept loudly. It wrenched their hearts, but Deborah, Miriam, and Rivkah all knew this was right. Mrs. Stern vowed to support her daughter through this difficult time.

William drove them home, and in the backseat Deborah and Miriam discussed what to call this still unnamed baby since Rivkah had changed her mind about naming her. They wished they could name the child after the young mother who bore her, but it wasn't within Jewish law to name a child after someone who was still alive.

"I think we should call her Golda, after my mother, whose name was Gila. They'd have the same Hebrew name," said Miriam, looking at the newborn's light-colored hair.

"I think it would be awful for a child with blond hair to be called 'Goldie,'" insisted Deborah. "That would be like calling a dark-haired child 'Blackie.'"

"Sarah was named after Mother's sister, and Hannah named her second baby, Mendel, of blessed memory, after Mother's father. I think Mother would have loved to have a baby named after her," said Miriam.

Deborah raised her eyebrows and said, "Certainly, but so would Bubbie. And since Bubbie was older, I think the baby should be named after her, to show respect."

After much discussion, they finally decided to name her Ida Rose, after Bubbie, whose name was Idit, and Rivkah's brother Robert.

Once home with this new baby, nothing felt familiar. Deborah and Miriam both struggled with the newborn responsibilities. Although they had taken Sylvia for extended periods when she was tiny, they'd had time to rest between visits, something that didn't happen with full-time parenting.

"I'm exhausted," said Miriam on their third morning together. "It's difficult to take care of all of Ida's needs and still give Sylvia her share of attention. I don't know how we would manage without Rachel, who has sweetly offered to extend her work time."

"I know. We're managing with little sleep. Ida hasn't slept for more than two hours at a time. I wonder how women manage who care for their children alone or with husbands who provide no help. At least we have each other," Deborah said as she put the baby down for another short nap.

Miriam, amid yawns, said, "Have you noticed Sylvia's behaving differently since we brought the baby home?"

"I think she's acting more like she did last year, making baby sounds instead of using words," said Deborah.

"And I noticed her crawling instead of walking. She hasn't done that in a long time."

"I wonder if it's normal for a big sister to behave like that."

"I suspect it is," said Miriam in the middle of another huge yawn.

"Susan and Helen have offered to watch the baby for us, and I think we should take advantage of their kindness."

Deborah giggled. "I don't think they're being kind. I think they desperately want to spend time with Ida. They're watching us with envy, and I think the kindness would be to give them some time with the baby."

"We should probably plan to both take a nap when Ida is with them. I'm certain we can ask them to watch Sylvia, too."

"I like your plan. I'll spend all day anticipating my nap with you. We've not had any time in bed together since we've been sleeping in shifts."

Miriam looked at her askance, hoping Deborah had nothing in mind other than sleep, as she was desperately needing rest.

Deborah and Miriam managed with little continuous sleep. To complicate their schedules, a constant stream of guests came to see the new baby for the first few weeks. Marilyn and Julie arrived with great excitement, though they had little experience with newborns. When Miriam had to ask them to leave at naptime, they were embarrassed, but not offended. Chava and Esther came several times, but they were welcome guests. They focused on Sylvia, understanding she needed the attention more than the baby. Rachel often stayed after her childminder hours to spend time with the infant. When Aaron came to pick her up each day, she invited him inside. He was awkward, obviously not experienced with new babies. Miriam noticed Rachel instructing him how to hold the baby, probably in preparation for when they had their own children.

Hannah and William spent time with Ida daily, enjoying time with the newborn to fill a bit of their emptiness. One day, they arrived with Marjorie and a surprise. William had hitched up the cart behind the car, and they brought Micah for a visit. Deborah was pleased to bring Ida to see him, happy the weather was perfect for an outdoor visit.

The most surprising visit of all was on a Sunday afternoon, two weeks after Ida was born. Miriam opened the door, never imagining the guests waiting at her door. "Please come in," she said to the same group of women from the Temple Sisterhood who had come to visit with rejection in their hearts a few years earlier. The three women settled into the same seats they had sat in before in the parlor, and each reached out for her turn, holding the new baby with great pleasure.

One of the women, while holding Ida, spoke up. "Miriam, your mother would be proud of you, knowing you took in another child who needed a family. She'd have loved having a new baby in her home, and I'm sad she never got to share this great joy with you."

Miriam hardly knew what to say. She was touched by this woman's words.

One of the other women turned to Deborah, saying words Deborah never imagined she would hear. "Deborah, you're a wonderful woman. We were wrong about you." Deborah's tear-filled eyes were the only answer they needed.

Deborah and Miriam went back to work, not wanting to get far behind. Miriam depended on rides from William, so worked full days for two days. Deborah, since she had the car, worked shorter hours for three days.

Gradually, Ida got on a schedule, sleeping for longer periods. Sylvia adjusted to having a baby sister, returning to walking instead of crawling. Also, the progress she'd made toward toilet training resumed. She no longer messed her diaper regularly as when Ida first entered the family.

"I'm so grateful you decided to accept the responsibility of having a second child. Our family is complete now," said Miriam. "No need to worry that I'll request taking another child if one is offered to us."

"Sure. If someone offered you another baby, I'm certain you would be pouting if I said no."

"I feel complete now. Sylvia has a sister and we have another child," said Miriam.

"And, are you also thinking 'a normal one'? I must admit that thought has gone through my head many times."

"Yes. I'll admit to thinking that, too. Even though I love Sylvia with all my heart, it will be wonderful to watch this baby grow like other children and see all the stages babies go through. Thank you for letting this happen." Miriam hugged Deborah, holding the infant on her hip.

"And thank you. I'm pleased Rivkah, whom we will now call Doda, will be part of our ever-growing family."

Deborah's Journal, June 26, 1916

I can hardly believe how much our lives have changed with a second child. I had no idea how much a small infant fills up every available hour of the day; feeding, rocking, and laundry seem endless. Yet, every time I look at Ida, or smell her wonderful baby smells, I feel more certain I made the right choice. And I'm thrilled when I look at Miriam, who, through her yawns, is smiling all the time.

Lately, Sylvia seems more needy, but I am happy to offer her the extra attention. She will always have a special place in my heart, being our first-born.

Work feels less important right now, and I almost resent it taking away time from my family. Though when I walk through the doors, I am fully engaged. What has changed is that I don't think of work issues when I am home.

And writing has taken a back seat. I often write a bit each day to calm me down, yet this is the first time I've taken time to write at all since Ida's birth. I'm certain I will return to writing as soon as I return to regular sleeping. At least, I hope so.

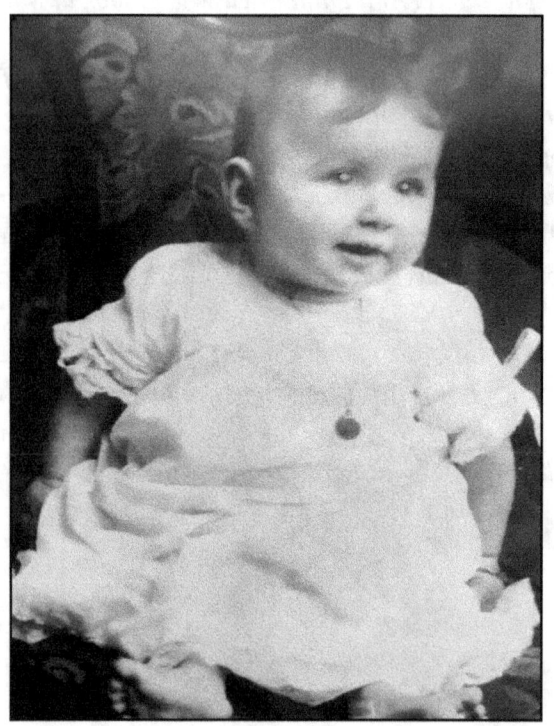

Ida

CHAPTER 19

Benjamin

June 1916

"Who's Benjamin?" Deborah asked with a quizzical look.

"Ida's father," Miriam said as she looked at Deborah, who was spending Sunday afternoon reading.

"He wants to see the baby? Do we have to let him? He certainly didn't do right by Rivkah. I think he lost his rights to see this child."

"I really don't know what we should do," said Miriam. "He's downstairs, requesting we bring the baby to him."

"I don't feel good about this," said Deborah.

"Can we deny him seeing the child he fathered?"

Deborah put Ida down in the bassinet. "Helen told me he's quite insistent, and Rivkah isn't with him."

Just then they heard a young male voice calling up the stairs. "I want to see my baby. I've a right to see her."

Deborah and Miriam looked at each other, stunned.

"I'll take care of this," said Deborah, walking toward the stairs.

"Be careful."

"I will."

An adolescent was waiting at the bottom of the stairs.

"Where's my baby? I've a right to see her," insisted the young man.

"Hello, Benjamin. I'm Deborah. Nice to meet you," she said with an outstretched arm.

Benjamin didn't shake her hand, but glanced up the stairs.

"Where is she? I have rights you know."

"Benjamin, the baby's sleeping. I don't want to wake her from her nap or you'll see a screaming infant. Come sit in the parlor and we can talk," Deborah said with a calm voice.

"I don't want to talk. I want to see my baby. She's mine. I can take her from you."

"Benjamin, Benjamin. You need to calm down. I can't consider turning the baby over to someone so distraught. It would upset her. You need to be relaxed with a newborn."

"I'm not relaxed. I found out that I have a daughter, and I've the right to see her and to take her if I choose."

"So that's the problem. Rivkah just told you that you're a father?"

"She's stupid. That's why I stopped seeing her. I didn't know she was with child. I thought she was fat and cranky."

Deborah motioned to the chair in the parlor, walking that way in hopes this angry young man would follow. He didn't. Instead, he started up the stairs.

Deborah turned to him and said forcefully, "Benjamin, I insist that you come down the stairs. You don't have my permission to go up, and this is my house."

"Who are you to tell me what to do? You're the slut who is living off the girl who lives here. You're living in sin."

Deborah's face reddened. Although it would typically be her nature to yell back when spoken to in such a manner, her voice remained calm. "You're not behaving in a way that gives you any rights, Benjamin. Come down the stairs this instant, or I'll be forced to call an officer."

Reluctantly, at this threat Benjamin came down the stairs. "I'm the one who should be calling the police. I have rights you know. You have no rights to this child. Maybe I'll have you arrested for indecent behavior."

"Calm down, Benjamin. You're not helping yourself by threatening me. I think you should go now."

"I'll leave now, but you should expect an officer to show up at your door very soon. When he arrests you, I'll take the baby who's rightfully mine."

"I hope you calm down before talking to the police. They wouldn't give custody of a small child to someone so distraught."

"We'll see who gets custody." Benjamin slammed the door.

Helen came out of her hiding place where she had remained during the entire confrontation. "Thank God he's gone."

Miriam came rushing down the stairs, with pale skin and rapid breathing. "Deborah, how awful! I listened to the whole thing. You handled him perfectly, but what will happen? Does he have rights to see his daughter? Can he have us arrested and take Ida from us?"

Deborah took Miriam and Ida into her arms. "I don't know. I'm unsure what his rights are, but I fear he could have us arrested—not for taking his baby but for being together."

"What can we do? How can we protect Ida? He clearly isn't capable of being a parent. Any judge would see that," said Miriam.

"Let's not talk of judges and courts. I hope Benjamin doesn't do anything foolish."

Miriam had tears in her eyes. "I thought it might be a problem that Rivkah never told him about her condition. He must have been shocked to find out he has a child. Maybe he'll calm down."

"You knew she hadn't told him?" Deborah blurted out.

"Right now you both need to calm down," said Helen.

The three of them talked about all the potential problems Benjamin could raise and their fears he could take the baby away from them. Susan joined them in the discussion when she got home from her errands. They encouraged Deborah to call her father for his legal opinion.

"I'm not a child advocate, so I'll need to talk with some of my colleagues who know more than I do," said Mr. Levine.

"Father, tell us what you do know. I don't think we can wait another minute for some information," Deborah said in a strangled voice.

"I know the legal rights of a fifteen-year-old are limited; he isn't yet considered an adult. He has constitutional rights as a parent, yet I don't know if his age precludes him from protection."

"And what about his threat that he could have us arrested for indecent behavior?"

"Again, I'm not an expert in this field, and I don't know anyone who is. From my understanding, the indecent behavior laws apply only to men and only if they're caught in a sexual act. I'm not certain."

"Thank you, Father. Please see what else you can find out," said Deborah.

"Do you want me to retain legal counsel for you?" asked Mr. Levine.

"No. Not right now. We don't know if this boy will actually follow through with his threats. He may have been merely distraught, and was saying things to frighten us."

Deborah ended the call with as many questions as answers, but with hope Benjamin was too young to have any rights.

During the next few days, the girls lived in constant fear, awaiting another knock at the door. They expected Benjamin again, maybe with his parents, a lawyer, or a policeman. Or maybe an officer would arrive to take the baby or to arrest them. The girls went off to work each day with warnings for Rachel to stay at home and not to answer the door under any circumstance.

Deborah and Miriam arrived home from work one day to a surprise visitor: Rivkah. She was crying, barely managing "I'm sorry" between sobs. At her side was her sister, Rachel, holding the baby.

Once Rivkah calmed down enough to talk, she said, "I'm so ashamed. I didn't tell Benjamin anything about the baby until this week. He came by, saying he missed me and wanted to get back together. Somehow, when we were talking, I told him about the baby. He became furious."

"We saw that anger," said Deborah. "I wonder if he came right here after leaving you."

"I think he did. He said he was going get his baby."

"He tried, and he threatened us."

"He's a good boy. I don't think he'll try to take the baby," Rivkah said.

"I wish we knew for certain," said Deborah.

Sensing there was no resolution to this current situation, Miriam changed the subject. "How are you, Rivkah? We've missed seeing you."

"I've not been doing very well, and I didn't think you'd ever want to see me again now that you have the baby."

Miriam responded quickly. "You're wrong, Rivkah. We miss seeing you. You're welcome here any time."

"I am? I'd love to come visit with you and the baby. I thought you wouldn't want me around."

"We definitely want you to visit," said Deborah.

"Would you like to hold the baby? This is the first time you've seen her since we brought her here," Miriam said.

"Well, actually, this isn't the first time I've seen her. I've come over a few times when Rachel was here. I hope you're not angry about that."

"No, Rivkah. It's fine. How is it for you, seeing her?" asked Miriam with concern.

"She's so adorable. It's clear I could never have taken care of her, so I'm pleased you have her. And it's really nice my sister gets to be with her every day, and I know she's with people who love her."

"You're welcome to see her all you want. Remember, you're Doda Rivkah."

"I like that and want to be part of her life."

Still, Deborah and Miriam could not help but wonder whether life would ever seem normal again.

Their worst fears came true. The dreaded knock at the door came exactly one week after Benjamin's threats. They had let their guard down a bit, thinking the possibility of repercussions had lessened as time passed. Miriam answered the door, thinking it was Hannah stopping by with cookies she had baked. But there stood two police officers in full uniform.

Miriam stood still, unable to move. The policemen introduced themselves and asked to come inside, but Miriam did not react. They asked a second time if they could come in, but Miriam stood frozen. Deborah came down the stairs, thinking of the treats Hannah had offered to bring them, and she too was overwhelmed by the sight of the officers. She was glad she had left the girls upstairs in their bedroom, suddenly fearing the police would take them right from her arms.

"May I help you, Officer?" asked Deborah, with as much calm as she could possibly muster.

"We have a complaint filed against Miriam Cohen and Deborah Levine. Are you two these same women?"

"Yes," Deborah said, not inviting them past her door.

The officers, aware they were not to be invited in, handed a paper to Deborah and turned away. Deborah and Miriam stood still, watching them walk down the walkway and climb into their vehicle, a bicycle-like contraption with a side car, which accommodated the two policemen. Deborah was glad they had not arrived with a paddy wagon for them and their children.

Once the police were gone, Deborah and Miriam sat in the parlor and reviewed the *Investigation Report* they had been handed. It stated their names and Benjamin's name. The only information they could decipher in the sloppy handwriting was "refusal to allow the father to see his child, which was taken unlawfully from him."

Panic set in.

Miriam's Diary, July 30, 1916

What is going to happen? I'm so frightened. Can Benjamin take our baby away?

I don't think I'd ever recover from losing her.

Deborah tries to be strong for me, but I can see the stress in her eyes. I know she is concerned about Ida yet I suspect her fears go beyond that. Although she has not talked about it, I think she is worrying that we could also lose Sylvia if the authorities get involved.

I finally have the family I have dreamed about my whole life, but it all seems so precarious now.

CHAPTER 20

Family of Choice
July 1916

Deborah and Miriam were distraught, but their friends and family provided support. Everyone understood how critical the situation with Benjamin might be, though no one had any idea what might happen following the *Investigation Report*. There were no guidelines as to when or how the police would follow up, and neither Deborah nor Miriam thought to ask questions, naively hoping the whole situation would just go away.

Deborah kept in touch with her father regarding his offer to find them legal representation. Deborah was increasingly worried because he was unable to find a lawyer experienced in custody issues with two women. During these nightly chats it was clear he was more concerned with their legal risks as a couple living in a sinful and illegal relationship than with the custody issues. Deborah discussed with Miriam only Benjamin's rights regarding Ida. She worried that Sylvia could also be taken from them—or that they could be jailed.

Hannah talked with Miriam every day at work. Hannah, though still despondent over the loss of her own child, was a caring sister. She comforted Miriam, reminding her how their mother would have approved of their taking in this new baby. William said little. His assistance was better when there was a task that needed doing, rather than someone needing emotional support. Hannah and William took Sylvia home with them on several occasions, giving Deborah and Miriam some time alone with Ida.

Susan and Helen were wonderful. They talked with Deborah and Miriam night after night, never tiring of hearing the same concerns repeatedly. They reached out to women at their suffrage meetings, asking for information about local lawyers. Some of the women had lost custody of their children due to their involvement in the movement. Despite their best efforts, they found scant information about custody issues that mimicked the desperate situation Deborah and Miriam were facing. Even young Mildred was sweet, drawing them pictures to cheer them up.

Chava and Esther stopped by several times, each time explaining they had consulted with another friend or neighbor. They had no information that helped, but Deborah and Miriam were grateful for their encouragement.

Marjorie, despite her own concerns about her husband, and her recent sickness in the mornings (which she and Miriam giggled about, assuming she was with child) wanted to do anything she could to help, explaining that Miriam had been there for her in her time of need, and she wanted badly to repay the favor. Miriam was comforted by Marjorie's visits, and thoughts of another baby added a spark of happiness during this challenging time.

Marilyn and Julie were surprisingly exceedingly helpful. Marilyn's job as a social worker at Denison House gave her access to many lawyers who helped families negotiate legal issues. Marilyn connected Deborah and Miriam with a local attorney who, because he was a homosexual, was motivated to assist them. He reviewed the *Investigation Report* and took immediate action. At the police station he demanded information about progress on the case regarding Benjamin's complaint. He discovered that after the police served papers to Deborah and Miriam, no one had followed up. They did not take the needs of a fifteen-year-old boy seriously, nor did they suspect that these beautiful young women were engaging in lascivious behavior. They never considered the crisis that ensued because of the nonexistent investigation.

When this lawyer provided this information to Deborah and Miriam, they had difficulty believing there was nothing to worry about. They asked him question after question, wondering what Benjamin's rights were and whether the baby could be taken from them. Deborah talked to the lawyer privately one day when Miriam was busy and told him of her concerns that they could also lose Sylvia. He assured her this would not happen; it was unlikely that the police would ever investigate this case.

"But we were given an *Investigation Report*," Deborah argued.

The lawyer assured her there was to be no investigation and there was no interest in pursuing this matter. He had researched the rights of a fifteen-year-old father and found no evidence that Benjamin, as a minor, had any rights. Also, the only criminal proceedings regarding homosexuality he could find were regarding sexuality between men. The only custody cases that involved men were against fathers who abandoned their families when pursuing homosexual escapades. He did find the few cases on record regarding women homosexuals; the courts deemed them insane, requiring their admission to a mental institution. Their children were awarded to their husbands as the more fit parents. He did not share information about these cases with Deborah and Miriam.

Tension continued, despite having a lawyer on their side. Then one day, the greatest assistance of all arrived with another unexpected knock at the door. Miriam greeted the group of visitors politely and asked Deborah loudly to join her.

Deborah came rushing into the room, worried there was a serious problem. She found a group of familiar people, including the same group of Sisterhood women who had been there on two previous occasions, and also several men she recognized from the Temple Brotherhood. There were not enough seats to accommodate everyone, so the women sat and the men stood in a circle.

"We have heard of your woes," one of the men began, "and we would like to help."

Deborah and Miriam glanced at each other, then sat back to listen to their proposal. The men, all lawyers, were anxious to take on the case, explaining that the essence of Talmudic law was to ensure a child's Jewish upbringing. They quoted the Talmud's teachings regarding taking in an unwanted child as they had done. "Scripture ascribes it to him as though he had begotten him," one man explained. The men talked of the research they had undertaken in behalf of Deborah and Miriam's rights to their children and their willingness to take this to court if necessary.

The Sisterhood women said nothing, nodding in agreement, though Deborah assumed they were the initiators of this group action.

The men talked in language that was foreign to Deborah and Miriam, but by the end of their presentation it seemed they were far more experienced than the sweet homosexual lawyer Marilyn had found at Denison House. Deborah mentioned they had already consulted with him, and the men surprisingly offered to work with him.

During that week, one or two of the lawyers arrived each day, with questions. Though none of the lawyers had experience with a situation like theirs, they focused on the lack of rights of the young man, rather than the rights of this young lesbian couple. Like the young lawyer, they learned of the two unsuccessful laws in 1914 regarding "unnatural and lascivious acts," though they found nothing regarding women. The lawyers from the shul listened to his research, returning their focus to the limited rights of a fifteen-year-old.

By the time Shabbos arrived, the Brotherhood lawyers made plans to approach the police the following week to evaluate any planned action. They assumed the police would scoff at the idea of two women together, thinking women unlikely to have any sexual desires that would warrant censure. And, pleased that Benjamin was so young, they were certain that he had no rights.

While Deborah and Miriam were still overwhelmed, Rivkah arrived at the house to discuss Benjamin. Deborah was hesitant; Miriam wanted to support the distressed young girl.

"Shall I talk with him and find out his intentions regarding the baby?" Rivkah asked.

"What good will that do?" asked Deborah.

"I bet I could calm him down. I think he was shocked to hear he has a daughter. Do you think he could come here calmly to visit her?"

"He'd be welcome if he wasn't threatening." Miriam said.

"I don't want him here. He wasn't a pleasant visitor and threatened us," said Deborah.

"I guess we need to talk this over," Miriam said. "I spoke too soon without consulting the boss."

Deborah cocked her head to the side and looked at her askance. "The boss?"

"Well, maybe the authority."

They smiled at each other, a rare occurrence these days.

One evening, following their daily meeting with the lawyers, there was a knock at the door. Deborah and Miriam looked at each other, still worried about another police officer visit. Deborah took in a deep breath and headed to the door. There in front of them stood Rivkah and Benjamin.

"May we come in?" asked Rivkah.

"I don't know," said Deborah.

"I'm calm now," announced Benjamin. "I'm sorry for the way I behaved last week."

"Let them in," encouraged Miriam. "We accept your apology, Benjamin."

Deborah, less certain, opened the door for the young couple, who she noticed were holding hands.

"Come sit in the parlor," suggested Miriam as Deborah stood at attention, ready to forestall an attack.

When the three of them sat calmly, Deborah joined them.

"I was full of rage when I came over last time," said Benjamin with a soft voice and down-turned eyes. "Rivkah had told me about the baby, and I was really upset."

"I noticed," said Deborah.

"Would it be possible for Benjamin to meet his daughter?" Rivkah asked hesitantly.

Deborah and Miriam looked at each other, wide-eyed. Deborah said nothing, trying to believe this was a truce of sorts. Miriam nodded slightly and said, "I'll go upstairs and check on her. If she's awakened from her nap, I'll bring her down."

"We don't like to wake her from a sleep. You may remember that from your last visit, Benjamin," Deborah said sarcastically.

The three of them sat quietly while Miriam went upstairs to check on the baby. After a few minutes, she arrived with Ida in her arms. Benjamin stood as soon as they got to the landing, peering at the bundle she was carrying. She started to hand the infant to Benjamin who backed off and said, "I never held a tiny baby before."

"Come sit on the divan. I'll hand her to you once you're settled," Miriam said reassuringly.

Rivkah sat next to him and watched as Miriam lowered the baby into his arms. He looked so frightened that their fears of him running off with the baby dissipated.

Deborah got Sylvia from her nap and they sat with the two children, talking calmly. It seemed that Benjamin might actually be a nice boy who had had the most shocking news of his young life. Once he was no longer angry, neither Deborah nor Miriam worried he'd follow through on his threats. They felt safe. By the end of this unexpected visit, Ida had a *Dod* Benjamin, Uncle Benjamin, and their chosen family had just expanded.

After talking with the lawyers the next day, Deborah approached Benjamin directly when he stopped by. The discussion was as peaceful as it was satisfying. As he had promised, within twenty-four hours, Benjamin withdrew his complaint, and the *Investigation Report* had been put to rest.

Deborah's Journal, July 30, 1916

What a relief! Benjamin really scared us. Now I realize he was actually more frightened than we were. When I imagine what it would have been like for him, finding out after the fact he was a father, I understand his anguish. I'm amazed he was able to forgive Rivkah for not telling him.

I've no more fears he'll try to take Ida away from us. He's much too young to want to be a father. He seems barely old enough to have a girlfriend. I wonder if the bond between these two young folks is strong enough to keep them together. Only time will tell.

My father was greatly relieved when I told him the situation was resolved. He'd been continuously researching parental rights and calling colleagues with experience in child custody cases. He'd learned there was a great risk we'd lose Ida in a court of law because we're two girls, rather than a married couple.

This incident made it clear how much we've connected to our new baby. I love being her mother, and I'd fight endlessly for her. I know Miriam felt that way from the first moment Rivkah asked her to take the baby while I took a while to catch up.

CHAPTER 21

Reflections

December 1916

Deborah's Journal, December 30, 1916

1916 is coming to an end. When I think about the past year and the difficulties we faced, I marvel at how Miriam and I weathered our problems together. Stress has brought us closer.

Happily, life has also taken many wonderful turns, the most significant being the addition of our new baby. How fortunate we are. Ida Rose is a great joy in our lives, made even more special by the temporary fear we might have lost her. It's wonderful to watch Ida make strides in her development. I wonder how soon she'll surpass Sylvia. Will Sylvia be frustrated when her little sister can do things she can't? Or will Ida provide Sylvia with goals to achieve?

Also, of great importance this past year was my writing. Dr. Hubbard's coaching has turned my talent into success beyond anything I imagined. Now I might write a book! I'm clear it won't be about Ruth, but the world is full of other subjects. I might write about parenting, the richest part of my life, other than loving Miriam, which could never be the subject of something in print.

And there is the business. We've turned Miriam's father's little Yiddish printing shop into a thriving success. I'm now the manager of Mordechai S. Cohen Publishing Company. What an accomplishment! I'm proud of my business talents. Everyone looks to me for guidance and advice, even though I'm only twenty-four.

Most important in my life is my relationship with Miriam, which has matured of late. I no longer worry she'll run off with someone else, and I trust we'll be together forever. My sense of security has made me a much easier person to live with. Had I continued my jealous tirade, I'd certainly have lost the greatest love of my life. Although I'm still sometimes impulsive or irritable, I'm generally calmer.

I'm proud of the woman I have become. Yes, I can now call myself a woman instead of a girl. I'm the mother of two, the owner of a successful business, and a partner to the most wonderful young woman I ever met. I feel blessed.

Miriam's Diary, December 30, 1916

I'm pleased with my life. Despite losing my father, mother, and Bubbie, I've found a strong footing in the world. I'm no longer a young girl who feels insecure. My fears about not being enough and my desire to be more than a wife and mother have worked themselves out.

I am now a wife, of sorts, and a mother to two little girls. The world has provided for me in ways I couldn't have imagined six years ago when I first met Deborah. I feel complete.

I adore Sylvia and Ida more than I ever imagined I could. I never understood the depth of emotion attached to motherhood. Had I comprehended my mother's emotions, I might have behaved differently. If I knew the depth of pain my father must have felt when dismissing me from his life, would I have tried to reconcile with him?

My daughters are central to my existence now. Fears about Sylvia's health have wracked me to the core, as had my fright Ida might be taken from us. I don't know how parents, like my sister, exist after losing a child. The girls feel like part of me.

Deborah also is part of my very being. We make decisions together, turning to each other in tenderness, finding ways to let our love win every time. I trust we will be together until our dying days.

Deborah and Miriam were now settled adults, experiencing tremendous change and making great strides in their personal lives. They were enriched by their children and by those people who surrounded them. They were influential with many others, some who relied on them like Hannah and William, and others who benefited from their wisdom and kindness, like Rachel and Rivkah. They set an example for other women by managing a successful business, highly unusual for women of this era, and by creating an enriched family of choice.

As time moved on, Deborah and Miriam were influenced greatly by the larger world. They would have more stories to tell and to experience, like the Great War, the Spanish Flu, and the culmination of the suffrage movement. Many experiences they could not yet imagine awaited this chosen family and the family members they had come to love.

Addendum

Florence: The Girl with Pellagra

I grew up in Boston with one sister and four brothers. My parents had trouble feeding us and finding us clothes. We were a bad bunch, always getting into trouble. Papa would not let any of the boys stay in school past sixth grade so they could earn money for the family. Every day they had to beg on the streets and were not allowed back in the house until they had earned at least ten cents. Most people gave them one penny, so it was a lot of work to get enough. My sister stayed in school until eighth grade. She left because she was with child. I do not want to be like her.

I was the quiet one, barely talking, never asking for anything. I still was in trouble all the time, mostly for wetting the bed. I never went outside at night because I was afraid one of my brothers would do bad things to me if he saw me going to the privy. My oldest brother caught me once when I was seven and took me into the woods. After that, I stayed in the house after dark even if it meant I would wake up with wet sheets. My father beat me when I wet the bed, but I did not dare go out in the dark.

When I was eight, I got sick and everything got worse. No one knew what was wrong with me. All of a sudden, I messed my panties with poops, and I could not be in school because of it. And I began to quarrel with everyone. Then the skin on my hands got really red and my hair started to fall out. The worst time was when I was outside in the sunshine. When my mother made me stand on the corner to beg for money, like my brothers, I screamed. I could not stand being in the sun long enough to make my pennies, so I hid under the bushes. Many men wanted to give me extra money if I would go behind the building with them, but I always refused and ran away. My parents let me come inside the house at night even when I did not make my share, but I was always scared they would make me stay out.

When summer came and the sun was out for long hours, I became wild. I fought with my parents, wanting to stay in the house all the time. They said they would send me away if I did not go outside, but I just could not do it. So, they sent me to a place with a funny name, The Experimental School for Feeble-Minded Children.

When I got to this awful school, I was miserable. The other children were very strange. Most of them could not talk, and a lot of them looked really ugly. I guess I looked pretty funny too with my swollen red hands and bald head. They tried to teach me how to make brooms, but I screamed. They tied me up when I got upset, but that did not help.

Then, after I was at this school just one month, I started to get better. A bit of my hair started growing back, and my hands became pink instead of red. And my diarrhea got a little better. I was very lucky that my grown-up friend, Eugenia, who worked there, saw the changes in me. She thought the doctor could figure out what my problem was, but no one wanted to send a wild girl like me to the doctor. Eugenia made them pay attention. She talked about me over and over. Finally, I think they just wanted her to shut up and they agreed to send me to see the doctor.

When it was time to see the doctor, I was really scared. I had never seen one before, and I did not know what he would do to me. He made me undress, and I was afraid that he would do the same things to me that my brother did when I was seven, but he did not. He was really nice and checked me all over, real gentle. He told me that he needed to take blood from me, and I got frightened. But he said what he was going to do, and he promised he would not take it all. After he talked nice, I was not so scared. I let him take some of my blood and it only hurt a little.

About a week after he took out my blood, the doctor wanted to see me again. I was frightened, thinking that this time he would want to do bad things to me. But when I got to his office, he was dressed in the same coat and pants and white shirt he wore the first time, and he did not take them off as I was afraid he would. He sat behind his big desk, and he asked me to sit in the big chair on the other side. He told me that he had figured out what was wrong with me. He used words I never heard before, and that was the first time I heard the name pellagra. He told me that was my sickness and he was going to fix me. I could hardly believe my ears. I did not believe he could make me better.

The doctor gave me some pills that he called niacin. And he wanted me to eat extra meat and eggs. He gave me some peanuts, saying they would be good for me too, and he gave me some extra ones to put in my pocket. I did not have a pocket, so I held them in my hand. He would tell the people who watched me that I was to have extra food that he wanted me to eat. I was certain that they would not do that, and the other kids would hate me for getting extra. But the other kids did not care when they fed me lots of extra meat.

And what happened was a miracle. First, I stopped making messes in my pants. Then my hands got better, and my hair started to grow back. Real hair not just little strands. Most amazing of all, I stopped being angry. Eugenia was really excited. She said that I did not belong at this school anymore. I did not want to be begging on the streets, and I did not want to wet my bed again, and I did not want to be around my big brother so he could do nasty things to me anymore. Eugenia said she would see what she could do. I did not know what that meant.

After a long time, Eugenia came to talk with me, and she told me that I would be leaving. I was scared that I had to go home, but she told me that I would be going to this place called Denison House. I thought it would be another place for kids with problems, but when I got here, everyone was really nice. They put me in a room with two girls who said funny words I could not understand because they came from a place called Italy. They moved me to a room with girls I could talk with and they put me in school. I never went to school after I was eight, so I had to be with the little children.

I still cannot write enough to tell my story, so this nice lady, Deborah, has helped me write this down. Maybe someday I will be able to read what she put on the paper. She read it to me, and it sounds really good. I am very glad to be at Denison House. I hope they let me stay until I am really old. I do not want to go home ever again.

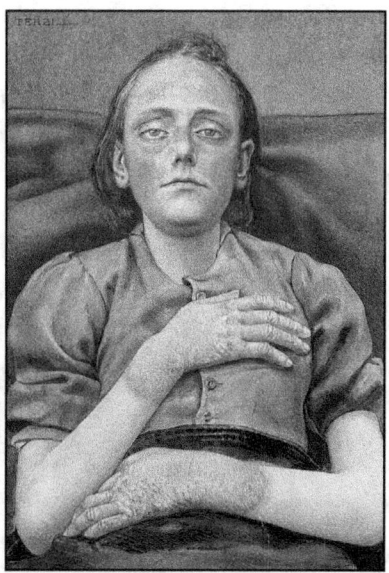

Florence, the girl with pellagra

George: Unintended Victim of War

I am just a kid, only ten years old. I never did anything wrong. I am angry because of this stupid war. It is not fair.

A man who said he was a soldier came to our room at Denison House one day to talk to my mother. Mother did not know the man and he did not look like a soldier, so she was a little scared of him. When this solider man opened his mouth, a really bad smell came out, like the smell of rotten meat, and I could see his crooked, yellow teeth. And his words were a little funny, as if he had a mouthful of toffee. He was hardly able to stand up. He tipped to the side a little and had to hold on to something so he would not fall onto the floor. Ma tried to scoot him out the door, but he said that he needed to tell her something. She did not want to listen, but he said he used to live in Liverpool in England, just like us, so she said she would listen.

The man said he was a soldier in the Great War in England. Father was a soldier, too. That is why he wanted to talk to us. He knew Father when they were both on a boat, a really big boat, called the Lusitania. Even though the boat was not supposed to be in the war, they put some soldiers on board, in case there was a problem.

When this war happened, my father worried about us. He had cousins who came to The States and he thought we should come too to be safe. He made me and my mother leave Liverpool and get on a big boat to come to Boston. Our boat was not the Lusitania. Father said we could stay with his cousins when we got here until he finished with the war. We did not even know the cousins, but Father was sure they would let us stay with them. He wrote down the place they lived and we saved that piece of paper, even when everything else got ruined. When Mother got sick on the boat, she made sure that she did not spit up on the piece of paper with their house on it. When we finally got here, Mother was afraid they would take her piece of paper so she hid it somewhere inside her panties. She was sure they would never look there but I worried that she would get pee on the paper. Or maybe even poop.

We had a terrible ride on the boat ride from England. Lots of people got sick and some people died. I only got sick one day. Mother says it was because I am really strong. Mother got sick a lot, but I took good care of her. I brought her water to drink every time she spit up because they let us have water if we got sick. She always shared it with me.

We were real lucky and made it to The States. When we got here, we could only think of how nice it would be to sleep in a real bed with no water underneath us. But when we went to the place where the cousins from the piece of paper were, they said we could not stay with them. They had a tiny place they called a tenement, and they said it was already full up. They said we would have to find a new place in Boston to stay, but we did not know where to go. Our cousins said many people died of consumption, and we better be careful or we might get sick and die. That made us more scared.

Even though we did not have much stuff, we were shaky and tired. Our bags felt very heavy so we left our bundles in a park and started to walk. We were hungry and did not know where we were going. A policeman called loudly and scared us. We tried to run away, but Mother was so weak she could not run very fast. He caught us and asked what we were doing. We looked awful so he might think we were bad people. Mother started to cry and talked real fast, telling the policeman about Father being on the Lusitania and the cousins not having enough room for us, and us having nowhere to go. We were lucky that he was a nice policeman. He took us to Denison House and not to the jail. That is how we got here. When we were here, Mother sent a letter to the cousins in the tenement, telling them we were fine. I did not think they were worried about us.

But now I have to tell you about this soldier who came to see us. The man kept talking in his funny way. He told us that he was on the same boat as Father and they were friends. Father told him all about Mother and me. They talked a lot while they were on their big boat. But one day, when this boat was floating, there was something called a torpedo that hit the boat. It was because of the war. This soldier and Father were in the water together after the boat fell into the ocean. They were shivering cold, and they were watching people die. Father was afraid he would die too. Father said if he died, this man had to promise to find us to tell us he loved us. The soldier was alive after the boat sank, but Father was dead.

The soldier got better, and he came to Boston to find us. He said something that sounded like, "The drink almost got the better of me, but I had to keep my promise." He went to the tenement my father told him about to find us. The cousins told him we were at Denison House. I was really glad my mother sent them that letter. He came to find us to tell us that Father was dead but he loved us, right to the end.

I do not understand war. My father did nothing wrong. Why did he have to die? Did those people who hit the boat with the torpedo think about all the people who were on the boat? Maybe, when I am grown up, I will be a soldier so I can kill those people who made my father's boat sink. But I do not want to die. I miss my father.

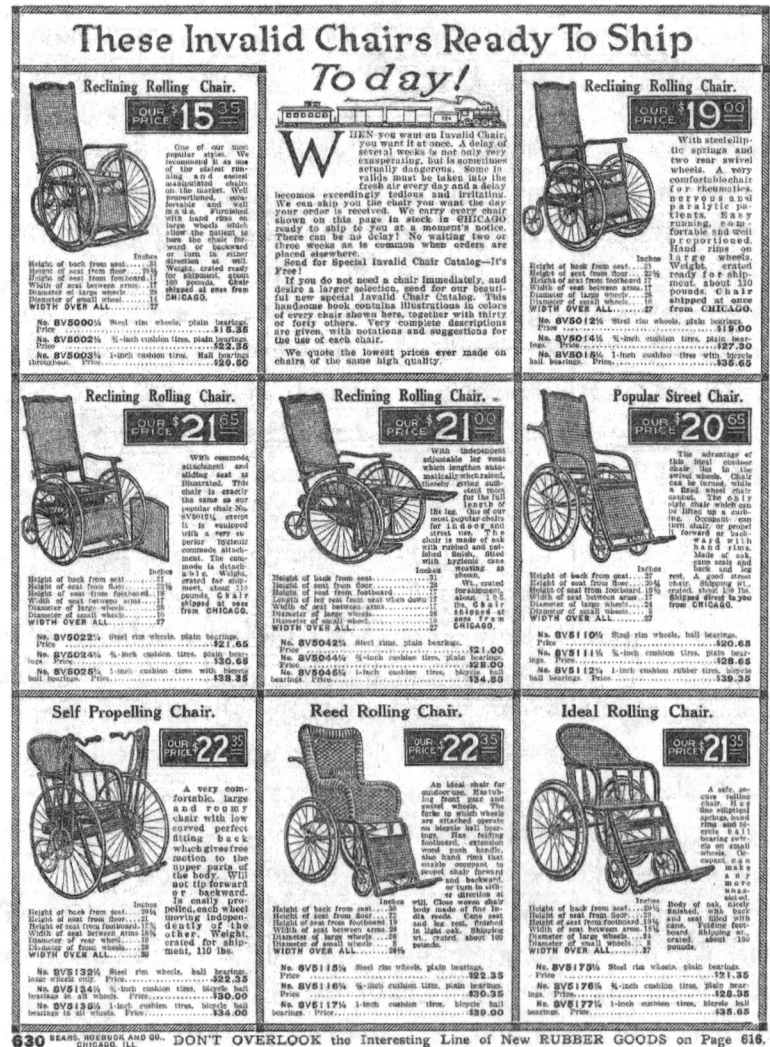

Sears & Roebuck mail-order catalog, 1914

Invalid Chairs

Wheeled furniture, mostly for children, dates back as far as the fifth century in Greece. In the eighth century in China, chairs resembling wheelbarrows were the first known to carry disabled people. Europeans developed extravagant contraptions to carry royalty, a portable throne of sorts. The first self-propelling chair, which looked more like a hand-bike, was developed in the 1660s. The bathchair, an uncomfortable contraption, was created in 1790.

After the Civil War, disabled men that had survived the ravages of war lacked the ability to move around on their own, creating the first market for rolling chairs. First called "Nursery chairs," they were patented in the mid-1800s to aid soldiers with mobility. There were varied designs, including a rocker chair that could be outfitted with wheels. Later improvements included hollow rubber tires, like those on bicycles, with self-propelled push-rims.

Years later, following the Great War, many soldiers had been disabled during the battles. They found the "rolling chair" or "invalid chair" to be helpful in readjusting to civilian life. The American Relief Clearing House for the Society of Mutilated Soldiers distributed these chairs to maimed European soldiers. The first motorized wheelchair was manufactured in London in 1916.

The biggest shift in popularity of these chairs was in Atlantic City, New Jersey. Rather than being constructed for the disabled, there were public rolling chairs for rent on the boardwalk. Initially, healthy people feigned problems walking, but gradually they became a popular way to view the attractions for anyone who had the money to rent the chair. As with most gadgets, their popularity faded. By the 1930s folding portable chairs became popular for traveling. These were the first mass-marketed wheelchairs.

In 1984, an enterprising hotel clerk found a discarded pile of the Atlantic City chairs in a back room and created an entrepreneurial enterprise. Wealthy, yet lazy people impressed others by rolling along the boardwalk, pushed by the unfortunate souls hired to propel them. This added status to wheelchairs, further removing the stigma previously associated with their use exclusively by people with disabilities.

Mobility scooters, a recent adaptation of the invalid chair, aid people with mobility limitations. Further adjustments include single-arm drive chairs, and tilting and reclining chairs. Standing wheelchairs can now allow someone who cannot otherwise stand the option to be upright, and sports wheelchairs allow the disabled to be athletes. Technology has improved the old-fashioned invalid chair in ways those in earlier generations could never have imagined.

Mezuzah

A mezuzah declares: The people who dwell here live Jewish lives.

Before affixing the mezuzah to the doorpost, the following blessing should be recited:

בָּרוּךְ אַתָּה יְיָ אֱלֹהֵינוּ מֶלֶךְ הָעוֹלָם

Barukh atah Adonai, Eloheinu, melekh ha'olam
Blessed are you, Lord, our God, sovereign of the universe

אֲשֶׁר קִדְּשָׁנוּ בְּמִצְוֹתָיו וְצִוָּנוּ לִקְבֹּעַ מְזוּזָה

asher kidishanu b'mitz'votav v'tzivanu lik'bo'a m'zuzah
Who has sanctified us with His commandments and
commanded us to affix a mezuzah.

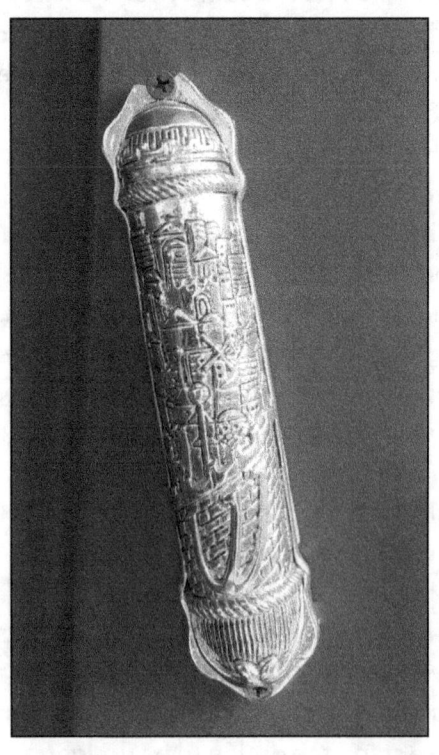

Elizabeth's Mother's Arrest

I am embarrassed that I need assistance in writing my story. I am a thirty-five-year-old woman who is literate, yet I do not write well enough to craft my tale of being a Suffragette. But it is important for me to tell my story, and I am appreciative I have been offered assistance to write this down.

My story begins like that of many others. I was brought up in a decent family, with more affection than money. When I was still in school, I fell in love with a classmate and I put marriage ahead of education. Looking back, I wish I had listened to my parents when they begged me to finish school before marriage. But my heart was deeply touched by this bright young man with irresistible blond curls, who promised me a wonderful life, full of happiness and riches.

Nathan and I were wed right after I turned sixteen, and we soon began our family. We had three girls. Nathan went to school in the morning, then spent many hours in a factory, earning enough to buy clothes and food for our growing clan. I stayed home and made wonderful meals from the little we could afford. I was proud that my girls were always clean and happy. Once the girls were in school and Nathan had finished his studies, he was able to get a wonderful job in a prestigious law firm and our lives were on the way to fulfilling the dreams he promised.

I had many available hours during the daytime, so I was thrilled when a neighbor invited me to join her at a suffrage meeting. I immediately found my calling in life. Surrounded by a group of intelligent women, I became a true believer in the rights of women. Why was it that women were not able to vote? Why were they looked down on by men, even those of lesser breeding or education, who thought that a woman's place was at home, not involved in making our country a better place in which to live?

My neighbor, Bertha, invited me to join her at rallies where bold women stood strong for their beliefs. I agreed with them that women should have a say in the running of our government. I wondered if this would be a more just world with women working toward justice in our society. A woman's right to vote should be valued, since women understand that if people work in harmony, rather than relying on warfare, we might be able to solve the world's ills. Before I knew it, I was carrying banners at marches and organizing campaigns for women's suffrage. I considered myself a suffragette, though I feared the ramifications of claiming that title.

Then one day, at a suffrage parade in Boston, I heard a talk by Alice Paul, the leader of the Congressional Union, a militant branch of the National American Woman Suffrage Association. I was so overtaken by her words that I knew I needed to dedicate myself to this cause.

But the cost of this new focus of my life was that my home-life suffered. My husband had always been a wonderful provider yet he threatened that he would withdraw my monthly stipend unless I desisted from the political meetings I was attending on a regular basis. He claimed that I was no longer caring for our home at the same standard to which he had become accustomed, and on this point he was accurate. He said our girls were suffering when I attended meetings instead of prioritizing their needs, a statement that hurt my heart. I believed I was ensuring their future by earning them the right to cast a vote for the beliefs I was instilling in them. Occasionally my resolve faded, and there were times when I put my girls' needs above those of the movement.

When Nathan withdrew my allowance as he threatened, I relied on the money I had saved in the empty honey jar I hid in the cabinet above the sink. He was astonished that I continued to feed our girls. In a frenzy, he threatened to throw us into the streets if I did not stop putting suffrage above my family's needs. But how could I? The movement needed articulate women like me to ensure that voting was the right of both men and women.

One day Nathan followed through on his threats. He locked us out of our home, and I had to sleep in the park with my girls. Suddenly, my daughters, who had always supported me in my actions, were angered with me for taking my resolve this far. We moved into Denison House, a settlement house that took in needy families, offering us shelter and support. From this place I could continue my work, knowing that my girls' basic needs were being cared for.

But everything changed during the suffrage parade of October 23, 2015. I joined a large group of women I admired and trusted who traveled from Boston to join thousands of others to walk down Fifth Avenue in New York City. We stood in solidarity when the police threatened us. I stayed firm in my convictions, and I proudly held the banner, "Mr. President, How Long Must Women Wait for Liberty?" believing it to be the most important action I had ever taken. Although I knew that it was likely I would be arrested, I had no choice. This issue was too important for my girls' future.

We were not treated well. Many women were beaten by the police and needed to be taken to area hospitals. Many of us were arrested, the most demeaning experience of my life. We were shoved into a police wagon with no concern for our welfare and taken to the Jefferson Market Prison, the women's prison in Greenwich Village. The building's brick exterior and ornate Gothic details made it appear more like a church than a jail. Its tower stood high above all the other buildings in the area, but once we were brought to the basement holding area, we no longer noticed the building's beauty. We were made to wait in the overcrowded building with prostitutes and other undesirables, with no food or access to conveniences. Many women soiled their clothing and others fainted from hunger as the long hours passed. Some women were grabbed, dragged, beaten, pinched or kicked, or worse. I was lucky to be ignored as the guards focused on the younger, more beautiful women. I thought this was the worst treatment I would ever see, but I was so very wrong.

The cells we were transferred to, once we were processed and stripped of our clothing and given shapeless dresses to wear, were dark and moldy. There were fewer beds than women and one toilet in which we needed to do our business in front of all the other women. We had to beg for tissues and to have the toilets flushed. The prostitutes shared their bodies, right in front of us, in exchange for free access to these basic needs. Cockroaches scurried around the floor, and often climbed onto us as we slept on the cold floor, with no pillows or blankets to protect us. We were fed nothing but bread and water for every meal, so our stomachs ached and our heads pounded. The only relief was when we were allowed to clean up before approaching the courtroom. We were asked to plead guilty to unknown charges at which time we would be released to the care of our husbands, many of whom would surely inflict their own punishments.

When standing at the bench, in front of the judge, I stole a glance around the room, spotting Nathan in the second row. As a lawyer, he had found his way into the courtroom. I am certain he expected me to plead guilty to a misdemeanor and return to our home and desist from my suffrage activities. But seeing him made me feel stronger in my resolve. I could not let men like him rule our lives. What would this accomplish in creating a better world for my daughters?

After vowing with my fellow suffragettes to continue this fight until women were treated as equals, I was thrown into a new cell, with conditions as bad as the first. I was told that I would spend the rest of my days in this bare room, with no access to the light of day or to my girls.

The Jefferson Market Courthouse, 1905 (above) is today a Landmark Building in NYC

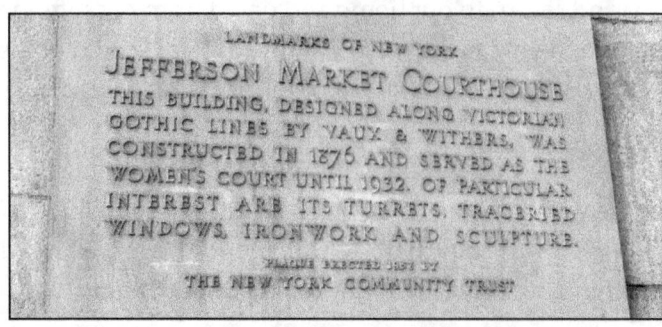

What had I done? Would I ever see my daughters again? How could I provide for their welfare from the confines of these dirty walls? Was I gaining anything for them by sleeping in filth and having no ability to pursue the men who had imprisoned us? Would our rights be heard?

Days went by, then weeks. Life in jail had no meaning. I was not doing any good for other women. I was only hurting myself. Then one day, after about a month of this subhuman life, several of us were sent to a small room where we were cleaned up. We no longer had the strength to wash our own bodies. Our clothes fell off our diminished frames, and our eyes were sallow. We filed into the courthouse as a bunch of broken women. I hardly heard the words being spoken, but when they were done, we were set free.

Nathan was not waiting for me. I would not have returned to him even if he had been waiting with fresh food and clothing. All I could think of was my girls. When I arrived back in Boston, I began the long walk to Denison House, where I knew they were being cared for. All the way there I paid no attention to my dirty body or bloody feet. I tried to dredge up some remorse for the pain I had caused my children, but I knew that I had done the right thing.

As I reached our room at Denison House, I was greeted by my daughter Elizabeth with a flood of tears. My eyes barely dripped a single tear as she stripped me of my filthy clothing, which she rolled into a ball to be thrown out. She draped me in the one towel that we had taken from our house before we were locked out and had used for a pad on the bare ground as we slept in the park. She walked me to the room where she could clean me up before my other girls could see me. She fed me a biscuit she had taken from lunch one day, saving it until the day I returned. The sweetness brought tears to my eyes, both for the overwhelming taste of real food, and for the loving gesture.

I'm now living with my precious girls again. They tell me every day how scared they were they would not see me again. They also tell me of their pride in me because I stood firm for my beliefs. This was the only way they would get what every girl deserves. I believe in the right of suffrage.

Sally: The Mail-Order Girl

The Post Office Parcel Post service began in 1913, allowing Americans to mail large packages. An unexpected consequence was when some parents sent their children through the mail.

Hi. My name is Sally and I am seven years old. I have a funny story to tell you about how I got to Denison House. I will stay here until my daddy gets out of jail, which the lawyer man says will be real soon.

The story started when my grandma and grandpa moved to the countryside. They got a farm in Worcester. That is a long way away, too far for us to visit from Boston. I missed my grandma and grandpa a whole lot, and I wanted really, really bad to visit them. My daddy said he would find a way, but he could not figure it out because he had to work every day. And my mommy needed to stay home because she was going to have a baby and she was not feeling real good.

But I missed my grandma and grandpa. I cried a lot and my daddy told me over and over he would find a way. One day he heard a story that helped him figure out how I could visit with Grandma and Grandpa. He would mail me.

Daddy heard about a family with a lady named Mary who mailed her girl to her grandpa. They used a railway mail train. The father paid 53 cents for stamps, and he put them on his little girl's coat. My daddy decided that is what he would do with me. He said it would be cheaper to pay for the stamps than to pay for a ticket on the train.

So that is just what my daddy did. He took me to the post office, and he bought two bunches of stamps for 53 cents. He put some stamps in a little bag in the pocket of my coat. He said those stamps would get me home. He did not want to mess up my coat, so he put a shirt on top of my coat and he stuck the other stamps on the shirt. He made funny faces when we had to lick all those stamps. Mommy made me some sandwiches to take with me. Daddy worried that the sandwiches would make me weigh more and he would need to buy more stamps, so he had me eat all the sandwiches right at the post office station. My tummy hurt from eating so many sandwiches. But I was so excited about going to see my grandma that I did not care. I kissed my daddy good-bye and thanked him for finding a way to get me to see my grandma.

The post office man said he had never mailed a little girl before. But he would make sure that I was taken good care of. He talked to the mailman who would stay with all the mail, including me, in one of the railroad cars near the back of the train. The mailman made a special spot for me to sit, on top of a whole bunch of soft packages.

I never went on a train before so I was really excited and happy that I would get to see Grandma and Grandpa soon. But all that excitement and all those sandwiches made my stomach make lots of noises. I did not know if they had a toilet on the train, but I told the mailman that he had to find me one or I was going to make a mess right on top of his mail. So, he made the train wait while he took me to find a toilet.

There was a policeman waiting when I got out of the toilet, and I was scared that I did something wrong. He said it was not good to mail a little girl, but I told him that I wanted to see my grandma and grandpa real bad. He thought it was wrong to put stamps on a person.

The train took off before he could find out anything, and I got to travel with the nice mailman the whole way to Worcester. There were no windows on the train, and it was very bumpy, and it took a long time. Sort of like a whole day. I held my pee, like a big girl, but I thought a lot about finding another toilet when we got off the train.

When we finally got to the train station, I was really happy to see my grandma and grandpa. There was another policeman waiting for me. He said it was not good to mail a girl. I showed him that my daddy bought the stamps. He was not happy, but he let me run to my grandpa to give him a big kiss. My grandpa took me right to the toilet at the train station, 'cause I really had to go.

There were seven cases of children being mailed before a law was passed to prohibit it. Mary was the first person to mail her child. These photos are actual mail-order children.

I spent a bunch of days visiting the farm and helping Grandma bake pies. I had a nice visit. I liked the chickens the best. And the worst was when I had to bend over a lot when we picked the berries off the little bushes. But they tasted real good.

When it was time to go home, I put a different shirt over my coat. Grandpa licked the stamps to get me home. He made the same funny faces Daddy did when he licked the stamps. The nice mailman was at the train station, and he took me to the toilet before we even got on the train. I was the only little girl with the mail this time, too. The mailman told me stories of the other little children who had been mailed like a package. He told me that I was number eight, and he knew the stories of all the other little girls who were mailed. Oh, and one boy.

When we got back to Boston, I could not see my daddy. Instead, I could see a whole bunch of policemen. They told me that Daddy was in trouble because he mailed me. There was a new law saying it was not okay. They told me they were going to take my daddy to the jail. I cried a lot. I wanted to see my daddy, and I was scared that he was going to the jail. And then I worried that I could not get home. But the policeman said he would give me a ride. I told him that I did not have any more stamps to pay him, but he said that this part of the trip was free.

When I got home, my mommy was crying. She held her big belly and let out some very big cries. The policeman told Mommy that Daddy had to go to jail because it was not good to put stamps on a girl. He said they would get a lawyer for my daddy and I would get to stay with my mommy. He told me he was glad that I had a nice trip, but I could not go that way again. I wondered what kind of ideas my daddy would have the next time I wanted to visit the farm.

So, my daddy is still in jail and we are living at Denison House because we could not pay for our flat without Daddy here. A nice lawyer man comes to visit us a lot, and he talks to mommy about all kinds of things I do not understand. The lawyer told me there was no real rule about mailing a child so he hoped that Daddy would come home very soon. Mommy talks to the baby in her belly and tells my little sister inside (I hope it's a sister) that she has to wait to come out. I hope Daddy gets out real soon because that baby is in a rush, my mommy says.

I am glad I got to see Grandma and Grandpa, but I am sad that my daddy had to go to jail because of it. I hope he gets out soon and the baby waits for him. Then we can all take a trip to see them, to show them the new baby after it comes out. When Daddy gets home, we can leave Denison House.

Cleo: The Sharecropper's Daughter

I'm Cleo and I'm from Mississippi, which is a long way away. My dad was a sharecropper, which he always said was like owning the soil. He got to work the land for the Smith family, who he used to say was a fine family. They lived in the big house, and we got to go sometimes when they invited us. Like on Christmas, when they invited all the sharecroppers to come for a dinner that they made special for us. We all sat around big tables in the yard, and they made us a great big meal. They had turkeys and ham and corn right on the cob. They let us smother it with lots of butter. And then they made us special cookies, which they said were for Christmas. And we got to sing lots of songs together. It was real nice.

When it wasn't Christmas, we never got to go to the big house but we sometimes got to go to the barn that was real close to the house. Sometimes they had extra food and they would let us come get some. And when their special peach trees had more peaches than they could eat by themselves, they let us pick up the ones on the ground.

I asked my papa if sharecropping was good. He said he got some money when he sold the food and the cotton we growed on the farm. But he said it wasn't fair 'cause the Smith family got most of the money, even when we did all the work. He said it was much better than when his daddy was a slave, when all the negroes were treated real bad. Now he gets to work on his own piece of the farm and he can keep some of the money when he sells the crops. And both the negro and the white sharecroppers got treated the same way. It wasn't real good, like friends, but the Smiths were nice, like I told you, on Christmas and special days like that.

My papa goes every single day to pick the cotton. Well, on Sundays he got to go to church before he goes to the field. He says it is back-breaking work, but I never saw his back break. When he comes home, he is hot and sweaty and he won't talk to any of us till he got himself clean.

A lot of days we get to help him. I like to help 'cause then I don't have to do the arithmetic Mama makes me do if I'm at home. Mama is in the fields every day except when she is sick from having a baby. And that was a lot 'cause there are six of us kids. The last baby she had was dead when he came out and Mama cried a lot. Even after the baby was gone to the grave a long time, she still cried a lot.

And then Mama had more to cry about. My big sister, Erline, started getting sick and fat and Mama figured out that she was going to have a baby.

But Erline wouldn't tell anybody who the baby daddy was. When Ernest was born, he was the lightest negro baby I ever seen. He made Mama cry some more. Erline cried a lot and so did little baby Ernest. Some days it seemed the whole house was cryin'.

Everything in the cryin' house was all right until one of the big Mr. Smiths started coming around. He seemed real interested in Erline and her baby, but Papa said he couldn't come no more. I saw my Papa stand up real tall, and he had a gun in his hand that scared Mr. Smith. Papa never pointed the gun at him, and never said bad words against him, but that Mr. Smith never come by again. After that day, Papa talked a lot about wanting to leave the sharecropping.

One day Papa got us all excited. He said lots of people wanted cotton because of the war that was going to happen. I told him I don't understand what fightin' got to do with cotton, so he said the cotton was for uniforms. Papa said we were goin' to get rich. He said he was going to make more money than we would know what to do with it, but that was confusin'. I know what I'd do with lots a money. I'd buy a big house for Mama and Papa and all us kids. And I'd make sure that we always had a lot of food and we could go shopping and buy fancy clothes. I think I'd like that, getting fancy things to wear. Then I could look like those colored girls in the magazines who have tall men all around them. I don't think I'd want all those men. I'd want one nice man who would make me happy all the time. Mama says I'm still too young to have those thoughts.

But when Papa started to get more money, he was real angry. He said that he couldn't spend it. He went to buy us a car, and the man said he wouldn't sell to a negro man. Papa tried to buy us fancy new clothes, and they only wanted to sell him the same stuff we always had. Papa was real mad.

So one day, when Papa had saved some money, he decided we needed to move north. He said his money would be good in the north. I didn't know where north was, but I didn't want to move away. But I am just a kid so I don't get to make those big decisions. Just the grownups can do that.

So Mama started packing all our stuff. And Papa went to lots of stores to buy us a big car so we could leave. No one wanted to sell him a nice car so one day he came home with a good old truck with these wood sides we could peek out from. It wasn't a nice one, but he seemed proud that he got it, and now we could go north.

Going north wasn't such a good idea it turned out. Papa drove a long way, with all of us in the back making lots of noise, especially baby Ernest.

And we made him stop every time there was a colored toilet. If we stopped somewhere that was for whites only we had to wait. One time my sister Shirley wet herself 'cause there was not a colored toilet for a long time. It made Papa mad.

When we got to New York, it was real scary. That's where folks told Papa that he could make lots of money, but we were all too scared to get out of the car when we saw all those people and all those big buildings. We told Papa that we didn't like his up north. He said he would find us somewhere else to go so we kept driving.

Then we got to this place called "Chusetts," or something like that. People told us to go to a big city so Papa could find work. The next stop was Boston, which wasn't too scary. They had some tall buildings and lots of people, but it didn't scare us like New York did. We got out of the car and walked around in the park to get a big stretch. And they let us go to toilets wherever we wanted, not just with the negro signs. I liked that a lot, and so did my sister Shirley. She didn't have to worry about messing herself again.

But Papa couldn't find any work, 'cause they didn't have farms in the city, and all he knew how to do was to raise vegetables and cotton. Nobody told him that they didn't grow cotton in the north. And none of us was big enough to get a job, so all the money he got from his job as a sharecropper was running out. And we was all tuckered out from sleeping in the car. Then the car broke down and it took almost all the money to get it fixed.

Sharecropper working on rented land

That's when we got really lucky. A nice negro man told us that we could all go to Denison House and they would help us out. Mama said he was crazy to think that they would take all of us, six kids and a mama and a papa. But when we got there we must have looked real bad, 'cause they invited us to come inside to have some food. It was the best food we had since we left the farm.

Even though Papa said he was too proud to stay there, Mama made plans for us all to sleep in one room together. It is really hard to fit that many people in one room, so they had to give us two rooms, one for the boys and one for the girls. Mama and Papa didn't like the idea of being split up, 'cause they always had one big bed to share. But now Mama stayed with the girls and Papa stayed with the boys, and some days that made Papa spitting mad.

The folks at Denison House were real nice to us. They helped Papa find a job working for a rich family. He was to tend their horses and carriages and to drive them anywhere they wanted to go. He had this special jacket and hat to wear every day, even if it was hot or cold. He always needed to look perfect and to say nice words, like "Yes, Ma'am." And when it got real cold, he would take a big shovel and get rid of the snow everywhere they wanted to walk. He liked his job because he was outside. I wouldn't like it because I get cold real easy.

Papa didn't complain and we all got good food and we didn't have to sleep in the car anymore. Now Papa says he is saving money so he can get us a farm. He says he won't be like a sharecropper 'cause they don't have 'em in the North, but he will get to keep all the money he makes when he sells the crops. But they got no cotton and the vegetables are different. And they got no peaches in the winter, my favorite food.

So, Denison House is good, even if Mama and Papa aren't liking to live in different rooms. I hope we get to have a whole house for ourselves real soon. Maybe we can get a big house, like the Smith house. But the big houses here all seem close together. My brother says that is 'cause we're in a city. Maybe we can move away to a little city when Papa get lots of money. I'll be sad to leave, 'cause I really like the molasses cookies they make at Denison House.

Henry Ford and Antisemitism

Henry Ford was an antisemite.

When Miriam and Hannah's father purchased a 1910 Ford Model T, America's most popular car, Henry Ford was becoming one of the most influential people in the United States. From the time these cars were first produced in 1908, they were affordable, due to Ford's innovative assembly-line production of these popular black beauties. The Model T was symbol of the rising middle-class in this era of modernization. Mr. Cohen could never have imagined that the automobile maker would later become one of the best-known antisemites and followers of eugenics in the country.

Henry Ford's upbringing in rural Michigan probably influenced his attitude toward Jews. He might have learned in church the popular belief that Jews killed Christ, and his father and other farmers may have intimated that Jewish merchants would cheat you in business. During his early years building cars, his attention was focused on developing one of the most influential companies of the time, not on his attitude toward Jews.

But as Ford's business and the Ku Klux Klan grew, his thoughts focused on Jewish capitalists, whom he blamed for all evils. He developed a belief that Jews were "mentally immoral." As the eugenics movement peaked, he was in agreement with their position on selective breeding to enhance the genetic quality of the human race. Also, he believed Jews were at fault for the Great War, due to an international plot by Jewish bankers.

It was not until 1919 when Henry Ford purchased his small hometown newspaper, *The Dearborn Independent*, that his beliefs became public. In this paper, he published the "Protocols of the Elders of Zion," claiming the existence of an international Jewish conspiracy to plan the fate of the world, and a series of ninety-one articles denigrating Jews. He later bound these articles into four volumes, titled *The International Jew*. He distributed a half million copies to his dealerships. Sometimes people buying a Ford Model T would find a copy of his newspaper tucked into their new automobile.

Had Mr. Cohen learned of Henry Ford's beliefs, he would have discarded his car, despite it being his most prized possession. Deborah and Miriam, had they learned of Mr. Ford's attitudes towards eugenics, and being aware that his beliefs were also focused on mentally defective people like their daughter Sylvia, would have turned in their car for a model from another car company.

By World War II Ford was entranced by Nazi Germany, doing business in the Third Reich. He and his friend Charles Lindbergh became obsessed with Hitler and Nazism. Hitler's manifesto, *Mein Kampf*, reflected Ford and Lindbergh's beliefs regarding eugenics. Hitler kept a portrait of Henry Ford on his office wall.

In 1938, on his seventy-fifth birthday, Ford received an award from the Nazi regime called the "Grand Cross of the German Eagle," usually given to foreign diplomats. Documents later showed that Ford converted his German plants to military production, at a time he resisted doing so at his plants in the U.S. Later, he fought a civil case regarding cash settlements from banks and insurance companies accused of defrauding Holocaust victims. He remained an enemy of the Jews until his death in 1947.

Henry Ford

YIDDISH
(spoken language transliterated)

A dank	Thank you
babka	Sweet braided bread
gay ga zinta hate	Go in good health (said in parting)
gefilte fish	Minced fish patty
hamantashen	"Haman's hat," triangular filled pocket cookie
kugel	Puffed up pudding
kvelling	Displaying pride in someone close
lesbisnke	Lesbian
mandel bread	Almond bread cookie
Munn or mohn	Poppy seeds
naches	Pride
rugelach	Filled pastry
tsoris	Trouble, suffering
shaina meidel	Pretty girl
shpilkes	State of impatience or agitation
yente	Jewish matchmaker (common usage), also, busybody
Zal es zayn azoy	May it be so

GLOSSARY
HEBREW

אַבָּא	*abba*	Father
אֲפִיקוֹמָן	*afikomen*	Half-piece of matzo for dessert after the Passover meal
אֲרוֹן קֹדֶשׁ	*aron kodesh*	Holy ark
בַּר מִצְוָה	*Bar Mitzvah*	Coming of age celebration Jewish 13 year old boy
חמץ	*chametz*	Anything not Kosher for Passover
דוֹד	*dod*	Uncle
דּוֹדָה	*doda*	Aunt
אִמָּא	*ema*	Mother
עֶרֶב	*erev*	Evening (before holiday)
יהוה	*Hashem*	Unspoken name of G-d
הַבְדָּלָה	*Havdalah*	Separation, service at end of Shabbos
ימים נוראים	*High holidays*	Days of Awe
חוּפָּה	*huppah*	Canopy for wedding ceremony
כָּל נִדְרֵי	*Kol Nidre*	Declaration recited before the beginning of Yom Kippur
כָּשֵׁר	*Kosher*	Fit for dietary restrictions
כשר לפסח	*Kosher for Passover*	Fit for Passover dietary restrictions
שנה טובה	*L'Shana Tova*	Common greeting at Rosh Hashanah holiday
מה נשתנה	*Ma nishtana*	The Four Questions, as recited for Passover
מַצָּה	*matzo*	Unleavened flatbread
קנײדלעך	*matzoh balls*	Soup dumplings
מַצָּה פַאַרפֿל	*matzoh farfel*	Broken matzoh for cooking
מזל טוב	*Mazel Tov*	Good fortune, Congratulations
מגילה	*Megillah*	Scroll, refers to Book of Esther on Purim

מְזוּזָה	*Mezuzah*	Decorative case, inscribed with Hebrew verses, at doorway
מִי שֶׁבֵּרַךְ	*Mi Sheberach*	Public prayer for healing
מִצְוָה	*mitzvah*	Deed performed as commandment, act of kindness
פֶּסַח	*Pesach*	Passover holiday
סֵדֶר	*seder*	Ritual service and feast at Passover
שַׁבָּת שָׁלוֹם	*Shabbat Shalom*	Peaceful Sabbath, a greeting for Shabbos
שהחינו	*Shehecheyanu*	Prayer to celebrate special occasions, gratitude
שְׁמַע יִשְׂרָאֵל	*Shema Yisrael*	"Hear, O Israel," centerpiece of morning and evening prayers
שמירה	*shemira*	Guarding the body of deceased, to protect it as the soul hovers
מְחַת תּוֹרָה	*Simchat Torah*	Holiday marking end of annual cycle of Torah readings
שִׁבְעָה	*shiva*	Literally "seven," week-long mourning period
שׁוּל	*shul*	Synagogue
סֻכּוֹת	*Sukkos*	Feast of Tabernacles, harvest pilgrimage festival
טו בשבט	*Tu Bishvat*	New Year of the Trees
תשובה	*teshuva*	Literally "return," commonly: to ask forgiveness
אָרצייט	*yahrzeit*	Anniversary of person's death
ישיבה	*Yeshiva*	Hebrew university

Romance at Stonegate
(Deborah and Miriam's Boston Marriage Series)
ISBN Paperback: 978-1-63765-674-7

Deborah and Miriam, young Jewish girls vacationing in Massachusetts the summer of 1910, are immediately attracted to one another. As they explore their intense connection, they face challenges in their families, community, religion, and within themselves. These young women are products of turn-of-the-century values yet fall in love, a rarely accepted behavior in post-Victorian America. They explore ways to fit into a culture that is unforgiving of the choices they make, discovering what it means to be lesbian in a world which is not ready for them.

Struggles in a Boston Marriage
(Deborah and Miriam's Boston Marriage Series)
ISBN Paperback: 978-1-63765-675-4

True love knows no bounds . . .Deborah and Miriam are two young women whose love has survived the many obstacles life has thrown their way in their first years together. Now they find themselves in Boston, raising a young child whose been diagnosed as a Mongoloid Idiot, in an era where little was known about how to care for such a child at home. Deborah's thrilled that her writing is due to become published and she also pleased to be part of a growing and thriving business. Despite having found the woman of her dreams, she finds herself irritable and untrusting of Miriam's love.Miriam has given her heart and soul to Deborah and feels fulfilled now that she has a child and has meaningful volunteer work. She is proud of all their accomplishments at the printing and publishing shop and with her own ability to stand firm in her beliefs, even when Deborah challenges her. The world around them is changing. The Suffrage movement is trying to give women the freedom to vote and they feel guilty that they do not have enough time to continue their work for this cause. Also, people fear their country may go to war. During this time of uproar, Deborah and Miriam find their relationship becomes tested by an outsider. Will their love be strong enough to endure?

Victory, Virus, Votes: 1917-1920
(Deborah and Miriam's Boston Marriage Series)
ISBN Paperback: 978-1-63765-587-0
ISBN Hardcover: 978-1-63765-657-0

The end of World War I sees an upheaval in American society—the Great Migration of Black Americans, the devastation of the Spanish Flu, and women's struggle for the vote. *Victory, Virus, and Votes: 1917–1920* brings history to life through the lens of two young Jewish lovers fighting to find their place in a turbulent world. The continuing saga of Deborah Levine and Miriam Cohen explores key historical occurrences such as the suffragists' Night of Terror, the Great Molasses Flood, and the Women's Land Army. This fourth book in the *Jewish Boston Marriage* series will enrich and thrill readers as they witness the power of love and integrity in the chaotic beginning of the Modern Age.

Let's Connect

Get to know Ellen M. Levy

Email: ellenlevyauthor@gmail.com

Website: https://www.ellenlevy.net

Facebook: Ellen M Levy author

Instagram: Ellen M Levy author

www.ingramcontent.com/pod-product-compliance
Lightning Source LLC
Chambersburg PA
CBHW071147260626
47162CB00003B/945